CODY'S BOOKS

CODY'S BOOKS

*The life and times of a Berkeley
bookstore, 1956 to 1977*

Pat *and* Fred Cody

CHRONICLE BOOKS

SAN FRANCISCO

Printed in the United States of America.

ISBN 0-8118-0140-3

Library of Congress Cataloging-in-Publication Data

Cody, Pat, 1923–
    Cody's Books : the life and times of a Berkeley bookstore,
    1956–1977 / Pat and Fred Cody.
        p.   cm.
    Includes bibliographical references and index.
    ISBN 0-8118-0220-5. — ISBN 0-8118-0140-3 (pbk.)
    1. Cody's Books. 2. Cody, Fred, 1916–1983. 3. Cody, Pat, 1923–
    4. Booksellers and bookselling—California—Berkeley—
    History—20th century. 5. Booksellers and bookselling—United
    States—Biography. 6. Berkeley (Calif.)—Intellectual life.
    I. Cody, Fred, 1916–1983. II. Title.
    Z473.C63C64   1992
    381'.45002'0979467—dc20   92-3964
                                                                   CIP

A Yolla Bolly Press Book
This book was produced in association with the publisher at The
Yolla Bolly Press, Covelo, California, under the supervision of
James Robertson and Carolyn Robertson, with assistance from
Diana Fairbanks, Mary McDermott, and Renee Menge.
Composition by Wilsted & Taylor, Oakland, California.

Acknowledgments
Grateful acknowledgment is made for permission to reprint the
following: Excerpt from "Print Freaks" from *The Berkeley Monthly*,
June 1, 1978. Excerpt from 1982 tape interview with Mark
Kitchell, director and producer of "Berkeley in the 60s." Tribute by
Alan Soldofsky from *Poetry Flash*, August, 1983.

Distributed in Canada by Raincoast Books,
112 East Third Avenue, Vancouver, B.C. V5T 1C8

10 9 8 7 6 5 4 3 2 1

Chronicle Books
275 Fifth Street
San Francisco, CA 94103

For our family

CONTENTS

If he be a seller of books,
he is no meere Bookseller, one who selleth
merely ynck and paper bundled up together for
his own advantage only; but he is the Chapman of Arts,
of wisdom, and of much experience.

GEORGE WITHER, 1588-1667

PREFACE

It has been thirty-six years since my late husband Fred and I started Cody's Books in July of 1956. A good part of the twenty-one years we owned the store were years of social ferment and transformation—not just in Berkeley—in America and in the book business. When we began, the copying machine was a mimeograph; we used it to inform our customers about new books. Inventory control and book ordering were done from publishers' lists, using that modern improvement, the electric typewriter.

Cody's was an adventure and a challenge. We built it during years of great change in the United States. Luck, serendipity, the paperback "revolution," hard work, and some inspiration all played a part. I don't think it could have turned out as it did in very many other communities. We had the advantages of a large university with its questing scholars and eager students, as well as location in the Bay Area, one of the leading book markets in the United States. I think all the people who sustained Cody's during those years will want to know some of its history.

The story of the aspirations and development of Cody's is found in letters we wrote to my brother Bob Herbert and his wife Fi, and in reminiscences and essays Fred wrote. I have added my recollections about the store and some notes on what was going on in Berkeley at the time.

CODY'S BOOKS

INTRODUCTION

BEFORE THE STORE   BOOKS IN OUR LIVES

I cannot live without books.

THOMAS JEFFERSON, IN A LETTER TO JOHN ADAMS, 1815

Books were a part of our lives almost beyond remembering. Fred grew up in the 1920's on a farm in Scott's Run, West Virginia. His father supplemented his pay as a rural mail-carrier by raising vegetables, chickens, a cow, and some pigs. Old Doc and Betsy were the irascible horses used by Fred's father for plowing and sometimes by the boys for bareback riding through the woods. Fred, older brother John, and younger brother Mart helped with farm work. Fred's mother and the cow were not in harmony and halfway through each milking, Bossy had the habit of putting her hoof into the bucket so the milk had to be thrown to the pigs. "Let me try, Mom," said Fred, and he got Bossy in a relaxed mood by singing Methodist hymns to her. He always got a full bucket, so milking became his chore.

Scott's Run had no library, but his mother taught in the one-room schoolhouse and she brought the McGuffey Readers home for her three boys. Summertime visits to the richer farm of Aunt Margaret meant access to an attic where Fred could lose himself in old volumes of Horatio Alger and tales of the Civil War.

Later, his father, by then a leaser for the gas utility, moved the family to the city of Huntington. This offered new horizons, as Fred recalled in an essay on "Print Freaks" he wrote for the Berkeley Monthly:

As time has passed I have come to feel that the *Saturday Evening Post* was more interesting as a profitable exploitation of orthodoxy than as an adventurous contribution to the national culture, but it was not so at the beginning. It would be hard to put into words just how I felt when it was shoved into the galvanized metal mailbox of a northern West Virginia farm. I was zealous in following all the seri-

als—oh, Clarence Budington Kelland! ah, Mary Roberts Rinehart!—
and I never missed one of the exploits of Alexander Botts, the intrepid
Earthworm Caterpillar salesman. Above my bed I pasted the illustrations by Anton Fischer for the sea stories of Guy Gilpatric, and it
never occurred to me to doubt that the *Post* had discovered a titan of
the brush in Norman Rockwell. I am afraid I even pored over the
four-color ads with much the same fascination I now see lavished on
their counterparts on the tube.

When, several years later, we moved to an urban scene, a wider
world unfolded. Just down the street from the soiled classic pillars of
the Carnegie Library—itself a house of wonders—was a cavern
packed to overflowing with an array of periodicals I knew at once
would take me years of browsing to explore. When I was not feeding
yet another fierce appetite, that for the movies at the triple-feature
flea trap nearby (ten cents before 6 P.M., fifteen cents thereafter) I applied myself to this holy calling. I played fair, it seems to me. I made
certain I spent all my carefully hoarded magazine money at Pete's
newsstand, and I solidified my position by minding the store while
he slipped out to the nearest restaurant to grab a sandwich and a cup
of coffee.

Pete was almost as fabulous to me as his wares. He had come to
our golden shores as a young man from Yugoslavia, so English was
his second language. He spoke it, however, with a rich raunchy gusto
acquired in the coal mines he had had to leave after an injury drove
him to a less demanding occupation. A life of hard work and struggle
was written on his dark face and he often broke out with spluttering
denunciations of the coal and steel barons, provoked by the head-
lines of a newly delivered newspaper.

The owner of the stand, although his sympathies were decidedly
in Pete's camp, sometimes had to deliver a mild injunction to his employee to damp down the fire of his invective lest he drive most of the
trade from the stand. In the absence of the boss, however, Pete was
likely to forget his promises. His finest displays were reserved for
anyone brash enough to bespeak a copy of the *Chicago Tribune*, a
newspaper Pete held in special scorn. "For God's sake, man, calm

down," one customer remarked mildly as he threw most of the paper back to him, "I only get the damn thing for the sports section."

Fred's appreciation for reading and writing led to a journalism major at Marshall College and then a job on the local Huntington paper. From his meager pay of $15 a week he saved enough for an annual visit to New York where he would go to a museum in the morning, a foreign movie in the afternoon, and the theatre or opera in the evening, every day for as long as he could afford to stay—usually a week.

This life did not go on for long. When Fred registered for the draft, he was classified 4-F because of nearsightedness. But after Pearl Harbor, December 7, 1941, the armed forces became less fussy, and Fred was able to enlist in the Air Force on December 8. He had nearly four years of ground duty, two of them in England, until he was demobilized in August 1945. After a week in Huntington and turning down an offer from the Associated Press to be their West Virginia reporter at $45 a week, he came up to New York in September to go to college on the G. I. Bill and $1,500 he had saved while in the service.

For me, breaking my left arm at four is memorable because my older sister Rosemary read stories especially to me, a treat, since she had four younger siblings. That same year I caught diphtheria, and one of my clear memories from 1927 is my sorrow when my mother, on doctor's orders, had to burn all the books I had in my sick bed. Rosemary taught me the alphabet and numbers before I started school—no kindergartens in 1928 Oxford, Massachusetts—so that I was indeed in high anticipation of learning to read when I began first grade.

All during that time, the town library was my favorite place. Those were Depression years, so it was open only on Tuesday, Thursday, and Saturday. I was limited to checking out two books at a time, but even so, by the age of eleven I had completed the children's room and been admitted to the adult section—books selected for me by the librarian. She confined her choices, however, to the saccharine romances of Grace Livingston Hill.

Ever since then, libraries have had special significance in my life. In my large family of three older sisters, three younger brothers, and a youngest sister, we had only a few books my mother grew up with such as Children's Stories from Dickens with its account of the death of Jo the cross-

ing sweeper that always made me weep. There were no bookstores in Oxford, nor in the town we lived in when I went to high school, West Mystic, Connecticut. I doubt I would have visited a bookstore anyway, since I had no money.

I had an unsettling experience with a library during my high school years. My father, a Republican and a Catholic, listened every night to the radio commentary by Fulton Lewis, Jr. It might well have been from this program that I caught wind of the furor surrounding the publication in 1939 of Steinbeck's Grapes of Wrath. I asked Dad about this book and he told me that he had heard that Steinbeck's portrayal of the farm workers was full of coarse and vulgar language. "I go to the toilet three times a day, but if I were writing a book, I wouldn't find it necessary to put that in."

My curiosity thoroughly aroused, I went to our town librarian, elderly Miss Fish, when I did not find Steinbeck on the shelf. She looked severely at me. "The Library Board reviewed that book and decided it was not the kind of book we want in our library." A chill came over that room and over my spirit. I never went back to the Mystic Library again.

From high school I went to teachers college in 1940—the only college in Connecticut with no tuition. The other factor in my being able to go was the improvement in the depressed economy because of defense industries. Employment rose so that part-time jobs for college students became available. And I had to work; my family's support lay in letting me go and not requiring me to get a job and contribute to the household income. I landed in Willimantic, Connecticut, site of the teachers college, with $23 and my mother's old Gladstone bag for my clothes. Throughout college, I worked for my room, board, and books.

I started there the week after my seventeenth birthday. College was a revelation, and I replaced my Catholic and Republican outlook with the left perspective of my new friends and the faculty. There was a shortage of grammar school teachers so we were put on an accelerated no-summer-off schedule and I graduated in December 1943. I had no intention of teaching and getting stuck in some small town where all of a wretched salary would go for living expenses. Instead, I went back home for a year as an electrician in the submarine shipyard at Groton in order to make money to go to graduate school. Early in 1945, I joyfully made the move to the magnet for many aspiring young people, New York, and Columbia University for a master's degree in economics.

I met Fred at Columbia that September, a week after he arrived in New York, and we were married in 1946. He got a job at the United Nations. I worked in the public relations section of the United Electrical, Radio, and Machine Workers Union (UE) while completing the writing of my thesis. Three years later, Fred decided to use the G.I. Bill to see some of the world, and we joined friends who had gone to Mexico to school. We had two years in Mexico City, Fred as an M.A. student in history and I as a reporter on a little tourist paper. This was followed by two years in London where Fred got a Ph.D. in Latin American history, while I worked in the American Survey section of The Economist weekly and also did economic reports on Latin America for their business research section, The Economist Intelligence Unit (EIU).

Our move to Berkeley in 1954 came about as a result of a trip to Paris at Christmas 1951 to visit my brother Bob Herbert, then a Fulbright fellow in the field of art history. On our way back to London we crossed the channel in a terrible gale. We had both taken Dramamine so I was able to concentrate on the ever-present book, in this case Emma by Jane Austen. Bill Rouverol, a young Berkeley professor, was on that ship with his wife Bea, and later told us he had to meet someone who could read Jane Austen in a raging storm. We all broke the usual rule of young Americans abroad of never speaking to other Americans, and by voyage's end were learning how much we had in common.

The friendship that began on that trip flourished, and in 1952, when the Rouverols returned to Berkeley from a year at Oxford, they started a campaign to get us to come there. They argued that California was a logical choice for teaching opportunities in Latin American history. Neither of us had ever been to California, but its reputation for beauty, a fine climate, and room for a range of thought appealed to us.

We arrived in April 1954 on the California Zephyr with two trunks of our possessions and our savings of $854. Once in Berkeley, we made our living through the economic reports I continued for the EIU and by Fred's

temporary jobs, until he was hired to do promotional and marketing work
for a paperback book club in Palo Alto. As for the teaching job he had imag-
ined for himself, here is his description of those days:

It was then I discovered that my own lack of interest in an academic career seemed to be shared by those to whom I offered my
services and, besides, I thought it demeaning to begin such a life by
signing some kind of oath supposedly attesting to my political orthodoxy. So, as I observe is still quite usual among people in similar situations, I thought of opening a bookstore.

This was in the mid-fifties. They were not years when the Republic
was bubbling over with enthusiasm for the strenuous life of the mind,
but it was perhaps a fortunate time to enter the retail book business
because of a new development in publishing. This was the period
when publishers first began to exploit what we call the trade or "quality" paperback. Mass paperbacks had gotten a start at the end of the
thirties but it was not until the fifties that the trade and university
presses began to issue their paperback lines—Anchor, Vintage, Col-
lier, Meridian, Noonday and the rest. The publishers and the book
reviews were brimming with enthusiasm over the phenomenon
which some of them went so far as to call the "paperback revolution."

Well, a good many of the established bookstores were not eager to
spring to the barricades since their commitment was to the hardbound book. This was not entirely because of the price differential
between paperbacks and hardbounds but also because they had difficulty in regarding the paperback as, properly speaking, a book at
all. So they resisted stocking them or grudgingly gave them limited
display. Stores like City Lights in San Francisco and Kepler's in Menlo
Park, however, welcomed the advent of paperbacks as a means of
making books available to a wide audience receptive to literary and
political currents. And they began to prosper as they became known
as bookstores specializing in paperbacks.

Some of this enthusiasm was communicated to me when I met the
owners of those stores while working for a paperback book club and
wholesaler on the Peninsula. When the club went bankrupt that
spring I described my reactions in a letter to my brother-in-law Bob:

"A sturm und drang period of great dimensions has recently occurred with us and the end is not yet. In short and in fine, my friends,
I have no job. The great reorganization took some time to clean the
slate of the old retainers but that proverbial new broom has finally
swept me off into the refuse heap of the non-essential to the new operation, as it is expressed. Well, the tension and stress was nigh making a wreck of me anyway so when I was offered, in a very confused
way, a job at much less pay and of menial aspect, I quit. Later on, it
might have been possible to have a series of negotiations to try to
clarify the muddle of just what the future held for me there, but by
that time the weight of the past finagling was too heavy and I was glad
to get out from under it and leave.

"So now the future lies before us just like the commencement
speeches that soon will restore to brief life the old platitudes that
everyone had thought were dead. We have decided that for us the
future holds the destiny of being small businesspeople. I am under-
taking to shrink myself to the proper dimensions in every way and
we are pushing ahead with plans as quickly as we can. More specifically, the plans are for a small bookshop specializing in paperbacks.
The location is not yet determined. Fortunately, I have a good friend
already operating a successful bookshop (Kepler's Books in Menlo
Park) who is being endlessly helpful in guiding me. Pat will handle
the financial side where I am recognizably somewhat faltering. In
fact, it will be a partnership and when it comes to disbursements of
money and financial policy, she will have veto power. I regard this as
one of the most hopeful portents for the future. Of course I can hear
you saying that we are making a terrible mistake and making fools of
ourselves into the bargain. The lot of the small businessman is hard
and rocky altogether and we will go through the tortures of hell. And
I wouldn't argue with you too much as to the accuracy of the argument. It is probably true. But after surveying all the prospects and
searching our souls this was what we came up with and the die is cast.

"It will take a minimum of $3,000 to start. This we plan to raise by
hook and crook wherever we can. We are going to have very rigid
budgeting for as long as needed. In the home, I mean. I have a place

for you in our organization but I know that you are so busy with your own affairs that you probably haven't time to do much. However, I'll mention it just in case. I wonder if you could take a little time while you are buzzing around Europe to pick up the names, addresses and details of what is produced by outfits that are printing low-price books, prints, etc. No time would be required to look at the stuff but if you could assemble this information as you go around it would be very helpful, since I could then write to the people myself. There are three bookshops in the area who are interested in going together to do as much group buying as possible, thus getting the very best terms. One of the group will be going to New York in the fall and he will grab everything he can. Since we are all non-competitive, it ought to work out pretty well. So far as the more immediate prospects are concerned, I have been surveying possible locations with considerable intensity and have found two that will bear further looking into, I think."

Here is my view on it, from letters we sent to my brother Bob and his wife Fi. Bob was working for his Ph.D. in art history at Yale, specializing in nineteenth-century French art. Fi was getting her Ph.D. in intellectual history.

Meanwhile, back at the ranch house—the book club, after suffering such acute growing pains that an early demise was expected, has passed into the control of "outside interests" whose ideas and principles are very different from those of the original group. They are concentrating on wholesale rather than retail distribution so Fred's job got lost in the shuffle. They offered him a reduced post at reduced pay, but we couldn't see any future in it so he has left them and—o pioneers—on to greater things. He has had a good year's experience there and knows the paperback field thoroughly—so—we are going into business for ourselves. We are going to open a book shop. Fred is busy scouting locations, and we will have the close counsel of a friend who opened one a year ago and has made a success of it. It will deal *only* in paperbacks, also art prints probably. I will do the book-keeping and so on, and Fred will run it—twelve hours a day, seven days a week until it gets going well enough to hire occasional help.

Since we have (naturally) no capital we will have to borrow on personal loans (not "investments" where people might lose) from friends and relatives.

Fred visited several towns in northern California, looking at possible locations. He visited the library in Santa Cruz and discovered the fact that it had one of the highest circulations per capita of any library in the state was a poor omen for the success of a bookstore. This was before the University of California built a campus there, and it was known as a retirement community for those of modest means.

Our friends in Berkeley were, of course, urging that city upon us. They pointed out that there was only one bookstore specializing in paperbacks. Its stock was limited and—fatal flaw in our eyes—was arranged by publisher, for the convenience of the store, rather than by subject, for the convenience of customers. The University, with its very large student body, provided a ready market for a general bookstore, since the student bookstore concentrated on textbooks. And finally, from his work at the wholesaler, Fred knew that American publishing was on the edge of the paperback explosion. At that time there were few "quality" or "trade" paperbacks, as distinct from the mass-market books or "slicks" from Bantam, Dell, Avon, and so on. We got in at the beginning of the paperback phenomenon and the timing had a lot to do with our success.

Later that month—May 1956—Fred wrote to Bob, then in France:

Here, I, Doubleday Brentano Scribner Cody, interrupt. At Pat's suggestion. If I get the location I have in mind it is going to be necessary to work very hard on stocking it with things that are (1) different and (2) things that will sell. In large part the two things chime in together. But as you probably know, Berkeley is one of the livelier towns culturally in America. It has two theaters for art films, a very fine amateur theater group which gives excellent performances of classic plays and opera—their "Marriage of Figaro" in English is said to be a very fine job. Of course, the University is the nucleus for a lot more cultural activity. In short, it has a varied and stimulating cultural program on a year-round basis.

Since it is such a town, naturally the bookshops have proliferated at quite a rate and it would be foolish to open up with more of the same. So every effort has to be made to get in stuff that, because no other shop is featuring it, will bring in trade. Of course, the domestic paperbacks will be a solid stock in trade but they are far from being enough. In any event, there simply won't be space to put in a complete stock of these which would put the shop on a competitive level with others in the town. If you have any friends who have connections in publishing, it is possible that they can come up with the names of export jobbers who offer the wares of European publishers to people over here. These are handy people to deal with because they cut down on the paper work and often do a quicker job than do the publishers themselves. I agree with you, Robert, that some of the smaller art books ought to do well. With an emphasis on the reproductions, rather than the content, although good content won't hurt.

As I see the store, it will have the best-sellers in paperbacks (domestic) and a bang-up order service for those not in stock. We can do this because our jobber for these is just a day away. Then, since the neighborhood is in part a middle-class one, we will try out a table of the best-sellers in hardbound and we'll order those we don't have in stock. In the magazine and periodical line, we will do the ten or fifteen most popular magazines among students (domestic), and for the rest, we will go in very strongly for foreign magazines and periodicals, and domestic quarterlies and such. Children's books will be given special attention.

And finally, we will do all we can in the field of good but inexpensive art books and reproductions of all kinds. That will be our stock, as I see it now. In almost every case, we will be doing something that is either being done very sloppily now or not being done at all. This applies in particular to children's books, foreign paperbacks, inexpensive paperbound art books, reproductions and prints.

I couldn't be more enthusiastic about this venture. As you say, Robert, small business can gobble up all your time and take it out of you. But my buddy who is running the successful shop has slowly built his business to the point where he can now afford to take two afternoons off a week and usually two evenings. He anticipates, after being in business about a year, that another six months should give him more free time and allow a couple of weeks each year in New York to combine business with pleasure on a theater-going, stock-shopping trip. Both Pat and I feel that this is a goal well worth working for.

Looking over your letter again, Bob, I notice that you say everything in France and Italy is cheap and paperbound. Right. So the thing we would want you to keep in mind is what you think will sell in Berkeley, California. These low-price art books are a case in point; so are the editions of the really well known (in the U.S.) French and Italian writers of the present day. And the children's books, too, of course. These should have a very heavy emphasis on illustration preferably.

We had no savings and, in fact, owed the hospital $500 for the delivery of our first child, Martha, in February 1956. I worked at home doing economic reports on Latin American countries for the EIU in London. This brought in some money, but not enough to live on. We borrowed $1,000 each from three friends and from Fred's parents, and took out a loan of $1,000 on Fred's life insurance, for a total of $5,000. By mid-June, Fred had leased a place at 1838 Euclid Avenue on the north side of the University campus. It was small, 16' by 29', on the left street-corner side of a courtyard. Over the door was the marquee for an art film theater inside the courtyard. There was no heat, office, or bathroom space. This first Cody's, where we were to stay for four and a half years of our apprenticeship, is now one corner of a pizzeria.

PART ONE
The Euclid Store

CHAPTER ONE 1956 TO 1957

THE FIRST STORE   BUILDING OUR STOCK   CENSORSHIP
IN DEFENSE OF SMALL BUSINESS

. . . with reference to this habit of reading . . . it is your pass to the greatest, the purest, and the most perfect pleasures that God has created for his creatures. . . . The habit of reading is the only enjoyment I know, in which there is no alloy. It lasts when all other pleasures fade.

ANTHONY TROLLOPE, 1815–1882

These early days are described in letters to Bob and Fi where we brought them up-to-date and, at the same time, it now seems, cheered ourselves up by voicing our plans:

Fred is at Berkeley; the long and torturous negotiations for the lease have finally concluded and he is actually going ahead with fixing the place up. Within two weeks we will be open for business. We are really doing it on a wispy budget, in fact as of now we're only sure of $2,500 of the necessary $4,000 (a bare minimum). Faint-heartedness was never one of our failings so we are ploughing on, and our next weeks will be busy—keeping up with my work, doing the books for the shop, taking care of Martha, and so on. . . .

We moved up from the Peninsula June 30, spent the next week hectically finishing up all sorts of details at the shop, and finally on July 9 at 2 P.M. opened up. Our stock is not complete by a long shot but Fred wanted to open anyhow to start cutting the overhead, no sense sitting around waiting till every last book and card is in place. Considering that a) we didn't do one iota of publicity b) our stock is not at all what it will be—not over 700 titles, no magazines or cards yet, c) it is summer session at the University, 5,000–8,000 students compared to the usual 17,000—we are more than gratified at the results. Location is everything in a shop like ours, and it is clear that we have an excellent one.

As you can imagine, we are frantically busy. Fred is at the shop from 9–6:30 (takes his lunch) and from 7:30–10:30 or 11, six days a week and Sunday from 5 P.M.–10:30, and will continue on that schedule until we make enough to hire some help. Here at home, I do all the bookkeeping for the store, all the letters to publishers, etc., the banking, write my reports for London, take care of Martha, the housework, meals to get, etc.

We will get a portable t-writer for the shop so Fred can write up his orders, publicity, etc., and he will have time to write you. Maybe we will get one for free, if the demonstration we have had of the solidarity of the middle class continues. Every shopkeeper around has been so helpful. One gave us an old counter and also a long counter we use for storing art prints, let us use his electric saw. Another letters our signs for us. Across the way the photographer lends us his electric floor waxer and polisher, and next door, the hamburger place gave us a cash register that is so old it has tone. Fred painted it gold all over to make it look even sillier—it has a Victorian ring to it every time he marks up a sale.

I kept the ledger sheet for our first month in business, July 1956. We opened at 2 P.M. on July 9 and took in $36.18. Our sales for the month, $801.93, led me to write:

We have just concluded the first month of business, and I made up a profit and loss statement which shows that we about broke even, which is much better than we expected for the initial period. We can't wait till the fall term when business should pick up and we can order in a lot more stuff. Then there will be Xmas to get ready for. I think I told you Fred's hours—10 A.M. to 11 P.M. with one hour for supper six days a week. On Sundays he has to go down to Palo Alto in the A.M. to pick up books, and opens shop at 5 P.M., so the only time we see each other is breakfast and supper and then it's mostly to discuss business. Once we are more established of course we can hire some help. But not for awhile, not with this debt we have. . . .

The reference to going to Palo Alto to pick up books needs an explanation, a footnote to the economic history of bookselling. At this time, all the mass-market books—and they were the majority of paperbacks pub-

lished—*were distributed through wholesalers, each of whom had an exclusive territory. Bookstores, unless they were very large and had special muscle, could not buy directly from the publisher at the usual wholesale discount. When we tried to do this we got polite letters back telling us that we should contact our local distributor.*

These distributors gave us a 20% discount. A supermarket can make money on 20% because of their large volume and rapid turnover. The 20% pattern came about because these distributors originally handled just magazines, where the turnover is twelve times a year for monthlies and fifty-two times for weeklies. Unsold copies are cover-stripped, the magazines are thrown away, and the covers are returned for credit. Paperback books, with publishers issuing eight or ten new titles monthly (books out of copyright, or especially commissioned, or rights purchased from the hardback publisher) were treated the same way. They came "on the rack" every month, just as the magazines did, had thirty days to sell, and were pulled and stripped at the end of the month to make room for the new ones.

But we were not a supermarket. We did not want a lot of the trashy paperbacks. We needed the quality book and access to the back list for steady supplies. We needed a 40% discount. If we had to pay 80¢ for a book we sold for $1, we ran at a loss: our rent, supplies, phone, electricity, and survival wages cost us at least 35¢. Our response to the publishers who refused to sell directly to us was, to say the least, quixotic. Our pride would not let us open an account with the distributor. So, we got our friend Roy Kepler of Kepler's Books in Menlo Park, who did have an account with the distributor in his area at a slightly better than 20% discount, to order for us, too. The book club for which Fred had worked, Paper Editions, had become a wholesaler of the few but growing quality paperback lines available. So, on Sunday mornings Fred would drive down and visit both the wholesaler and Kepler's to get our supply of books for the week.

Late in September, Fred wrote:

Having labored like a slave in this bookstore for the past umpteen hours I am in a nice relaxed mood to write you a line or two. I am having some difficulty in retaining my conviction that Books Are Important. After you pack and unpack and order and re-order and watch the fads make the trash go—well, it is a chastening and bewildering experience. I have much to do across the counter with students of some divinity schools nearby. And there are times when I wonder whether they exercise Christian forbearance on everyone but booksellers. Still, they buy so we love them.

In fact, business goes better each week so we have few complaints money-wise. We are getting lots of dollar prints and posters from Marboro and they sell as fast as they come in. Lautrec and Vincent are the boys but Chagall, Klee and even Seurat do well. Very advanced crowd. Retarded types buy the bullfight posters upon each of which I spit as I send it out of the store. I wish you would look out for very good silk screen prints for me. I have two now from the Museum of Fine Arts, Boston, which are lovely—Van Gogh "House at Auvers" and Daumier's "Horseman." Prices twelve and fifteen bucks. Should go well at Christmas.

I shared Fred's optimism in a November letter:

The store is going along well. Christmas trade started in earnest this week and we hope it keeps up so we can pile up a little capital to invest in expanding our stock, which has been our big problem. As a new business, a lot of places wouldn't give us credit and when you have to wait till you sell something before you have money to buy it, well, you see where it leads. Fred is a born bookstore proprietor if ever I saw one, he has a real knack for picking things that will sell, and then promoting them in original ways; and also he is something of a novelty in Berkeley, a bookstore owner who knows something about books. We are building a regular roster of faithful customers.

Sales for our first six months in business, July through December 1956, totalled $10,031. As the new year began, I wrote:

Our accountant, Abe Brumer, went over our status as of January 1, after six months of operations. He is a friend as well as professional counselor. He told us that when we first talked with him (early October) he didn't think we'd make a go of it—I guess because he's seen so many struggling retailers, and of course we are woefully undercapitalized. He now says—"you're doing much better than I thought you could—you're a going enterprise." Of course we knew that but it was good to learn that there weren't some awful traps I had forgotten. He said most new businesses lose money the first year—not only have we avoided that, but we've lived off the store for six months. Of course we couldn't have if I weren't working, and the general prosperity in the U.S. has helped. Who knows, we might get back east next year for a visit. . . . Right now we are reinvesting everything we can since our sales volume is directly proportionate to our stock. Then we have to start repayment on our debts in June. By March 1959 we will be out of debt.

In March 1957 I wrote:

Yesterday I thought I would give Fred a rest, so I worked at the store in the daytime and left him with Martha. It was very salutary for me, I didn't realize what a tremendous amount of work he has to do. Even when people aren't there, there are lots of little things to do so you are on the go—and on your feet—most of the day. I'm still exhausted from it.

But one nice redeeming feature—in the mail came a shipment from the New York Graphic Society. They had sent us their catalog on the UNESCO series of national art, so we took a chance and ordered one of the books—*Norway* ($16.50)—and separate plates from the other books. In the first place, we picked very well because the book is just terrific, if you haven't seen it, when you get near a bookstore or library do so. Well, it is such a gigantic thing that I had it on the counter for lack of a better place, and a woman who came up with an armload of books noticed it, and looked at the separate plates I showed her, and just like that bought five of them (at $1.95 each) to make a total sale of $18. Well that may not sound like much but we seldom get such a big sale; usually it takes three hours or so to take in that much, so I was very pleased, also happy to have our judgment confirmed. We had bought them on the chance people would like them, which meant tying up our money in a risk venture.

Fred was equally sanguine:

The store goeth its way. We have pretty well stocked the thing now and built up the take so that it ought to go along fairly well. Our latest acquisition is the Modern Library and now we just haven't space for much of anything else. People—at least some people—complain that the joint is crowded. But they still come back and they buy so what the hell? I enjoy fooling around in the store and the hours, long as they are, go pretty quickly. And I enjoy listening to the kids rattle off their learned opinions about everything under the sun. They remind me so much of myself when young that sometimes I'm between tears and laughter listening to them.

About time to give out a bulletin: progressing satisfactorily. We started out during our early days pulling in a gross of thirty-five to forty bucks a day. We are now up to an average of around eighty. It is true that we have too much in the place and it is a little cluttered. But people seem to like to prowl around in the corners so it doesn't seem to hurt much.

Come this summer, I hope and plan to open at noon and close at ten in the evening. This will give me a couple of hours in the morning to put in at writing. I still harbor the delusion that I will be able to turn out something a publisher will regard as humor and I'm determined to try this summer to test the hypothesis. I hope to get a room away from the house to do this. I'd do it in the store but there is no hiding place in there with all them windows.

Fred never did get around to writing that summer. The store was too demanding. But his urge did not fade. And much later, when we had help and the store was stronger financially, he did get the time.

Within a year, we managed to get the mass-market distributor to give us a 25% discount, so with the thought that we could later push that up even more, we began to deal with them and end the punishing round-trips on Sundays to Menlo Park after what was already a sixty-hour week.

We also began importing books from France and Germany. Looking back I have an appreciation for the spirit that moved us in trying to make that cracker-box of a place into a true window on the world. Neither of us read French or German, but the idea was to have a sampling of the classics in those languages anyway. We did not try to keep up with contemporary European publishing.

Among the books Fred ordered, almost as a joke, was Aphrodite by Pierre Louÿs, considered a bit daring in the 1890's but very staid by 1957 standards. Imagine our perplexity when we received a letter from U.S.

Customs telling us that the books had been seized as obscene and would be returned to France within thirty days. We had no money for lawyers, and besides, we thought the American Civil Liberties Union would like something a bit lighter than the cases they usually dealt with, so we told our story to them. They wrote to Customs and also told the San Francisco Chronicle *about it. In response, we got a story in the paper, and our books, as well as a letter that was a marvel of bureaucratese:*

Treasury Department
Bureau of Customs
April 10, 1957

American Civil Liberties Union
Attn: Mr Ernest Besig
Re: Mr. William F. Cody, Our Case No. 3104

Reference is made to your letter of April 8, 1957, relative to the detention of three copies of a book entitled *Aphrodite* by Pierre Louys under section 305 of the Tariff Act of 1930.

You are advised that the initial detention was made on a translation accomplished by a customs translator in the Customs Mail Division. Upon receipt of your letter further translation by another customs translator was accomplished and additional consideration was given to the books.

We did not agree unanimously that the books were unquestionably obscene. They are, therefore, being submitted to the Bureau of Customs in Washington, D.C., for their opinion.

You will be notified of the Bureau's reply.

There was, however, a more serious attempt at censorship. Here is my letter on the subject to Bob:

We sent you a press clipping on the Customs seizure of some books we ordered, didn't we? That was part of an entire story unfolding here. Prior to it, Customs seized *Howl,* a long poem published by a fellow bookseller in S.F. and printed in England, and a magazine, *Miscellaneous Man,* published in Berkeley by a poet, very avant garde, also printed in UK to save money. The Customs in Washington ordered the fools here to release these publications. Then, the censorship forces (who they are hasn't come out) went to U.S. Attorney here, but he refused to act. So, the local S.F. police—and of all divisions, the *juvenile* bureau took it up. Yesterday our friend the bookseller and his clerk were arrested for selling *Miscellaneous Man* and *Howl,* on the grounds they were obscene, and not fit for children to read.

Quite a furor, with lead editorial, cartoon and book review column in *S.F. Chronicle* vigorously angry over it. ACLU taking it up. Police say they have list of "other" books but waiting to see court outcome of this case. Today Fred fixed up a window display of *Decameron,* Sartre, etc., entitled "Not fit for children to read." I'll bet we're the only booksellers in town to do anything about it. The paper said that in several large bookstores in S.F., the offending poem was removed by the stores the day after the story broke. Some guts, huh?

Fred's remarks on other concerns we had in mid-1957:

Well, the old store is undergoing many changes. I am going in much stronger for the cheaper paperbacks and the place is lousy with greeting cards. This is not as bad as it sounds. The flippant studio cards have a terrific profit margin and enable the books to survive— yes, it almost comes to that. In addition, I have now established connections with the wholesale distributor of paperbacks (the cheaper ones) in the area and will be able to offer a much more complete selection and service on them than before—having refused to deal with them up to now because of the low mark-up.

Business-wise, May does not promise to be a very good month. Many of the grad students are bearing down now and even the undergrads are making last desperate attempts to stage comebacks. So it may be fairly slim pickings. Basically, however, we continue to feel optimistic about the store. It has been rough on both of us—not just me—because Pat does ordering and the bookkeeping, which is tough. Still, I think we both have gotten a lot of satisfaction out of building the thing and making it go.

I now conclude with a brace of titles from Berkley and Pyramid Books which are the nadir of the nadir in the paperbacks: *Strange Friends, Creep into thy Narrow Bed* (please, don't forget that comma),

Drinkers of Darkness, Give Me a Little Something, Sex Is Better in College, Passion in the Pines, The Pickup, and *Warped Women.*

Excerpts from Fred's letters in July and August:

Well, Bob, I'm afraid the great Cody is not doing much writing so far. The hell of it has been that I haven't been able to arrange with anyone to work on a regular schedule in the mornings which is when I need the time. In addition, the store has very perversely decided to do better business this summer than it did during part of the regular term time when all the students were here. And then there is a tremendous lot to do, going after books and putting them up, and selling and all the rest of it.

Don't get me wrong, I enjoy it, perhaps I even enjoy it too much for what is in it. Our stock is burgeoning. Dear old Doubleday offered delivery now on orders with billing on January 1/58 and we took advantage of that. Then I am dickering with a knowledgeable gal in the Berkeley art world to act as agent in putting in a fairly good selection of graphic art stuff by local people—and most of it at a modest price. We have lots of wall space and I think this will, if handled properly, go well at Christmas. And of course it will also be on consignment. A chance to help local artists, as well as ourselves.

Well, after a hard day at the store jiggling with the books and lights, I should be reclining for a short siesta or out watering the lawn, or cutting it for that matter, or doing a hundred other things besides writing you a letter. But I feel like writing so I will, and let all those fine chores go to hell. Anent the subject of jiggling the lights: I have never been satisfied with the lighting of the store and I guess I never will. Of course, it would really take a patch of coin to fix it up properly and I continually jiggle because I am trying to accomplish miracles with a faulty foundation. Still, I bestirred myself today and flooded the window fluorescently with a big long tube and then I twisted my spots around and replaced them. I suppose it is better. At least it's different.

You will be pleased to hear that I STILL haven't put up a sign, electric or otherwise. There is a salesman who comes around at three month intervals and talks signs. Fortunately for the budget, he is one of the most supercilious prigs I have ever encountered and every time I talk to him I stop wavering about a sign and decide that I'll NEVER have one of the damn things.

School starts late this year but business has been sooo very good this summer that it may just keep on right through the rest of this month and into September. Now you would think that good business is a fine reason for being certain about a vacation but if business is good, then the tendency is to stick right close so as to make certain that it is better. Which only goes to show that Pat's warnings (given on various occasions) that business is altering my attitudes somewhat are probably well based. Of course, my contention is that perhaps some of my attitudes needed changing anyway.

I am a hound on promoting the new paperbacks as they come out. And I hate to be away during the debutante time for these things which is latter August and up to mid-September. Pushing the new *Peanuts* now and happy to say that we did sixteen copies yesterday. A few books like that certainly help to pay the rent. Coming is *The Organization Man,* Anchor, $1.45, which ought to be another very hot number, indeed. We just received a batch of the new Dramabooks whose publisher is doing a bang-up job.

You should see the art books we are going to have on the shelves this Christmas season. All the Abrams books are being stocked—we get them on full return privileges and January billing. So we'll have all those wonders. Then we'll have the less expensive Skiras, the new Praegers, including the two new $5.75s which are such tremendous bargains. Other developments in the store: big stocking of French, German, Italian and Spanish paperbacks. Big stock of Christmas greetings with emphasis on museum and European cards—many of them at only a nickel, complete with envelope. Well, I tell you, Cody's is going to be a doggy place this fall and winter and I don't think it's too much to say that we've done ourselves proud. Oh yes, we'll have a big bunch of kids' books from England with a sprinkling of the better domestic product. Also Maurie has been helping me on his day off with new shelves, and we've invented some inexpensive racks that are joys to behold. He suggested we try using bolts with wing nuts on the back and with a few extra holes it makes the shelving completely adjustable. Maurie got a Skil saw and also an electric drill. I saw and he drills and we have a fine old time.

In September:

We're facing a real space problem with the store. The place is packed with stuff now and I've had to put racks in the damndest places. I'm hoping to have special outside racks built which can be locked at night. If these plans go through, it should relieve the congestion somewhat since we'll move the "slicks" outside and give more space and display to the higher price paperbacks and to the hardbounds now being stocked.

We've really gone all out on Christmas cards and I think we've got by far the best selection in town. One of the salesmen for the "studio cards" was around the other day and was surprised and offended when I said I thought he ought to drop a card which said, "May the bluebird of happiness crap on your Christmas tree." "Our best-seller," he said. "We have them for birthdays and Easter, too," he said. These cards are the damndest thing. We have a big rack outside now that is filled with little five-cent cards carrying such remarks as "I'm fascinated by work: I can sit and watch it for hours." Believe it or not, we sell three or four dollars worth of these a day.

Speaking of best-sellers, we are right in the national picture these days: our three big sellers are *Peyton Place, The Organization Man,* and *Good Ol' Charlie Brown.* Here, the Peanuts strip is amazingly popular. We've sold two hundred of the latest book and still going strong. Our German paperbacks are much stronger now, and we have a lot of French books coming from Hachette.

The fall season must have kept us so busy that I did not write Bob and Fi again until November:

The short-lived preseasonal slump has ended and we are up to our ears in Christmas cards, big fat art books, and so on. We've done more desperate rearranging of shelving to try to get a few more quarts into our pint, so we really haven't any more room at all, and use spare corners of the house as our stockroom. A few weeks ago we had about 100 French books under the bed.

That reminds me, we are now dealing direct with Hachette, instead of as before through French and European Publications of NYC. Consequently we are selling Gallimard, Garnier, etc. cheaper than anyone else in the U.S.—Livre de Poche for 50¢ and 80¢, and Pourpre for 75¢ for example. Books that we used to get from F & E to retail at $1.65 (our discount 1/3) we now retail at $1.25 after taking a 40% discount. One reason for that is that we pass on to our customers the devaluation of the franc but F & E doesn't. Well, aside from that, I want to tell you that never in our dealings with anyone domestic or foreign have we received such incredibly good service. I could go into ecstasies over it. I sent them an order on the twelfth September; acknowledgement the seventeenth; first shipment the twentieth; invoices in triplicate with multi-lingual notes on them; separate accounting for every title not shipped; and everything arrived by the middle of October, well packaged and undamaged.

In December, Fred wrote:

I gather from remarks scattered through family letters that ole Fred is now regarded as a benighted Babbitt lost forever to the great and aspiring things of this world and consigned eternally to the lower depths. Well, in a sense this is so, I suppose. The fact is that the store does take a hell of a lot of time. It is a mass of trivial detail for the most part that must be attended to or at least time must be allowed for sweeping it in the properly crafty way under the rug. The great question is whether just more than a year of it can completely undermine the habits of thought and general attitudes of a lifetime. I don't think so but who knows?

My contention has been and still is that as the store makes more money I will be able to hire help and then I can have time for things like letter writing and gallery going and the rest. It's quite true that a business grows upon what it doth feed upon and that it becomes very difficult not to get carried away by the momentum which builds up. However, I feel very grateful for this experience as a store proprietor.

It has taught me a great deal. It has also made me a more responsible person in the sense that it has forced me into a very sober routine and into organizing my time and my work much more efficiently than I have ever done in the past. All to the good, I think.

We had hoped that we could come east next year and it may be yet that I will fly east for the American Booksellers Association meeting which is being held in that old cultural center, Atlantic City. The main object would be to go through the trade part of the ABA meeting which is very good now and then to leave that place right away since I have no interest in hearing all the department store bookstore managers give their annual brags about how they sold out on *Auntie Mame*. But the ABA does have a good bunch of exhibits where a store like ours can pick up stuff that is off the beaten track. In any event, Pat couldn't make it this year with the new baby. So we will be looking forward most enthusiastically to a visit from you.

In 1957 our total sales were $30,364.

BEST-SELLERS FOR 1956
Camus, *The Fall*
Greene, *The Quiet American*
Whyte, *The Organization Man*

BEST-SELLERS FOR 1957
Cozzens, *By Love Possessed*
Rand, *Atlas Shrugged*
Packard, *The Hidden Persuaders*

But be that he were a philosophre
Yet hadde he but litel gold in cofre;
But al that he might of his frendes hente,
On bookes and his lernyng he it spent.
GEOFFREY CHAUCER, c. 1342–1400

When I look back at the Euclid store, I marvel that Fred could do so much to make a silk purse from that sow's ear. He got wonderfully enthusiastic about new books and wanted so much to communicate that interest to others. Here is his report on our first major promotion, which took place in April 1958.

Store promotion will be engrossing during the next two weeks. We are having a salute to Evergreen books and I have two organized events, the first of which is arranged. At the first, Barney Rosset, publisher of the books, will speak with a panel that includes local authors, Mark Schorer and James Schevill. The store will be lousy with Evergreen books and posters and circulars and pictures of authors. The whole thing should be fun in a peculiar kind of way. It's the first time I've done something like this so I'm suffering a bad case of stage fright over it. If it does go well, I will plan more things like it during the summer and for next fall.

After the events:

Our Evergreen promotion went off pretty well, I think. I personally don't think that it had an entirely satisfactory effect in promoting Evergreen titles. A good many of them are rather specialized and it is difficult to get people to look at more than the covers. However, it certainly did increase sales of their Reviews and of *The Subterraneans,* that awful book. I really went all out, though, and the result was that April business has been very good so that the promotion and the fuss it raised probably helped a lot more generally than it did in the case of the books featured.

The front window was given over to Evergreens; then I used the back wall to feature photos of authors, posters, and so on. On two big racks across the front of the store, we had every Evergreen in print with more posters. The half-page ad in the *Daily Cal* was plastered around. This ad, botched the first time by the omission of the artwork, was re-run gratis, with the cuts, so that we had a break through the awful incompetence of the university daily staff.

Then our meeting attracted about sixty people and we had a very good session. Rosset, publisher of Evergreens, is a very nice guy and so is his sales manager, Fred Jordan, who was also out. After the meeting we planted ourselves in our back patio and had beers and schmoozed for hours until it was time for them to make their plane. They were genuinely impressed by what we had done, and we've had a really fine letter from Jordan thanking us. In May, I will do somewhat the same kind of a promotion for New Directions books but on a more modest scale. Working in a small space, I tend to do too much with promotion, I suppose, but I would much rather do too much than not enough. I think, though, we are building the impression that the store is a lively one that really enjoys featuring books instead of just putting the damned things on the shelf and waiting. There should be a story with pictures in *Publishers Weekly* on the Evergreen promotion and if and when it appears we'll send you a copy.

The month of March, as I may have mentioned, was for the birds and I have had to put myself back on a pretty rigid schedule to recoup. It has been rough not to have a little more time off during the *frühlingstimme*. There is nothing like that old monster necessity to drive one on. The Great Question is whether summer will hold up. Ever the optimist, I am inclined to think it will now that we have the courtyard patio restaurants going full tilt and the movie theater has begun to book some movies that do more than draw disgruntled sneers from the passers-by.

Our son, Anthony Martin, was born in June 1958, and his crib joined Martha's bed in the room next to my office at home, where I did all the store business as well as my economic reports for London. We lived only three blocks from a business district in the low-rent flatlands, so I could walk to the bank with my store deposit tucked under the blanket in the stroller. Just after Anthony came, I wrote to the Herberts:

Store business has been going very well lately, and although September–February is the top half of the year for us, we are through the worst months (March, April). Summer last year held up well since although the university population drops from 19,000 to perhaps 6,000, the latter are in good part teachers and other adults who buy twice as many books as the under-grads. Financially, we are keeping afloat but only just—with income tax (I can get apoplectic about that), new baby, repayment of debt, and so on, we are in the usual small business position of a shortage of working capital. However, we're quite used to the idea that it is a continual struggle, and that we needn't expect to be in a position where we will have a backlog in the bank so that we can pay bills on time, for quite a while. It doesn't bother our puritan ethos as much as it did before our accountant got us used to the idea.

Financial difficulties continued, but we brightened our shop with innovative merchandise. Into that small store we crowded French books and German art calendars, one of the first stores in the U.S. to carry them. In those days, the only wall calendars were those given out by the local dry cleaner or perhaps a major corporation. We began to import art calendars directly from Germany. The Germans had not yet reached this market so the calendars were only in German. No matter. The quality of the reproductions and the variety available were outstanding, and we were certainly the first store in northern California to carry them. At the same time, Fred scouted out art Christmas cards that we could sell for 5¢ each. From a letter I wrote in October 1958:

During the weeks I don't have articles to do, I get caught up on store work. The August slump continued and even deepened for the first half of September so that we were really scared and wondering if the recession had finally hit us. I won't have you cliff-hanging, business did pick up and the last three weeks have been very good. However, it's a good thing we had the bank loan renewed or we would have been up the creek. By next summer when you come out again, we will be able to take off some time, for we finish our debt repayment schedule (aside from recent bank loan) in June and won't be quite as pressed—at least we won't if I can rein in some of Fred's dreams of glory on expansion of stock or premises. Our big shipment of French books is starting to arrive. Fred gets as excited over them as if it were Christmas and these were his presents. German art calendars also arriving—breathtaking.

Here is a remembrance Fred wrote many years later:

I was always enchanted by the profusion of catalogs and promotional material sent us by the German wholesale book distributors. They came in huge long over-size envelopes and, despite the fact that I never ordered more than paperbacks and these in very small quantities, there were elaborate catalogs from all the publishers, the most impressive being the gorgeous announcements of art books from Dumont and Hatje. I only had to spend a moment to translate the German price into dollars and cents to realize, with dismay, that they were far beyond my meagre resources. So I contented myself with ordering the lovely little Insel books and the superb little volumes published in the Piper series.

I made it a practice when I found a bundle of this material from Germany in the morning mail never to open it at the store. It gave me a pleasure almost indescribably intense to take it home with me and, after dinner, to open it and go through the tempting treasure during the course of a quiet evening. That was how I stumbled on the Kalendarliste in 1958.

It came as a total surprise to me that the Germans seemed to have ransacked the human mind for the purpose of matching a calendar—or a flood of them—to every interest and taste. There were scenic calendars, calendars for mountain climbers and winter ski enthusiasts, calendars for children and housewives, calendars for musicians, dancers, photographers and for architects. But what made my pulse race were the Kunstkalendars—column after column of listings.

Each of the art book publishers did calendars that were anthologies in calendar form of plates from their books. There were the calendars for many of the great art periods and movements—Renaissance, Baroque, Klassisch, Impressionisten, etc. Then there were calendars with reproductions of the work of major artists—Dürer, Rembrandt, Brueghel, Picasso, Matisse, Klee. . . . They were published in all sizes and prices from the slim Michel calendars at less than a dollar to huge, closer-to-poster size "magnums" which would have to sell for ten. Along with the lists came full color promotion pieces describing the calendars in detail and, often, with reproductions of some of the pictures.

We had to have calendars—there was no doubt of it. Far into the night I worked, marking up the list. The next morning I handed it to Pat to "figure up" the total and went blithely off to work. Her voice was tense when she called me in the early afternoon. "You won't believe it," she said, "if we did that order it would come to nearly five thousand dollars."

I was struck dumb.

"You can cut it when you get home," she said.

It was an evening of torture and anguish. It had seemed to me that my quantities, if they erred, had been in a conservative direction. But I bravely cut and I was, it seemed to me, especially severe with the higher-priced calendars. Finally, I handed the revised order over to Pat. Her fingers flew over the adding machine and, at the end of an hour, she grimly announced that I had succeeded only in cutting the order in half. So, because we had agreed it could not go over a thousand dollars, I again set to work on the task and, finally, the mutilated remnant of the original order was ready to be sent off to Germany.

Months later the cartons arrived—packed so expertly not a single calendar had been damaged on their long journey (no one, but no one, knows how to ship books better than the Germans). I opened a few packages and excitedly inspected a few of the calendars and then decided it would be impossible to "receive" the order properly in the store.

That exquisite labor was reserved for that evening at home after I had bundled them into the back of the car. As always, pricing of imported publications generated a delicate and prolonged debate. Perhaps what made pricing so difficult for me was that we were on a very slender budget ourselves. We were always looking at the price of books and now the calendars in terms of what we might find irresistible so far as price was concerned. The result was that we found ourselves painfully arriving at a price for each calendar, sometimes haggling with each other over differences of no more than five or ten cents. But at last the job was done and a month or so later—the day after Thanksgiving—I took them to the store to put them on display. (It's now common practice to begin displaying calendars in October. It seemed to us that this was, for a number of reasons, absurd. It still does.)

At this point, I nearly gave in to despair. How in the name of God was I ever going to display them now that I had them? There was nothing to be done except to start "spining" paperbacks to clear the top shelves. I also jammed a couple of card tables on to the floor on which I piled sample copies of the calendars.

I now found that I was going to have to keep the larger calendars in reserve. It took only a few inspections to give them a frayed and rumpled shopworn look. This worked fairly well, although, having no stock room, I had to sacrifice precious space behind the register to stock them.

But oh how they sold! They were indisputably a hit, a most palpable hit. With practically no advertising except for word of mouth, the customers streamed in to make their selections. By Christmas we had sold all but the display copies. And they went when I offered to sell them at one-third off.

From then on calendars were the biggest feature of our Christmas season. Encouraged by the growing demand, we upped the order each year and the selection as well as the size of the order increased. "I haf never," said one elderly lady staring about her, "seen zo many calendars, even in Chermany." My heart nearly burst with pride.

But even with calendars the Euclid Avenue store limped along, taking in just enough to keep going but never enough to be a success.

Perhaps most irritatingly, many of the people who were our regulars liked it that way. They were very fond of a bookstore that was cozy and it pleased them that the selection of books was small. "I don't like," one woman said, "those big stores: all those books to choose from! It confuses me."

It was also true, I guess, that the store, for those who really liked books, was entertaining. Every time they came by they were likely to find that we were pushing a new paperback discovery. When Dell put Brian Moore's *Judith Hearne* into paperback I was jubilant. I made placards with quotes from reviews, filled the window with it, and tried to wheedle everyone who entered the store into buying a copy. The book still sticks in my mind as a portrait of a wan and desperately deprived woman. I felt that anyone who read it could never see an unmarried woman in her middle years as that cruel cliché "the old maid." I suppose that, in the period of a month or so, we sold fifty copies of *Judith Hearne* and people did come back to talk with me about it in terms of the highest praise.

Then there was Grove. It's hard to recall now how exciting Grove and its paperback line Evergreen seemed in the late fifties and early sixties. Barney Rosset had come into publishing like a hurricane. The books poured out—Genet, Ionesco, Beckett, Henry Miller gone public, the uncensored *Lady Chatterley* . . . The yahoos and the bluenoses mounted the attack but Grove went into court to bear the horrendous expense of fighting the good fight.

By and large, it never seemed to me then or later that Grove (and Rosset) got the measure of support or credit for its publishing policy that it deserved. Perhaps it was because Grove revived and put into mass circulation some of the underground classics of Victorian porn like *My Secret Life*. I'm sure Rosset didn't take such books very seriously and, in fact, probably considered them little more than amusing erotic literary curiosities. But they offered a convenient bludgeon for attacking Grove when, in a number of instances, it was the entire approach Rosset brought to publishing that was the real target of the assaults.

Anyway, I was on fire with enthusiasm for what Grove was doing.

We strained our limited budget to stock the books as heavily as possible. Evergreens were so prominently displayed everywhere in the store that some people said we ought to change the name to the Evergreen Book Store.

In the same period, Lawrence Ferlinghetti's City Lights Books was making turbulent waves in the courts and elsewhere with Allen Ginsberg's *Howl*. We filled the window with it and featured it prominently. I felt a chill when a Berkeley police officer came into the store and said, "I notice you're featuring that book," but we went on displaying it.

Those were the days—it seems difficult to believe—when books like *Howl* and the uncensored version of *Lady Chatterley* were still being treated as under-the-counter porn by most stores. They kept the books in stock but copies of the Lawrence or Ginsberg, when asked for, were delivered to the customer in a brown paper wrapper. I guess you could say that Rosset and Grove must be given a major share of credit for taking such books out of wrappers.

By that November, we were making more new plans that I described in a letter:

Things are better at the store after a sorry September, and a disappointing October, that is, we are running ahead of last year, which we've been counting on. We got quite a few of the publishers to kick in on the new shelving. Also, we are having another full-page ad (with Kepler and City Lights) in the *Chronicle* on Sunday, November 30. We have done well with the French books and the German art calendars—they're terrific. The Hachette man was in the U.S. and stopped to see Fred. We now have a standing order arrangement for new Livre de Poche, Prix Goncourt, and other publishers.

We ended that year with sales only marginally improved from 1957. The 1958 total was $32,525. Nineteen fifty-nine was a better year. In fact, we made enough to hire some part-time help, a graduate student from the nearby theological school. Fred described the change in letters in February and March.

Well, business has picked up as expected and the season of hope and joy is at hand. It was unfortunate that your visit caught me at a time when the store was bound to be in the doldrums. However, it has made the expected recovery, and we are in great hopes that we can pay off all the bills and relax this summer. And also have time for work of our own. I grow more and more enthused about the prospects for the paperbacks. Did you see the big supplement that the *Herald-Tribune* got out on paperbacks? Thirty some pages it was and crammed with ads. When this orphan branch of publishing can support this kind of a supplement it must be going places. My fondest hopes are reserved for the lower-priced paperbacks, such as Dell, Bantam, Pocket, NAL and others. They are now going into the school market with a vengeance and doing tremendous books. For sheer delight and pleasure in the looking-at, touch and feel of books, I commend to you the Dell *Wings of the Dove* and the Bantam *Two Years Before the Mast,* the latter having a cover design that is the epitome of grace and elegance. I have been pressing both on all customers that I can and they are moving. I have dipped again into *Two Years* and what a wonderful book it is—perhaps the freshest, sweetest, purest book ever written by an American.

My hope is that these lower-price paperbacks will win such a wide public that eventually it will be possible for them to be sold to bookstores at a discount that will allow them to be given even wider distribution. If only, somehow, the paperbacks could make headway in some of the more backward sections of the country where, incidentally, they are needed most—then we would begin to have a really lively cultural milieu in this country. But then so many other things would have to happen to make it so. Still, despite everything, I have confidence that these little books can do a hell of a lot. I was so delighted with what a lab worker said who took *Two Years* on my determined recommendation. "What a fine book," she said. "Whenever I feel tired or worried, I pick it up and read another chapter." I don't suppose that Dana would have thought much of his book being a kind of pick-you-up but isn't that what most good books are?

Gad, what a session I had this afternoon! We have a co-op publishers' ad coming up, a double-page spread that will cost $900 in the special paperback supplement of *The Sunday Chronicle*. This afternoon Kepler, Ferlinghetti and I sat down together and tried to work out the copy of the ad. I only wish we could have taped it. It would make even Mort Sahl cry for mercy. The main fly in the ointment was Lawrence F., who, I fear, has lost contact with the grimy world of commerce.

It was perhaps the most peculiar ad conference in history, I should guess, because Larry was determined to make it look as little like an ad as possible. He absolutely refused to have any copy that praised the books we were advertising—any copy in the heading—the books of course have blurbs under the titles. We sweated over the thing for hours and finally ended up with one banner head and that is all. But then that is better than what Larry wanted which was simply quote Check-list unquote. Pat, when told about it, was irate. I just talked to Roy Kepler by phone and we are going to try to add just a little more copy even if we can only chisel in one small line somewhere. I'm afraid I feel the humor of the situation so much that I'm almost tempted to say the hell with it and let it go. But it isn't every day that publishers shell out 900 bucks and it will be many a month before we can round up another two-page spread so that it does demand a little sober thought.

I am happy to report that March—first half—has been tremendous, way over what we did last year. The movie theater is helping now that it has gone very fancy with a big brochure mailed out to thousands and a policy of really paying close attention to booking so as to get unusual films and so on. Also the store seems to appeal more and more to younger people and non-students—who are the ideal customers. The guy I have working at the store now is a marvel and has done tremendous things in neatening the place up. So I think this has helped. And he is a damned good salesman and understands very clearly just what I'm trying to do in the store. We have a hell of a lot of fun picking books to push and then seeing who can do the best job in getting rid of them. God help anybody who asks for a suggestion or a recommendation because we really work at making them take out an armload. But people like it and come back for more. We have even had a fan letter postcard praising the store. I would quote the text except that it is posted prominently on the premises. Come April we will have the double-page spread in the supplement and, in addition, we will go in with Kepler for forty spots on the main SF good music station, KSFR-FM. So we will be promoting very heavily with the idea of really trying to impress the store name on as many people as possible. I'll send you the supplement which will also contain an article by yours truly. And other lesser lights.

As you may gather from the tone of the above, I am feeling very good. With a little bit of luck, I think we can boost the store up to the place where it is quite a thriving enterprise. It has taken and will still take a lot of work but I am very encouraged about it.

We had what we felt was unfair competition from the student bookstore, but plugged away and looked forward to completion of our debt repayment, never very far from my mind as this May letter shows:

Things continue well at the store, despite such set-backs as the student bookstore having what they termed the first annual paperback sale with the cheaper ones at 20% off (i.e., at cost) and higher ones 25% off. Of course we were furious about it, the more so since this was done as a move to get student support for the ASUC, which is compulsory at $6 a year (thus providing a number of cushy paid jobs in various student organizations) but which has been recently threatened by a drive to have it voluntary. Right in the midst of the campaign on the latter, the ASUC executive board decided to have this sale to "return the benefits to the students of a student store." We thought of writing a letter to them but were advised by older and wiser heads not to do so since we would be pilloried as greedy merchants, etc., and it would enable them to show themselves as defenders of the downtrodden.

The ASUC is of course run by the fraternity crowd and is a stepping stone toward careers and politics later on. First they were going to have this sale for two weeks (all this taken without the knowledge of the manager of the bookstore) but I guess he protested so then it was ten days, just coinciding with Evergreen Book Week promotion designed by Grove Press to push their books in every store in the Bay

Area, and modeled on the Evergreen Week that Fred originated a year ago.

Well, the Evergreens are $1.45, $1.85 and so on, and with the ASUC store selling them at 25% off, our display just served as a browsing place and then people went over there and bought them. So we had to return a whole box of them to the wholesaler, and when Grove called from NY to find out how things were going Fred really burned up the wires. Theoretically those books are fair-traded but there can't be fair trade unless it is enforced by the publishers and, like manufacturers of refrigerators or washers, it seems that as long as they get theirs they don't give a damn about the retailer. Of course in the case of books this is a short-sighted policy since if discounting really gets going in books it will just wipe out a lot of small outlets like us. We actually operate on a margin of 30.4%, that is, though theoretically we get the higher priced books at 40% off list, our average for the whole store works out at 30.4%. We don't get the volume of traffic to make it pay to cut prices—that is, we would not sell twice as many books at 20% off as we do now—so we cannot afford to engage in any price wars.

However, despite the sale which is now happily over, we have been doing very well this year and Fred is pleased. This coming month will be the last payment on the personal debt we contracted in order to open the store.

In June, Fred could write that we had been able to hold our own:

The store has been well up over last year for the first five months of this one. We have had to buck some very fierce competition from the campus and other stores that have been selling paperbacks at one-fourth off, but we've been able to better our sales just by being our own sweet selves.

I added a footnote:

So it goes. Haven't even been out to the p.o. in days, and for why? Big coup at the store—the librarian of one of the "model" California prison farms, who has been in the store often, came in and picked out SEVEN HUNDRED DOLLARS worth of books. Fred brought them home to be invoiced (alphabetical by author, in six copies) and I just completed the job. This should make our usually sickly July sales figures look healthy.

By September 1959:

What has happened is that we are financially able to have a new schedule at the store where Fred works through until seven and then quits for the day, leaving our clerk there from 7–10:30 or so (before, you will recall, Fred had 6–8 off and went back and didn't get home till 11:30 or so). So, with Fred coming home at 7:15, we're not through dinner till eight, which shortens the evenings. Also, as he is free, we do go out more than we could before.

The grandeur of writing "our clerk"! In October, Fred wrote:

The house is also in a very disheveled state due to the store's overflowing. This has its advantages, though, because we can dip into them now and again. We are stocking most of the Abrams books for Christmas and those are especially delectable to have around.

The store has been doing well. We have added to our mail-order customers the Nevada State Prison, and we also receive orders regularly from South Africa, another kind of prison.

BEST-SELLERS FOR 1958
Amis, *Lucky Jim*
Kerouac, *The Subterraneans*
Seuss, *Cat in the Hat*

BEST-SELLERS FOR 1959
Pasternak, *Dr. Zhivago*
Lederer and Burdick, *The Ugly American*
Nabokov, *Lolita*
Connell, *Mrs. Bridge*
Faulkner, *The Mansion*

CHAPTER THREE 1960

Who does not love John Gutenberg? the man that with his leaden types has made the invisible thoughts and imagination of the soul visible and readable to all and by all, and secured for the worthy a double immortality? The birth of this person was an era in the world's history second to none save that of the Advent of Christ. The dawn of printing was the outburst of a new revelation, which, in its ultimate unfoldings and consequences, are alike inconceivable and immeasurable.

GEORGE SEARLE PHILLIPS, 1816–1882

Nineteen sixty proved to be a momentous year for us personally in the bookstore and for political events both locally and nationally. The early 1950's were marked by fear and repression of free speech. Universities that had often been centers for lively discourse in the past were quiet. Time magazine described students as the "button-down generation," a reference to the proper Oxford cloth shirt worn by young men eager to work at IBM.

But toward the end of the decade, other forces were at work. The momentous 1954 decision by the Supreme Court on segregation in schools had led to civil rights activities in the South that inspired white students to join in the struggle. In Berkeley, the response was to look at our own schools and how they were segregated because of housing patterns. On the national scene, the discrediting of Senator Joseph McCarthy made liberals somewhat less timid. In 1958, for the first time in seventy years, the Democrats won control of the state legislature. The Republican Congressman representing Berkeley and Oakland was defeated by a liberal Democrat.

Nineteen sixty was a presidential election year and the Democratic candidates were attacking the Republican administration and its candidate, Richard Nixon.

Students at the University of California seemingly woke from sleep and began to take an interest in politics. In February 1960 they were circulating petitions to the governor against compulsory ROTC for undergraduate men. In March, the ASUC voted to send a protest letter to Nashville officials over the arrest of seventy-eight Fisk students for sitting in at a lunch counter. Students took up the cause of Caryl Chessman, a convicted rapist (but not a murderer) sentenced to execution. Despite their efforts and appeals to Governor Pat Brown that included an appeal from his son Jerry, Chessman was executed on May 1.

Some of the anger and frustration over that event found a focus when the House Un-American Activities Committee (HUAC) came to San Francisco that same month, purportedly to save us from ourselves by "investigating" our teachers. Students for Civil Liberties was organized to oppose HUAC, and three hundred faculty signed a protest petition. Here is part of what I wrote to Bob and Fi:

I guess you know that the Un-Americans were scheduled to come here last year and subpoenaed 110 people, mostly teachers. There was such protest, including *S.F. Chronicle*, Bishop Pike of Episcopalians, etc., that the proposed hearings were postponed from June to September, then cancelled. So when they were set for last week, more protests—and with the experience of last year, people were better organized to do something about it. The Cal students re-activated a Students for Civil Liberties Committee, held a rally in SF on the day the hearings began, and then marched down to picket them. They were joined by SF State and San Jose State students. . . .

We attribute a lot of it—the origins of a voice from this "silent generation"—to the effects of the sit-ins in the south. The kids have seized on this as their political issue, and here in Berkeley there has been picketing of Woolworth and Kress for months now. Also a lot of activity on the Chessman case, and great disappointment when weak-kneed Governor Brown hid behind legal formalities. So the students were just boiling about things when these hearings came along.

Their demonstrations, and testimony by witnesses who refused to be cowed, routed the committee and heartened the political activists. We *watched this with sympathy, but our day-to-day energies were with our precarious enterprise. Sales in 1959 had risen by 27% to $41,389. And this was a real increase, for there was very little inflation in those years: under 2% a year until 1967 when it rose to 3.5% as military spending grew and financing it by printing more money became the national pattern. We began to think that we were on our way. Fred wrote in February 1960:*

The store was magnificent during Christmas but it limped during January. We can blame this on many things but it always ends a mystery. This month has gone better. I have bought a mimeograph machine and have already begun to turn out store propaganda on it. I've even had a couple of kids passing them out by the hundreds at the gates of the university. I plan to get out others from time to time. It seems a cheap way to advertise, and I find that, though many lists are quickly discarded, there are some people who can't throw such things away and who must check all book lists to see what is there. And then they come in, sometimes weeks later, and ask for a book on it.

We also plan on beating the bushes for library and school business. The largest bookstore in the East Bay has just built a new warehouse, and I was delighted to learn the other day that they mean to do absolutely nothing about stocking paperbacks either in the store or in the warehouse. That is good. I delight in the fine conservative instinct displayed there. Personally I think it takes a really dense intelligence not to see that the paperbacks have a tremendous future but I don't go into all the reasons for the opinion. Only to say that anyone who can look at the $1.35 editions of the University of Chicago *Greek Tragedies* and not get excited about paperbacks really shouldn't have anything to do with books in the first place.

A little more trade talk. We have been working with a few other bookstores on the old problem of getting the cheaper paperbacks at a decent discount. We now have a couple of leads, and I think that the little fire we have built has already stimulated two publishers of the mass distributed paperbacks to take their "class" books—in this case Laurel and Bantam Classics—away from the local magazine distributors and put them into the hands of the book distributors or jobbers at a better discount. But we're not satisfied with this and hope to get an even better arrangement. At least we have gotten this much action. And it should lead to a much wider use of the paperbounds in schools and a better display (and sale) for them in many stores. I'm amazed sometimes at how much a few unquiet spirits can do.

I have been punying around as we say in the hills. First, three days of the flu and then an attack of thrombo-phlebitis of one of my feet, or rather ankle. I have gotten into the habit of standing for as much as twelve hours in the store and it finally brought about an inflammation of the veins in my foot. There was a swelling and quite a bit of pain until finally I could hardly walk without limping like poor old Philip in *Of Human Bondage*. So I went to the doctor and he told me that I had to take two days off, stay off it, and soak it in scalding hot water. Which I did and now the swelling has gone away and I feel fine except for the fact that I realize at last that I am so very old. Now I sit more at work and this leads to reading and the first thing you know people will be stealing me blind or accusing me of not minding the business and the store will go broke. Then I will have to walk twelve hours a day to find another job and the phlebitis will come back. Life is very hard on the poor.

Then the blow fell, as Fred describes in a March letter:

The store hasn't been making enough money. Christmas was great, and then the University opened new dorms on the other side of campus, and a group of two or three hundred traitorous opportunists left their old landladies and went to the new residences. They left me with a very large stock of books and with a decreased haul. I have countered valiantly with sales and such and now am giving 20% off if cloth books are ordered from us when not in stock at the store. This seems to be having a good effect, and I am getting numerous orders. It is, however, an experiment because we aren't very sure whether or not the thing is feasible. We are also looking for another location for a branch on the more populous south side of campus. After feeling rather low about the whole thing I have perked up and I think we will weather the storm, after all.

I shared our woes in a letter in early May:

I had reports to do and a lot of store work; Fred very busy too but not, alas, because business is good—April was the worst month since August 1958 when you were here. Reason—new dorms on south side of campus that drained our area of students, or at least of those that read books. Recuperation is slow as they left all at once, and their little cubbyholes are only being filled by ones and twos. This impelled us to seek a Telegraph Avenue location but no luck though we have tenuous leads and something may come of it.

Did we tell you that in December we took on a new employee? He's a nice guy in a lot of ways—has problems, one of which is that he's a fairly hard drinker and went off on some benders, leaving Fred high and dry. After repeated warnings we finally said next time was it. There was a next time, so for a week and a half he was unemployed, then asked for one more chance. Since then he's been as dependable as can be. He's an excellent worker and I hope we get a better store so his prospects will be better as we can't afford much in the way of wages now.

No wonder. Business was faltering after a strong first quarter. For the April–June months we were down 21% and for July–September, 28%. It was time to get serious about moving. Here's what Fred wrote that June:

We had thought that we had a good chance of getting a store on the busier side of campus but it now looks as though Mr. Bittelheim, the owner, is such a procrastinator that it may be years before he makes up his mind to do anything. This week I went over in the morning and caught him in the act of having his breakfast. After sitting near him and waiting for some time for him to say hello, I finally got up and stood behind him. Then I put my hand on his shoulder and said, "Have you got anything to say to me, Mr. Bittelheim?" Pat and I agreed later that there is something very funny about this line and that it would almost be worth writing a whole play just so, at some point, a character could say: "Have you got anything to say to me, Mr. Bittelheim?" Anyway, Mr. B. quite obviously had forgotten who I was and fumbled around a while scanning various little cards in his memory file. Finally it came to him and he said, "Oh, you're Cody, aren't you? Well, you see, I haven't had a minute." Then he promised to come to see me. But I am not holding my breath. Inertia is a terrible thing. Well, if Mr. Bittelheim really *hasn't* anything to say to me, we still aren't in such a bad state. We have been going over various ways in which we can raise the volume at the store and I think we have come up with a number of ideas. So even though we aren't breaking any records now, better days are coming.

Meanwhile, I fear that we are not the store to which to refer aspiring workers. There just ain't any left over after I do my stint and Stan gets the minimum that's allowed him. We have cut everything to the bone and this will continue all through the summer which is not exactly our boom period.

At the end of August, we did have prospects in an area which was then a sedate neighborhood shopping district that has since become the lively "gourmet ghetto" of Berkeley, upper Shattuck Avenue. I wrote with enthusiasm:

I suppose the reason I didn't get to writing until now was that this August has been just abysmal for the store, as bad as it was when you were here two years ago, and though we try to divorce business from our personal lives, it is a little wearing, and I don't feel much like writing when in that worried frame of mind. But now September is at hand and we feel better.

Also, at last we have genuine prospects of a new store. A frequent customer for the past year is opening an art movie house (16 mm) and found an excellent location with an adjacent store. He's very anxious to have a bookstore there as the two types of business are helpful to each other. The property is one parcel, though it is two separate buildings. It was built as a theater in 1914, became a transport warehouse with office in 1915, and thus remained. There is considerable renovation necessary for the theater—removal of a loft, installation of a sloping floor, two bathrooms, projection booth, cashier's cage, and of course seats, plus an acceptable front entrance.

The retail space—11′ × 70′—is 60% greater than our present store space, the rent is less (probably it will be $100 month), and the opportunities are greater, which brings me to my third point, that of location. Shattuck Avenue is the main shopping street. This is located on upper Shattuck, which is far enough away from downtown Shattuck to support its own neighborhood area, but still on the main stream of traffic for a big professional middle-class residential area. There is loads of parking nearby so we can become a Berkeley store and not be restricted to neighborhood foot traffic.

The movie theater near our Euclid store has been a dismal failure, which has also been a factor in our decision to move. The new location with prospects of a well-run 300-seat theater next door, in whose program we can advertise, has us quite optimistic. Of course there are problems such as where we'll get the money for the renovation, etc., (an estimated $3,000–4,000) but we have the promise of loans of $250 each from four impoverished friends, hopes of a bank loan of $2,000, and perhaps a little help from Fred's father.

Fred picks up the story a month later and mentions the improvement we were able to get in our mass-market discount:

We had a rather lethargic summer business-wise but now things are popping again, and we are pushing ahead with the plans for Store No. 2 which, it now looks as though, will open around Christmas time. Pat must have written about the second store which will be next door to a new art movie house and which will be our bid to open up and draw upon those Younger Marrieds all the business analysts talk about. Planning for the new store kept us from thinking too much about the bad showing of the present store during the summer. It is all very well to say that one should just accustom oneself to the idea that business does go down in the summer. If it merely dipped rather than dived, all would be well. But the sad fact is that practically all the profits that come in during the good months go to pay off the losses for the bad ones. And only the most Olympian detachment suffices in viewing such a situation as that with perfect equanimity. The idea of the other store is to work on a clientele which will tend to support the store on a year-round basis.

Still, I must say I enjoy my little joint when things are going fairly well as they are now. There I am looking out the front window and who do I see loitering before my window but Sir Charles Snow, who has halted in his saunter down the hill toward the campus and the first meeting of his seminar. I had to restrain myself from going out and touching the hand that wrote *The Masters*.

And many of the students who come in are very lively and engaging company. Then, I have a lot of fun pushing my favorite stuff. Right now I'm forcing all the store regulars to buy *Saturday Night and Sunday Morning* which is now out in a paper edition. Which reminds me that we finally appear to have scored a major triumph in buying. The other day when I was picking up books at the local distributor's, the manager called me over and said that he was working out a better deal on the discount. I don't know exactly what it will be but anything at all helps a great deal. I have always felt that the lower-priced paperbacks are the real backbone of the paperback business because it is in them that the big volume business lies. So we've always carried them faithfully and now, during the good months, the bill for them goes well over a thousand a month. With a better deal we can push them harder yet and I hope in the new store we will be selling them at the rate of from three to four times that total. Even with the larger discount, we still won't be making a fortune, but I am interested in the challenge of taking the better of these books and doing a job of selling them.

Years later, Fred wrote this about his encounter with C. P. Snow:

The first signing I ever had at Cody's was private and didn't even take place in the store.

The author was C. P. Snow and the year was 1960. Snow, then at the height of his fame as the creator of the "Strangers and Brothers" sequence of novels, had come to UC Berkeley to do his stint as a visiting Regents professor. The University treated such visitors regally. They were installed in a fine house in the Berkeley hills with a terrific view and their duties were hardly exhausting since they were not required to do more than deliver a lecture or two and to devote a few hours a week to talk to students who dropped by a campus office. Sir Charles—as he then was, not having yet been made a peer—was in residence at a home a ten-minute walk from the store. It hardly seemed likely to me that I would be honored by his presence.

Nevertheless, looking up one afternoon from an order form, I was astonished to find myself staring into the famous face. Not only astonished but almost overwhelmed. I was also prepared for embarrassment, anticipating that he would ask for a copy of a new English novel or an esoteric study in history that I would have to confess was not in stock.

"I wonder," he said, looking around the cramped shop, while I waited anxiously, "I wonder if you have ever heard of something called *Classics Illustrated*?"

My face must have betrayed my shocked surprise at the question. But as the conjecture formed in my mind that this great novelist's idea of relaxation—his junk reading—was poring through the pages of *Classics Illustrated*—he spoke up quickly to correct me.

"Oh," he said, "I'm not asking for myself—it's for my son. I've looked through the things, and they're really quite well done."

I murmured an interjection that I supposed they were.

"You see," he explained, "the boy reads them—Homer or Virgil or Mark Twain—and that stimulates him to read the originals. I wonder where I could go to find them."

A mental snapshot of the vast stock of comic books at the distributor's warehouse in Oakland popped into my mind. I had a visit coming up the next day.

"I think I could have a bunch for you tomorrow afternoon," I said.

Sir Charles brightened. "That would be splendid. Shall I come at three?"

The next afternoon I waited eagerly for the return of my famous author. Moreover, I had prepared for his visit by carefully going through the stock of *Classics Illustrated* at the wholesaler and assembled a stack of the comic books—everything from Homer's *Odyssey* and Hugo's *Les Misérables* to Mark Twain's *Prince and the Pauper*.

I had also made certain during the morning to arrange for one of my friends to take command of the store while I was talking with Sir Charles. Ron was in place when the very solid and substantial figure came through the door.

After the polite preliminaries, I prevailed on Sir Charles to go to the nearby courtyard where we sat down at a table and I laid down the pile of *Classics Illustrated*. He was obviously delighted, proclaiming his satisfaction over each successive "book" as he went one-by-one through the stack.

"Well, I want the lot—the boy will be delighted. What do they come to?"

I was not about to allow him to pay. I said there was no charge but I wanted him to do something for me in return.

"I'd be very glad to pay," he said, but what could he do?

"Wait here for just a moment," I said.

I hurried into the store and then came running back with a stack of books which, when he saw them, brought a pleased smile to the author's face.

"Will you sign these for me?" I asked.

"Of course," he purred, reaching, with an expression of eager assent, for his pen. He took the book on the top of the pile and opened it to the fly-leaf.

"Could you sign them to Fred Cody?" I asked.

He nodded and began writing on the title page of *The New Men*, "to Fred Cody with best wishes from C. P. Snow, 29/9/60, Berkeley."

While he signed the other books he talked of doing signings at famous bookshops in London, New York, and Cambridge, Massachusetts. And then, when he had signed all of them, he took his stack of comic books and departed.

I thought I had seen the last of Sir Charles but a few days later Roy Kepler called from Menlo Park. He was honoring Snow with a luncheon at which he would be the principal speaker and would also sign copies of the Anchor paperback of *The Masters* and the Cambridge hardbound of *The Two Cultures*. If I liked, Roy would pick me up to be in the car when he brought Snow to and from his shop for the great occasion. I leaped at the chance and enjoyed it greatly. This was the glamorous side of bookselling—the opportunity to be with a famous writer, that made all the monotonous hours of "minding the store" worthwhile.

Still very much preoccupied with prospects for a new store, Fred wrote in October 1960:

The plans for the new store go forward. They've been held up by the fact that the lease for the building has not been signed, chiefly because of a southern-bred real estate woman who is straight out of Tennessee Williams. I met her twice and on each occasion I felt as though I had run into the mother in *The Glass Menagerie*.

Anyway, this sagging southern belle has finally collected herself and announced that she will bring negotiations to a close next week. After that, we will have to negotiate our lease, or rather sub-lease, but I don't anticipate that we will have anything like such protracted dealings on that head.

The reason you haven't clearly in mind just where we stand on the one or two store situation is that we haven't either. If we have an absolutely fantastic Christmas and late winter business, we will probably go on with the present store, though on a shorter lease basis. If we lay an egg during these periods, we will concentrate all our energies on the new store. As it stands, we will not go into the new store until just after Christmas. Which is very bad because it leaves us with some rather dreary months to look forward to. But there is absolutely no way to hurry it so we will have to make do.

On November 2, I wrote to the Herberts:

About the new store—*still* haven't signed the lease so that means we can't get in before Christmas which in our highly seasonal business means quite a different approach to the matter—we will now try to get a month-to-month lease so that if the lean months are too lean we can back out. If it is successful we will probably close Euclid since the lease expires in May. We have had a rough year, in recession since April, and the hoped-for fall upswing didn't occur.

In mid-November, Fred wrote:

All hell is breaking loose in publishing these days. Early this week, or was it late last week, a friend who was an editor at Dell called up from New York and said that he was leaving his job and would do all he could to get it for me and asked if I wanted to come to New York and try for it. Pat and I considered it but very quickly decided that we just didn't want to have that New York grind again, so I sent him a note saying to excuse me, please, but I wouldn't try. Dell is splitting off from Western and will have its own editorial staff now.

Then, later, along comes a good friend who is a salesman for Grove who said that Evergreen's sales and distribution are now to be done by Dell. Locally, the situation is boiling, too, with one paperback wholesaler apparently on the skids and a new one about to bow in. Tomorrow I have lunch with the Macmillan west coast salesman, and God knows what he has to tell. Coming up is a Wright Mills book written as a result of a stay of some weeks in Cuba. It's called *Listen Yankee,* and Ballantine will do the paper and McGraw-Hill the cloth in simultaneous publication. The salesman brought me the advanced mimeo of the book coming the last days of the month, and I read the first and concluding parts. As always, Mills writes very well and the book ought to make quite a stir. A commentator on our local high-brow FM station KPFA came along and begged the mimeo off me and will use it for a broadcast, which should also help sales.

Ballantine is a very interesting outfit and certainly one of the most enterprising of all the paperback publishers. All in all, the paperbacks still remain one of the most interesting and lively parts of the cultural scene. All kinds of changes in distribution are in the air and, although I waver in the faith at times, I still think that they will yet succeed in bringing books to the people in vaster quantity (and quality too, with luck) than has yet been dreamed of.

BEST-SELLERS FOR 1960
Lee, *To Kill a Mockingbird*
Schwarz-Bart, *Last of the Just*
Shirer, *The Rise and Fall of the Third Reich*
Goodman, *Growing Up Absurd*

PART TWO
The First Telegraph Avenue Store

CHAPTER FOUR 1961

When I get a little money, I buy books; and if any is left, I buy food and clothes.

DESIDERIUS ERASMUS, 1465–1536

Finally, after months of worry over falling sales and futile attempts for the Shattuck location, came the turn in the Cody fortunes. It is described in my letter of November 22, 1960:

Remember all we wrote last about the torturous negotiations for a new location near the new art movie? Forget all that. Today we signed a lease on a 35 × 100 store (present one is 16 × 29—how's that for expansion) on Telegraph, the hottest bookstore street in town, leading out from the main (south) campus entrance. We're four blocks down from campus. Rent is astronomical for us—$400 month—we are so excited we can't see straight. They've promised renovations (it was a grocery for past fifty-two years) ready for us to open December 5 so don't expect to hear from us, unless you've got $1,000 or so to lend in which case we will find time for a thank-you note. All of the store isn't display space—we'll have 35 × 80 with the balance as unfinished storage space susceptible of later improvement if needed. But 35 × 80 looks cavernous to us. Imagine the shelves we'll need to fill that and by December 5!, as we can't strip Euclid since lease there is to May '61.

This is how it happened. In order to do my economic reports, I had a housekeeper on Wednesdays so I could get to the University library for research. One day after my stint, I walked down Telegraph Avenue, not my usual path, and went by a vacant grocery store. I remembered reading that it had been closed in September after many years. Peering in, I could see the wooden bins against the wall where potatoes and onions had been stored, and the packaging string coming down from the ceiling—something of a time warp. I took down the number of the realtor and called. The place had been empty for weeks and that is why the likes of us, with no credit rating, were accepted.

I had to go to the Co-op Credit Union and get a signature loan for $750 in order to scrape up the first and last months' rent. The building owners promised to cover the wooden floors with vinyl, sheet-rock the walls, and install fluorescent lighting. This was done with great dispatch, and we opened there on Saturday, December 10, 1960. We could not really stock it properly, and we did not advertise. Nevertheless, we took in $3,671 there that December 10–31, and $10,659 for the entire month at the old store. For the year as a whole, we were down 15% from 1959.

What the move meant to us is also described in notes Fred made a few years later:

Our main problem was the unsatisfactory location. We were on the wrong side of the campus. Euclid Avenue has a small business district confined to one block. It attracted students who lived there, and some of the residents. Just above us there were three schools of theology and some of the students for the ministry liked the store. But there were not enough of them who read outside their field of special interest. The same seemed to be true of the engineering and architectural students whose schools were on the north side of the campus.

Despite all we could do, the store was not able to register sales of more than around $40,000 a year. Like many other retailers in the same situation, I felt a growing sense of desperation, working sixty hours a week in the store, with almost every evening at home marking order forms. There were two children now, Martha and Anthony, and only the money Pat earned with her research and writing enabled us to keep the household and store going.

Coming home one evening in my usual state of frustration, I found that Pat had some news. She had been on the south side of the campus in the famous 2400 block on Telegraph Avenue. A grocery that had been in business there since 1906 had closed its doors. If we acted quickly, we could get the store on a five-year lease. The rent was nearly four times what we paid at the old store, but Pat was certain that we would be fools if we didn't take this place.

The next morning we went to look at it. It was a dingy, run-down place, the floor worn and splintery, the paint peeling from the walls. The dim lighting made it like a dusty cave. Moreover, the three floors above, in as rundown a state as the store, were occupied by a transient population of colorful but irresponsible tenants who promised to make our lives a misery. But the space seemed to us almost limitless—35 × 80 feet with a curious storeroom in the back projecting from the rear of the ancient frame building. Its roof had probably not been repaired in a decade, and the gloomy interior had the atmosphere of a horror movie set. The most eerie feature were the vines that had found their way through gaps in the roof and hung in leafy festoons. It would have been an ideal place to have a book signing party for Edward Gorey. It certainly was an improbable place in which to store back-stock.

But Pat was indomitably sanguine. The owners had promised to make renovations in return for signing the lease, and it would look almost completely different when we moved in. And think of all the space! It was late in November, but the owners promised to have the new Cody's ready in less than a month. We would open in time for the Christmas season. It was irresistible. We signed.

Now we began to face the hard realities of making the move. We needed shelving and sales tables for the new store, and we needed stock to put on them. We got some shelving in place and began moving some of our stock over from the Euclid store. But even though practically every book was faced out, there were still empty spaces.

At this critical juncture the shipment of calendars arrived from Germany. For some reason my boundless optimism had prevailed over Pat's salutary restraint. It was for the former store an extravagantly large order. But what a magnificent show they made when they were displayed in all those empty places, mainly in the place of honor on the top shelves. There was enough space on the newly painted white walls to literally plaster sample pages of the most impressive calendars.

It soon became obvious that the new Cody's was a triumphant success, and the blessed calendars were leading the way. A week before Christmas we sold out our stock of many of them, and with the money, I rushed over to San Francisco to the wholesaler to buy hardbounds and paperbacks to take their place. Now we had the money to stock the store properly and make the most of our new opportunity. In the years that followed, calendars originated by American publishers began to appear. It was the beginning of a flood that now is one of the principal features of almost every bookstore's fall and Christmas stock. But to me, they always bring to mind the fortuitous way in which we were able to stock that first Telegraph Avenue store.

On another occasion, Fred described the changing area into which we moved:

It didn't take us long to realize that South Campus was in a state of transition. It had been a neighborhood business block with bohemian trimmings. The latter grew more pronounced when Maxine came over from North Beach in San Francisco and opened the first of Berkeley's expresso coffee shops, then called the Piccolo and later, when Maxine departed, the Mediterraneum, or the Med. We ourselves had somewhat altered the character of the block by moving into space which had been occupied by a very traditional independent grocery that had been in operation under the same ownership for fifty years. The Beatnik impact made itself felt in other ways. That part of Telegraph began more and more to attract youngsters in their teens and then the people, eccentric and otherwise, who found it a receptive and interesting scene.

I won't go into all the reasons the South Campus area became what was variously described as a youth ghetto, a hippie paradise, and a seed ground for the counter-culture and the New Politics. Even in the early sixties, though, no one could say we didn't have intimations of what was to come. I remember one perpetual grad student in his thirties who, when he wasn't practicing his remunerative sideline as a pool shark, circulated in the coffee shops distributing his business card. It identifed him as an Existentialist Counselor. . . .

I suppose the University itself was partly responsible for what happened to the area when it tore out large portions of what had been residential homes housing limited numbers of students and built residence halls which concentrated thousands of students there. The owners of business real estate in the area were not slow to realize that rents should reflect the new situation and that meant that many of the small restaurants and the modest places which provided services for a neighborhood clientele had to get out. In their place came a shifting pattern of retail shops and eating places directing their appeal almost exclusively to the young. I think the change was perhaps most noticeable in what happened to the record shops. The rather sedate shops with an emphasis on classical music first tried to adapt so as to compete with the chain outlets geared to pop and rock music, but then gave up the struggle and closed down.

It was just as well we had not waited for the upper Shattuck location. The movie entrepreneur, Mel Novikoff, was unable to come to an agreement with the owners. He went to San Francisco and opened The Surf, the first in what became a very successful chain of movie theaters in that city.

Once again, luck was on our side: we were able to get rid of the stock left at the Euclid store without having to pack up hundreds of boxes of some not-so-new books and bring them over to the new store. Fred describes this in a March 1961 letter:

First off, we have closed the old store. I have wept over the demise and can hardly bear to go and look at the bare walls with all the books on the floor. As I told Pat, explaining my feelings about the place, a lot of sweat and agony is smeared over the walls of that room. Of course, there are many good memories, too. But the feeling is mingled. Predominantly, though, it just makes me very sad to be there.

However, the sadness has been much alloyed by the circumstances of the closing. Down the street from the old store a fellow started a bookshop. He was interested in buying and taking over the store.

We gave him a figure and then handed him our books—financial books, I mean. After conferring with his backers, he finally came up with the idea that he would buy our old stock and move it down to his store and leave us with the old store to do with as we please. So we gave him the figures on *that,* and he signed an agreement to buy. We have taken the inventory of the stock remaining in the store which we will sell to him at two percent less than our cost. With the understanding that he will keep to the agreement, we should therefore have in our hands this coming Friday a check for a cool $6,000.

It will of course come in right handy-like. The lease on the vacated store runs out in June so it will stay vacant and we will pay it out and then mark it off the list of our properties. So endeth, almost before it began, that burgeoning chain of Cody's which had Doubleday trembling with fear. Cody's, it appears, will never be a Kress. We have many places where the six thou will prove very useful, mostly as a means of Making the Publishers Happy which is now one of the big objects of our life.

This sale was little short of a miracle, since close-out sales are usually on the order of 20¢ on the retail dollar, and we got about 66¢. In fact, when Fred visited me in the hospital the afternoon of Nora's birth on March 24, he brought with him the check for the sale.

With the worrisome little Euclid store now in the past, we went forward with zest. Fred wrote to Bob and Fi, now on fellowship in London, at the end of March:

Four blocks up the street the magnificent new University Student Commons or Union building has been opened. It looks and has the feel of all that I have seen pictured of the best examples of Soviet architectural genius. Indeed, it has no grace, no gaiety, none of the buoyancy you associate with youth and the longer I look at it the more I feel that the architects must have designed it originally as a recreation center for the executives of the Shell Oil Company. In the basement of this mistake, they have placed the University bookstore—the cafeteria and other such vital elements having pre-empted all the topside quarters. No expense has been spared to light the cave but it still looks like a cave. Money has been no object in fixtures, either, and they are all wonderfully public and institutional and ugly as hell. So I really feel happy about our joint which, though poor, has an honesty and a lightness to it that, I think, most people find appealing.

Among my files from this time is a sheet on which I had drafted a "profit and loss" statement for April 1961. Sales were $4,664 and after deducting for the cost of the books we had a gross profit of $1,633. Out of this had to come rent, loan payments, and so on. Labor costs were listed at $440 which covered Stan and one part-time person. The "proprietor's draw" was $300. I was not on the payroll, nor would I be for quite a few years. My work was part of the "sweat equity" we were creating.

But we were out of the little store, which we had come to learn could never have provided us with a living. And we needed to move for another reason: to accommodate the growing number of paperbacks as more and more major publishers added a paperback line to their production. As a larger store, we could become better acquainted with the publishing world, instead of looking on wistfully from the sidelines. This acquaintance sometimes depressed Fred, as this April 1961 letter reveals:

Ah, the publishers. I could write reams about publishers and about the book business in general. It is probably the most exasperating study in frustrating circumlocution since Mr. Dickens investigated the original enterprise. I am inclined to blame most of the shortcomings on the inadequacies of the gentlemen in charge of the publishing houses. The fact is that most of them are just plain stupid but skittish. The last is important. They are continually riding off in all directions in chase of the latest fad. In that respect they resemble the Hollywood clan. An instance was the Eichmann trial. There was a hot race to see who could add another Eichmann book to the list. The result was that at least five or six have appeared, none of them in the least good since all were prepared in a rush. Meanwhile, Mr. Shirer had finished his many years' labor on his book and produced something solid and thorough. And it is selling at the rate of thousands a week and making Simon & Schuster so pompously fat that it can hardly stand itself. But the number of publishers who will do the kind of sustained work that is needed to produce a really good book and then go on to see that the book reaches the public it should have is very small.

I'm reminded of an analogy. Growing up on a West Virginia farm, I early took note of an almost unanimous sentiment which formed the recurring theme of farmers' discussions whenever work or chance caused them to convene. This was that there was nothing they hated more than a goddamned chicken. They never tired of recounting stories of the unpredictable absurdities of their behavior, and they freely and frequently declared that, if they could carry into execution their most intoxicating fantasies, they would welcome the extermination of the species. There was, it was apparent, only one objection to embarking on the slaughter: the contrary, cantankerous, foolish and troublesome fowl laid eggs.

There is, it seems to me, a remarkable resemblance between the attitude of the farmer toward the hens and that of the booksellers' feelings concerning publishers.

Add to this the fact which I think is indisputable that no other industry in the country is content with a distribution and shipping system that is one long series of delays, mistakes and foul-ups. Publishers seem to revel in it. They blithely experiment with automation, putting in a new system that can't be expected to work for months, then refusing (or being unable because of the system) to answer any letters complaining about books not received. What other industry would thus finance IBM's fumbles? Publishers do, and seem to think their retail market should recognize that they are being very progressive even though money is lost every day because of their incompetence. I don't know how many publishers' representatives have said to me, when I've complained, "You think *you've* got problems. Why you. . . ."

The longer I stay in the book business the more depressed I get with people who talk about The Book meaning the limited edition kind of book, and who take as a personal affront the kind of book that, while perfectly produced, doesn't have all the qualities of the expensive hand-made edition. How damned silly to think of books like that. I *don't* think that paperbacks are the real answer to the inexpensive book. The "quality" paperbacks still aim far too much at an academic audience. No, what is wanted is a new approach to books, some brave publisher with a lot of backing who can carry on a campaign.

I detect signs that Penguin may be playing around with some such ideas. Their covers now are rather a mid-passage mark in the kind of book I'm thinking of. But they still keep to that small format, and they still keep either stitching or perfect binding. And of course a good many of them are reprints, Penguin having a particular aversion to spending anything on original fiction. And they still stick to paper covered with plastic for the covers and what I want is some publisher who will go all the way and really demonstrate the possibilities, practical and artistic, of using plastic as a book cover for a whole series of books. This, along with the advances in binding, together with the use of the most economic of present-day printing processes and others that should be developed, should finally bring about a book to meet our present-day needs.

We had started publishing on our own on the smallest imaginable scale: listings of new books. Fred described this and other promotions:

I want to go on with our paperback news (listing of new and forthcoming paperbacks) and try to keep improving it with every issue, learning as we go. Incidentally, the first issue was a roaring success from the standpoint of circulation. I did 750 of which we mailed out about 130. The rest were put on the counter and at another place in the store with signs saying Free, Take One. It took just about ten days for the 600-odd to be taken off. Our next number will run at least 1,000 copies, and I may go higher. Fun.

We will go on another radio station, probably in about ten days' time. Again, I will write the copy because I can't abide the kind of gook they turn out. I have an idea for a whole series of spots which will be very quiet and very restrained and perhaps even evocative. This new contract, six spots a week for about $15, will put us on this station for three months so we will have time to try to assess their effect with some accuracy. As you know, this challenge of trying to use radio to sell books is one that interests me very much. We will also be using the *Chronicle* on Sunday for thirteen weeks and again we will have a series of ads which hang together and have a kind of unifying thread. All this is very fascinating to me, at least, and I'll let you know what kind of results we get. On Madison Avenue, I suppose this would be called a Campaign. But it's more fun to do it yourself.

Once again we tackled the problem of the poor discount on mass-market books that we were forced to buy from a local jobber and could not purchase directly from the publisher. Here is a succinct account in a June letter that Fred wrote:

The curse of our existence as a business has been the fact that we have to carry a big stock of the lower-price paperbacks even though we get a discount which causes us to lose money on every sale of the blasted things. It has also been galling because of course all my sympathies are so much engaged by these books which offer so much promise in bringing good books to the millions instead of to the few.

Well, about two weeks ago we had a meeting in SF of quite a number of the paperback proprietors and talked mightily about how we might beat this jinx. Our hopes had been raised somewhat by the fact that the FTC had finally handed down rulings and decrees which prohibited publishers and distributors from doing discriminatory deals with separate stores and chains—fair treatment for all, that's the alleged aim. About all that came out of the meeting was a plan for everyone to decide to de-emphasize even more completely the low discount books and then to write letters to the publishers explaining why they had to do it and asking for fairer treatment. I don't know how the other brethren have done but we seem to have had fairly good luck. I wrote to the presidents of Bantam, New American Library, and Pocket. Of these, I've heard from two. NAL was first with a letter from their vice-president for sales, one of the most pusillanimous people in the book business. And his letter was true to type, full of half-truths, distortions and just plain lies.

Anyway, I had not expected much of NAL. They are famous for being congenital bruisers. Besides, once long ago, when enraged by the conduct of two of their salesmen, I wrote the president of the firm ordering him to command that these two worthies never come in the store again. However, since everyone I know in the business has had some sort of run-in with them, I thought I would see if time had mellowed them a little. But no.

Bantam hasn't answered yet. But Pocket Books, still the largest of all the paperback publishers, did. A letter from Leon Shimkin, president, and a nicer one I've never read. Saying that he sympathized and was working on the problem and that my letter had been passed on to his v-p for circulation. The latter wrote the next day and sent word that I was to see the head of the local distributing agency, and he would give me the word on a new arrangement he was sure would be perfectly satisfactory. So I went this morning to see this man, and he said by the first week of July he should have definite word and that we would then get close to 30% (up from 25%) on Pocket and some other lines including, he thought, Bantam. NAL was holding out, he said, but he thought they would come through now that Pocket had acted. The new discount will be retroactive for the last quarter ending July 1 and it couldn't be better than to have a nice little check coming in at mid-summer.

Perhaps all this is fatiguing to you but it is things like this—which seem minor—that can make a real difference in what kind of a store we have. Now we will be able to actively promote the lower-price lines. And I must say I would be very glad to see NAL come through with a better deal because no one is doing better on reprints than they are. The Signet Classics are an absolute model of what reprints should be. Their covers are magnificent, the paper is good quality, the introductions are of very high quality. In binding they leave something to be desired but, even so, there are one hell of a lot of fine books for fifty or seventy-five cents. And of course there are many fine books in the Mentors. This together with probably the finest fiction backlist in paperback makes them very formidable.

So far this month we have averaged a total take of $189 a day which is very good. The building we occupy is up for sale and the real estate man has praised it as a very good deal for us which no doubt it would be if we wanted to take up the burden. But we thought

it over and decided that we had no desire to become property owners, feeling that it tends to make one become too preoccupied with
things that are basically silly.

Our work at the store increased, our letter writing suffered. A brief note
I sent in August:

The store is doing very well, July the best month so far in the new
store (at Euclid, business always fell dreadfully in the summer), and
in the autumn we will have the equivalent of two full-time workers
plus Fred (Stan and two part-timers) so that there will be two on at
all times. Our present hours are noon to midnight, except Saturdays
10 A.M.–midnight; in September we may go back to 10 A.M. opening.
More than half our business is done after 6 P.M. With such a greater
volume, there's much more managerial work for Fred and paper
work for me.

There were also demands on our time from community and family con-
cerns. By September 1961 Martha was in kindergarten and Anthony in a
parent-participation nursery school. I did my nursery school stint on the
day I had a housekeeper/babysitter, going from the nursery school at noon
to the UC library for the research needed for the quarterly economic re-
ports on Latin American countries that I did for my London employers. It
was in fact at the nursery school that I met another mother who had re-
ceived a letter from a woman in Washington, D.C. The letter proposed that
women across the nation get together into a "Women for Peace" action day
protesting the nuclear arms race.

Many of us were worried about where our country was headed. Ken-
nedy had been in Berlin and on his return urged that fall-out shelters
should be built in back yards. I looked at my new baby and reflected: what
is the point of taking such good care, getting the regular check-up at the
pediatrician, if I do not also try to take care of what the outside world can
bring? With the store, the children, my economic reports, I had been taking
a sabbatical from politics. This letter struck a chord; it was time to get
active again. With some excitement I took this Washington letter to my
friend Frances Herring, who did research at the Institute of Governmental
Studies on campus. We agreed we wanted to join this "strike for peace" on
the proposed day of November 1. We drafted a list of women to invite to a

planning meeting, and Women for Peace was born. We decided to work from where we were: present petitions to our local officials as our closest representatives of government, asking them to speak for us to Congress and the President.

We were amazed at the response we got. We truly touched the spirits of many people, and the lethargy of the years of fear-engendered passivity fell away. At the evening meeting we'd advertised, there was standing room only and a consensus that we could not disband: we must continue our efforts (what we thought of as a one-day activity celebrates its thirty-first anniversary in 1992).

We were buoyed by other activists. In December SANE had full-page ads against nuclear testing. Over 500 faculty from ten Bay Area universities and colleges, including 249 from UC, sent a petition to Kennedy asking him to abandon the civil defense program and lead the nation to peace. His appearance at Charter Day ceremonies in March 1962 occasioned student demonstrations calling for an end to bomb testing and to the Vietnam "assistance," desegregation of federal housing, staying out of Cuba, and repeal of the McCarran Act. The struggles of the students to hold these demonstrations at all were part of an ongoing controversy with the UC administration about free speech, a struggle that would explode into the Free Speech Movement two and a half years later.

BEST-SELLERS FOR 1961
Salinger, *Franny and Zooey*
White, *The Making of the President 1960*
Tuchman, *The Guns of August*

CHAPTER FIVE 1962 TO 1963

BOOKS AND MORE BOOKS   SUCCESS IN THE NEW STORE
FRED BUYS ART IN NEW YORK   MORE CHILDREN
AND A NEW HOUSE   "SHRINKAGE"

The second part of the history of the world and the arts began with the invention of printing.

GOETHE, 1749–1832

At 2476 Telegraph we had the excitement of success and expansion. We also had the excitement of the beginning of the changes that marked the 1960's. We were direct witnesses of this fresh thinking in the new books that flooded into the store—and that we now had space to carry. Fred wrote in a February 1962 letter:

The overhaul of the store proceeds apace. We have completed twenty feet of new display shelving and it looks very fetching. So much so, it convinces me that once we have completed this renovation we will have one of the most attractive paperback stores in the country. As we go ahead we are much encouraged by the comments on the stocking and the arranging in the store. I don't think the store has ever looked more festive and attractive than it does now.

Our move to Telegraph Avenue and larger space made us visible. We began to get the kind of visits from publishers, editors, and sales representatives that meant so much to both of us, as Fred wrote in May:

The store is fine—we had the usual slump during April but picking up again now. All our extra help except Stan are leaving us for the summer but a very nice girl applied and I am putting her on. The trouble is that she can't start work until June 15 and that leaves two weeks where Stan and I will have to struggle along as best we can. I'm hopeful, though, I can get emergency help for those two weeks.

Ian Ballantine was here and we had lunch and a long talk. He is full of ideas but, like so many of us, hasn't much money to carry them out. Still, it seems to me he does well enough if he stays alive in the shark tank where he operates.

The store, the children, and work on peace issues took all our time. The Cuban missile crisis gripped us tight in a week of terror in October 1962: we were so tense we could not concentrate on anything but radio newscasts. One night we went to hear the British journalist and filmmaker Felix Greene speak. His apocalyptic view on the imminence of war upset us so much that we could not find our car when we got out of the Oakland high school where he spoke. We reported the car stolen and a few days later got a laconic phone call from a woman who said it had been parked in front of her house for four days and were we abandoning it? Trying times indeed.

We always looked forward to Christmas. Fred wrote in December:

We are in the charming position at the store of doing such a wonderful volume at the beginning of the Christmas retail season that we are worried about our stock running out. Since so much of it is imported this raises some nasty problems but I must say they are sort of nice problems. Perhaps the solution would be to sell everything out two weeks before Christmas and then hang up a sign saying "Closed—Gone East for Christmas." Which reminds me that I had a wonderful perverse idea the other day. This was to fix up the windows with the most tempting displays possible with everything marked down by at least one-half, put on all the brightest lights, and then lock and bar the doors and stay closed for one month. Maybe later on when we get a little ahead we can indulge in some of these satiric exercises in business-ship.

I added a postscript:

This was written a couple of weeks ago. Since then we have had two $1,000 days. It is going to our head.

The scope that a larger and more successful store offered to Fred is shown in this January 1963 letter on his shopping spree in New York:

I had quite a time in New York, mostly touring up and down Madison Avenue talking to people in galleries. If the N.Y. transit authority comes out ahead this year they can chalk it up to ole Fred because I must have been in and out of N.Y. buses a hundred times. Much of what I did was exasperating because no one could seem to get it through their heads that a paperback store could have any interest in graphics. A blessed few did get the idea though and I made some very promising contacts and bought batches of things from several people. Perhaps the best and most heart-warming reception came from the Picasso Arts people on Madison where there is a girl who is as charming as can be. I bought a little over a hundred dollars in Picasso graphics and then discussed with her the possibility of having some signed Picassos on consignment. To make a long story short I ended up with about a thousand dollars worth of signed stuff for an exhibition at the store. What is unsold has to be returned by the end of May. This is a very satisfactory arrangement indeed. They wished me all kinds of good luck and it was a very happy thing to have happen. Then I went to Peter Deitch who interrupted his poker game to tell me he was out of my class, which he is. Then he told me about Delphic Arts, an importer of graphics for galleries with offices in the Empire State Building. I went there and got some signed Buffets, Braques, Miros, and some stuff by people of the School of Paris contemporary.

After that, I went to Wittenborn to look around and there Mrs. W. inadvertently put in a kindly word about the Weyhe Gallery so I went there and talked to Martha Dickinson who runs the upstairs gallery. She asked for references and I gave Harper Row among others. She called Harper where an idiotic girl gave her to understand that we had owed $500 since March 1962. This was absolutely untrue, there being only a small invoice of the March date which Pat had skipped over and which had been lumped in with later purchases, none of which were overdue. Well, Miss Dickinson put on the deep freeze and said, civilly enough, that she was glad to have me choose what I wanted, that she would give me a discount, but that of course it would all have to be cash.

I gritted my teeth and said we would pay cash, picked up my stuff, wrote out traveler's checks for part of the purchase, asked her to send on an itemized statement on the rest, and left for Harper Row. There I threw one of the few really desk-pounding fits that I have ever permitted myself which ended in the assistant credit manager calling Miss D. and trying to undo the harm that had been done. But of course he couldn't and cash and coolness it will be until we work our passage through the hard way. It was a horrible thing and it made me nearly cave in for a short time but I bucked up and plugged on. At the Weyhe we bought mostly Frasconis and things by his wife and a selection of other woodblock prints that are in the lower price range.

A good bit of this was for a Spring Festival that we will have at the store in March. This should be quite a do. We will have potted trees in blossom all over the place and out on the sidewalk. We're getting an artist-teacher at the Cal School of Arts and Crafts who will do original decorations for the window and outside the store and then we'll have a graphics show with a heavy emphasis on graphics for children's rooms. I think it ought to be a really terrific thing. By the way, we also bought a signed Picasso for 200 bucks to give away on a raffle deal. All this, as you can imagine, is costing some money but I'm convinced that we can make it go.

We are still doing the New York Graphic reproductions and I went over their entire stock—except for the junk genre—and picked out some tremendous reproductions, including a number of new ones not yet in their catalogs. Some Van Goghs are particularly impressive. Some of the other stores in town are gaga over what we're doing and trying to keep pace but I think we have a good jump on them and can stay ahead if we keep at it.

We have had a hell of a good time promoting the new Baldwin book, *The Fire Next Time*. We did the window on it with an all black background, very stark, with a blown-up photograph of Baldwin staring out and then a blow-up of the ad from *Publishers Weekly* plus a blow-up of a passage from the book—the very stirring "not to be afraid" portion of his letter to his nephew. It got lots of attention, caused choleric people to come in and say they'd like to see a book about what the Negroes did to the whites, and it has sold sixty of the new books so far, and I don't know how many paperbacks by Baldwin.

I am very set up about the staff at the store. They did a tremendous job while I was away and it is so fine to see how they all pitch in and work so well. The guy in charge of the art, Steve, is a former Yalee and is bursting with ideas. All of us work together well and that is the strength of the store.

When Fred got home from that New York trip, work on our promotion included publishing a little booklet of poetry called Spring. *A copy somehow got to St. Louis and a bookstore there ordered fifteen copies "at usual trade discount," and asked to be informed of any future publications. An editor at McGraw-Hill wrote asking to buy ten copies. We loved getting mail like that, but our reality was the store, and how we were already outgrowing our space.*

The first hint of another move is in my February 1963 letter, and comments on work from my side:

As usual, we are full of a number of things, the art department being chief preoccupation. Also looming ahead is the fact that urban renewal is scheduled for Telegraph Ave. and our building will probably be condemned. This will more or less coincide with the expiration of our lease (December 1965). The owners have already offered to sell the building to us but there would be little profit in that since we'd be paying in effect just for the land. They are trying to pull a fast one, thinking that we don't realize the building is probably doomed—it is beyond the state where it can be brought up to code. So, we are keeping our eyes out for another location which is a problem since we must stay on Telegraph, and we must stay within the magic four blocks (four down from Sather Gate).

. . . plus the usual store work, which is growing because we no longer have our major wholesale supplier for quality paperbacks, they got too inefficient and out-of-stock too often so now we go direct which means a lot more invoices to post. I have sister Rosemary helping me with the bookkeeping, she comes over two nights a week and posts my ledgers for me (I have three of them to keep up, the accounts payable, the running inventory at retail, and the check disbursement ledger). Business is very good although we are now entering the six-week annual slump; the fellows at the store are determined that they will have a try at seeing if they can break this pattern, thus the Spring Festival which features the booklet we sent (250 to be numbered and sold at 95¢, rest given out with purchases); a $200 Picasso lithograph given away in a drawing on May 1; flowers and plants in the store and our art reproductions department featuring spring-like paintings.

Brother Bob, as a writer in the field of art history, and as a teacher with vexing problems in getting books for his students, had gripes about publishers, so we swapped complaints. Fred wrote in July 1963:

As bitter as you are with the publishers you could hardly have the heavy burden of disgust and contempt that I bear upon my tremblingly indignant shoulders. Taken as a group they are the most pretentiously self-bamboozled bunch of hypocrites in the country. But I will not enlarge upon the subject, tempting as it is, because I intend to send you a copy of the letter I am sending to Mr. Haynes, sales manager of Harper & Row, in which you will find more than enough material to substantiate my contention. I have grown so indignant on the subject that I am determined to get something published on it and, if the *Publishers Weekly* won't take it, I will try the middle-brow weeklies and monthlies, and if they don't want it, damned if I will not issue the thing myself and send it at my own expense into every one of their offices to menials high and low.

Mr. Haynes does not know it but I am relying upon him to engage with me in a dialogue in which he will advance the publishing point of view and I the common sense, rational, non-fettered approach to the matter.

Our little branch of this shoddy trade manages to do fairly well although we continue our struggle against terrific odds, mainly in getting the publishers to ship us books that are not battered beyond recognition and to avoid having to ship back half as many as we receive because of duplicate shipments. I will try to get you extra copies of the Viking and Doubleday lists for fall and Christmas this year so you can get the full flavor of the mediocrity that now obtains in publishing circles these days. Doubleday's list has to be seen to be believed; there is literally nothing worth a fuck on it; as for Viking, although it contains five or six books worth publishing, it also contains yet another of those "take you by the hand and I will show you the greatness of the great painters" books and a thing called *The Beach Book* which is an anthology of, you guessed it, pieces about going to the beach, headed with an introduction by no less a culture-monger than John Kenneth Galbraith and with end papers of solid silver foil so that you can reflect the sun in any way you choose. AHHHHHHH!

We had by now bought, for the first time, our own house, after facing eviction because our landlord was not comfortable with the color of our children's playmates. Again we financed with the kindness of friends and relatives, borrowing for the down payment. This was in the time before real estate inflation so our payments were only a little higher than our rent had been. The prosperity of the store meant we could afford a higher "proprietor's draw" to repay the friends who'd lent us money. We needed a larger house anyhow as I was pregnant with our fourth child. That August I wrote:

The store is prospering, as usual (so nice to be able to say that!). Sales the first half of this year were 48% higher than a year ago—I didn't expect the gain we had last year to continue at the same rate so it's been a pleasant surprise. One reason for it has been that we have the space for the increasing number of titles in paperback, unlike our rival down the street, UC Corner, which has been demoralized by our success and by the flood of books which they—not being book people—don't know how to choose among. Another reason is—and this sounds paternalistic but I don't know how else to describe it— the devotion and knowledge of our staff, three full time, one part time, besides Fred. As you know, we believe that we get what we pay for, and our wage scale is nearly double that of any other bookstore, in addition to which we started this year a monthly bonus, based on gross sales. I remember about three years ago the owner of UC Corner complaining to me that his wage bill was over $900 month (his hours are 7 A.M.–midnight). Ours runs over $1,700 month and we are open 10 A.M.–midnight.

The most difficult part of life in bookselling was the loss we had from theft, both internal and external. It was a constant pressing worry. We resented the attention it took from working to make the bookstore better.

We always felt that we were bookstore people, not cops, and we weren't good at being cops. It was our belief that people who would not steal from any other retailer had no qualms about stealing from bookstores. We thought they rationalized the act by telling themselves that books were intellectual property meant to be shared. We were the next thing to being a library, and besides, this large store had to be successful and would not miss a $1.95 paperback. Unfortunately for us, some of our employees had the same rationalizations.

"Shrinkage" nearly made us bankrupt over the years. Here is a comment I made in October 1963:

I'm glad to say that thanks to our policy of greater vigilance and more staffing, the shop-lifting has been drastically cut—it had to be or we would have gone bankrupt. Our losses were very heavy in 1961 and 1962, and concentrated in the April–June period when I presume the students are most out of cash and steal to re-sell or because they can't pay for the books.

The other bookstores in Berkeley have resorted to drastic methods such as uniformed "security" guards, store detectives who make public arrests daily (and catch some of the most unexpected people), measures which we feel don't do much good and really do more harm, since they alienate customers and make the thieving a challenge and also take away what conscience some people might have about it. Our method is prevention. We just try to have two people on duty at all times (thus our heavy payroll) and this year the loss was down to "normal." It still is our third biggest expense, after labor and rent.

Fred has been as busy as ever, this time getting out a fall promotion brochure and a separate publication, a sixteen-page selection of fables from LaFontaine and Aesop, illustrated by Grandville in an 1839 English edition that came our way in our antiquarian purchases. We just picked the ones we liked and are photo-offsetting them; the booklet will sell for 50¢.

This account is mostly about the store, books, and publishing. But the world of books was not our entire world. As new political realities made themselves evident, we both grew more and more concerned about the condition and direction of the nation. Here is a September 1963 letter Fred wrote to our friends John and Ruth Dunbar. John had worked in the West Virginia newspaper with Fred before the Second World War.

It is a pretty pickle that we are in in our brave land. This summer gave rise to a number of gloomy reflections as we passed through the countryside and observed along the way. Take California: cities sprawling helter-skelter with only a cruel parody of planning, with public utilities riding roughshod over the public interest, despoiling whole areas, with pickers poisoned by chemicals, with fish exploding in the streams from more of the same. When we went up to the mountains near Yosemite, we passed through the Sacramento Valley, one of the formidable agricultural producing areas of the world. The fields stretch out along the irrigation canals dotted with lone figures mounted on the mechanical monsters but somehow you are not conscious that these are farms mainly because it doesn't seem possible to see where the farmers live or indeed whether there are any farmers at all. All day and into the night the huge double trailer trucks thunder along the roads groaning with their loads of fruit and vegetables. At dusk the wind comes up and sweeps across the fields stirring up whirlwinds of dust from the topsoil. Somehow there is a sense of desolation in the midst of plenty, a feeling that man has set in motion a vast process of which he is now the victim rather than the boss. So big and so frightening.

Up in the mountains and the foothills a feeling of nostalgia is inescapable. There, where this vast apparatus cannot be made to function, there is something of the America that is past and of the kind of countryside with which most of us were familiar in gadding about West Virginia when we were in our teens. And of course, in the national forests, although you see the devastation of the past caused by mining of streams and forests, there is a blessed peace that acts as a balm. It is time we understood what has happened to our country. It has already been despoiled; the process of destroying a fair land has gone very, very far. So that from now on we must not deceive ourselves that we can accomplish much by saving small, isolated patches from the withering blight but must build a program of action to revive and restore as much as is possible what has already been blighted.

In the hospital where my mother was, I talked to people and was only cheered when I heard the older people talk. They at least had something to hold on to, some memories of hope and striving to cling to. The younger men yelled and griped about the politicians and the crooks but usually came back to the crucial importance of getting theirs. And when we drove out to Wayne County, it was just the same as it had been fifteen years before, a drab little nest of petty corruption. Of people who were getting theirs and joylessly sitting around the courthouse.

All this, as I reflected on it, is hardest on the kids and the women. Especially the latter. No one has even begun to write about the burdens that women have to bear in a society that has absolutely nothing to offer them except drudgery and monotony and helpless witnessing of suffering. It is the women who must bring a baby into this and see it grow up to a life that is wasted and damned and where success is measured by how strongly the child reacts to his environment and runs away from it.

I must say that in the face of all this I sometimes get rather irritated with my life. I am fortunate in that I seldom feel that quiet desperation in my own work that Thoreau spoke of. But I do feel a sense of desperation about the meaninglessness of it in relation to what is happening around me. Reading *Child of the Dark,* I mentioned something about it at the dinner table. "It's terrible to be hungry and have no food," said Pat. "Yes," said Martha (seven), "I'd hate to have to try it." So a child tells us the gist of the matter. So long as we can avoid it personally what the hell do we really care, or do, about the people who can't. And in talking about these things to children, what do people do except stir up a fierce striving to avoid personal deprivation at any cost? The unexamined life is not worth living and sometimes I think that a life that is unexampled is the same. I hardly know anyone who lives his life so that he teaches by example and without that, all the talk and the gesturing is empty and meaningless rhetoric.

This has been a somber letter, I suppose. And deceiving in that it would seem to indicate that practically all my time is spent in gloomy surveillance. It isn't. But don't you find that so much of life is tinged with pain these days? Music is a comfort, though. To listen to the "Trout Quintet" with the flashing and rippling notes bravely sounding out is somehow an affirmation. And Ray Charles singing. Looking at pictures is another solace. And the young. Our own kids and the kids I see. How is it possible that the old and highly placed can look at the kids and not have their compassions aroused and their imaginations stirred? Why are our eyes so blind our ears so deaf and our hands so idle?

When will Americans arrive at something like manhood and seize on to the tasks worthy of a man? I am sure they will and I take comfort in the conviction. This life is too senseless and the senselessness of it must come home at last to our people.

BEST-SELLERS FOR 1962
Gover, *One Hundred Dollar Misunderstanding*
Kroeber, *Ishi in Two Worlds*
Carson, *Silent Spring*

BEST-SELLERS FOR 1963
Solzhenitsyn, *One Day in the Life of Ivan Denisovich*
Baldwin, *The Fire Next Time*
McCarthy, *The Group*

PART THREE
The New Store on Telegraph Avenue

CHAPTER SIX 1964

PLANNING THE NEW STORE AT 2454 TELEGRAPH

For books are not absolutely dead things, but do contain a potentcy of life in them to be as active as that soule was whose progeny they are; nay, they do preserve as in a violl the purest efficacie and estraction of that living intellect that bred them . . . as good almost kill a man as kill a good book; who kills a man kills a reasonable creature, God's image; but he who destroys a good book, kills reason itself, kills the image of God, as it were in the eye. Many a man lives a burden to the earth; but a good book is the precious life-blood of a master spirit, imbalmed and treasured up on purpose to a life beyond life.

JOHN MILTON, *AREOPAGITICA*, 1644

We did our best, though, to shake off the gloom into which the semiannual inventory showing the extent of our losses plunged us. And we did have a lot to engage our interest. Our sales were rising and so were the quantities of books we stocked. We had a good staff that included a young man, Stevens Van Strum, whose passion for making Cody's a fine store equalled our own. The diversity of his interests was also an asset: French and German literature, poetry, art, small press publishing, gardening, philosophy. As they unpacked books, he and Fred had long talks on how we could get more space. In February 1964 Fred wrote:

We are all so busy and in such a state of anticipation that half the time we don't know what the hell we are doing. The store is going through a reorganization because our growing pains are really giving us the fits now. But I trust in the higher destiny to finally pull us through and prepare us for our translation into perhaps the largest bookstore in Northern California. Which is now a possibility. It remains to make it the best, not only here but in all the USA. And please don't say, with a sniff, "which isn't saying much."

We explored for space up and down the Avenue, in the four blocks be-

tween Dwight Way and the campus, to see if anything was available. The former Lucky supermarket on the southeast corner of Telegraph and Haste was on the market, but eluded us. I described the events in a letter to Bob written a couple of weeks after our daughter Celia Jane was born on March 8, 1964:

Plans for the new store are racing along. I think we told you of the need for one, since present store is in a building to be condemned under Urban Renewal, which is supposed to start in late '65 (lease ends December '65). Anyhow, the place is too small if we want to keep growing.

We tried to get the supermarket diagonally across the street from us—they leave in April—but someone got there ahead of us, reportedly a combination of Italian restaurant and billiard parlor. Then, Steve Van Strum and his father came into the picture. We may have told you his father is an investment counsellor on a grand scale—for banks, insurance companies, mutual funds, etc. Withal, he is rather a maverick capitalist—finds Wall Street full of stuffed shirts, hates insurance companies, etc. Steve is a fellow who came to work for us just about the time of your October 1962 visit, Bob—he's in charge of our art, French and German sections. He takes as strong an interest in the store as we do, and wants to continue working with us to develop it. It was his idea last year to have the Spring Festival, and he is now working on this year's festival which will center around poetry.

Anyhow, on the corner of Telegraph and Haste, i.e. half a block closer to campus than we are now, is a Shell gas station on which appeared four months ago a sign "For Sale or Lease, 85' × 100'." After a survey of the situation and talks with us, his father decided to buy it, using resources of a family holding corporation he set up some time ago. The sale was on sealed bidding and the bids were opened March 9. Following his real estate consultant's advice, Mr. Van Strum put in a bid of $110,000 and we—Steve and us—chewed our nails all weekend worrying—should it have been $112,000? or at least $110,050? Well, the next bid to ours was $108,000, so our way is clear.

Mr. V. S. is in accord with Steve's and our wish to make this the best store in the U.S., so Fred and Steve are to have a pretty freehand in specifying, to an architect of our choice, just what we want. That is, Mr. V. S. doesn't look at this as something that must have maximum profitability—it just has to cover its costs. That means the rent will not reflect the usual 8–10% net profit, we will not have to put up a rent deposit of four to six months (which would tie up our capital just when we need it most). We figure the building will cost around $100,000. The vague ideas we have so far are that the two street sides (and that is further good fortune, a corner lot which doubles display space) should be nearly all glass, floor to ceiling.

To the right, 6,500 square feet or so for us. To the left of that, two spaces to be let out for five years only, since we may want to expand into them. On the second story of that rental space will be our mezzanine, so that the main part of our store will be two stories high, with skylights or maybe entire roof of glass (is that possible? Anyway you get the idea—it will be used for lighting). The Van Strums will be putting up about $50,000 cash and the balance of lot and building costs will be on a mortgage. We are working out some arrangement whereby, after Abe Brumer, our accountant, works out what is called capitalization of our earnings and assets, we arrive at a figure of what our business is worth. It will probably be around $100,000 (that doesn't mean we could sell it for that, it's a projection of present growth trend, future earnings, etc.). Then, since we are going to incorporate, we will issue shares to Steve for that $50,000.

Steve's father's idea is that eventually Cody's Books should own the lot and the building, he is not especially interested in holding it. I told you he was a maverick. When he and Steve were discussing design, and Steve was saying that there are no models to go by in this country since book store architecture doesn't exist in the U.S., Mr. V. S. said to him, in the offhand way that real capitalists have, 'Why don't you go over to Europe and see what they're doing there?' with Scandinavia especially in mind. And he just may do that.

So you see it has been an exciting 1964 for us. We may be able to start construction in July and be in the building by September. We really feel like Horatio Alger heroes—did you ever hear of such incredible luck? By the way, all this about the new store is confidential, and I tell you that because I know you see lots of people and word could get back here quickly. Aside from prosaic business reasons, we want to keep it quiet for our own enjoyment of the surprise it will be when unbusinesslike Cody's goes into such glorious quarters. We don't have many enemies but there are the professional crepe-hangers who came around to the present store (1,992 square feet compared with 464 on Euclid) in the early days, looking about gloomily with such remarks as "Well, it sure is big, isn't it? Think you can get enough books to fill it? And enough customers? Heh-heh-heh." It will be the wonder of the week when we open, and the first *new* building on that part of Telegraph in many years.

A week later, Fred wrote on the same topic:

We are leaving the old store soon enough, I think. Our landlord is an incredible example of his species, always a nasty set. He sends us handwritten semi-literate letters full of the clumsy grace of a rhinoceros and resolutely refuses to take any responsibility for things like rain damage and so on. It will be a great pleasure to move out of his orful orbit. Not to mention the joy of not having to have a tizzy every time I'm away from the store and a fire siren goes screaming in the general direction of 2476 Telegraph. Of course we don't know whether he will hold us to the letter of the lease and make us pay rent for over a year even though we will not be occupying in all probability. Again, he may be glad to have us go so that he can get someone else and raise the rent now that the location has been established as a successful business site.

At first Steve's father, who is accustomed to putting up big office buildings, thought we should have a bookstore on rather a grand scale which would have cost upwards of $100,000. But as he has thought over the kind of store we have and what we actually need to fit our needs, he has come around to the much more sensible idea of a store that is simply a shell in which we can put our books. This will cut the cost in a number of ways. First, of course, it will keep the building out of the hands of one of the big architectural firms with their high fees and their rather pretentious ideas. But even better, it will also cut the rental considerably and enable us to buy the land and building back much more quickly. Both Steve and I envision a building that will look like a simple unpretentious gallery with good high ceilings, lots of light, and a minimum of frills. Inside we will use wood and textiles to achieve the softening effect that is needed around books and art.

The Germans have had to put up quite a few bookstores since the war and we were lucky enough to find an entire book devoted to them in the Architecture library at Cal. Most of these have that awful inhuman quality of much of modern German design but there are good details in many of them, particularly in the handling of lighting and display. In the latter, the Germans have probably been more inventive than anyone else, except possibly the Scandinavians. I am now scouting around for a really good book on Scandinavian retail design. We tend to feel that it is in the German and Scandinavian practice combined with the adventurous things being done by some of the smaller museums that offer our best tips.

An interesting thing in all I've seen on bookstores abroad, especially the German ones, is that ample provision is made for the customers to sit down at tables or stands. We are very anxious to incorporate that feature in the store but I can't figure out a way to do it without providing roosting places for people who would come in, establish themselves with a book, smoke merrily away making a mess, and be impossible to dislodge for hours. But it is very unfortunate that we can't offer that. I think perhaps what we can do is to have a room off to the side where we can invite people to sit down in seclusion there to look over the books they are interested in.

Store deportment is a matter I had never thought about until actually running one. We have a continual battle, for instance, to prevent people from coming in with ice cream cones, apples, oranges, soft drinks, beer, various kinds of gooey candy, and so on. The obviously startled look they give us when told that none of this is allowed is often followed by indignation. The problem is made more difficult by our competitor up the street who also sells soft drinks, hamburgers, hot dogs, candy, and who can't therefore forbid eating in an establishment where he is probably making more money out of the food than the books.

Brother Bob had written us about the small share of a book's retail price that went into the author's purse:

Pat and I chuckled over your characteristic authorial comments on the subject of publishing profits and the divvy of the spoils. There is something to be said in the bookseller's defense but this is not the place to say it, probably. I will only say that a good half of the cloth bound books that we get in (and that includes art books) have to be sold at considerably less than forty percent. Frequently, rather than return them, we mark them at cost to us and throw them on a sale table. Even then they often have a tendency to stay there for a long time. But when sold the author does get his royalty on the copy even though we have actually lost money handling the book. I wouldn't say that this is general bookstore practice and I have many thoughts (mostly damaging) about the average bookseller, but few people, including publishers, and never authors, understand that there are a few booksellers who consistently stock hundreds upon hundreds of books because they feel that they should be stocked and who don't apply to these books any rigorous turn-over check that would, in ordinary retail practice, chuck them out of the door or never allow them in in the first place.

We are building up our art book section at a great rate. Of course the Phaidon, Abrams, Skira books are the biggest sellers for us, particularly the Phaidon which sell surprisingly well. But we are also doing Shorewood, Braziller and other American publishers and bringing in quite a lot of books from France, Germany and Italy. We will have a way to go before we get anything like the stock that we want but it is beginning to shape up. The Dover books on Dürer and Brueghel and the Drawings book have sold amazingly. We have sold over 100 copies of the Dürer, which makes it one of the best-selling art books we've ever had.

Our old friends in Paris, Hachette, are giving us trouble. They wrote a letter complaining about our prices on the Livre de Poche which, they said, some of our competitors had characterized as dumping prices. They asked that we raise them to the going rate in America which is seventy-five cents for the singles and $1.25 for the double numbers. Our price now: fifty cents for the singles, seventy-five cents for the doubles. They seemed a little ashamed of bringing the matter up. The most galling aspect of the matter is that the damned college stores in this country—who should be most eager to keep prices down for their student trade—have gladly taken the opportunity to climb to the higher price which makes it possible for them to order from jobbers in this country rather than having the onerous chore of actually having to order them direct from Paris. And in our own case it is probably the student store at Cal that has raised the most hell with them about us and so brought the situation about.

We are writing a letter of the most courteous kind trying to explain to them that the market for French books can never be widened as it should and would be if booksellers have to sell at a price so jarringly out of line with what the books sell for in France. The assumption that people who can read French don't know enough math to figure out the approximate exchange value of the franc may seem plausible but isn't. On our side is the fact that the French book business with us has been growing at such a rate that perhaps Hachette will begin to get the idea that perhaps they hadn't better interfere too much with the "dumpers."

Early in April 1964, Fred wrote about the design for our new store:

I am hopeful that Claude Stoller will be our architect. He understands so well just exactly the kind of building we want. When I talked to him about it when it was merely a hazy dream, he always said that he felt that all that is needed in a bookstore is merely a pleasant structure to house them that is as unobtrusive as possible. Books are so wonderful in themselves, he said, that nothing should keep them from having the undisputed attention of those who come to the building.

There is a possibility, however, that the building will be designed by Owings of Skidmore, etc. But Steve's talks with him have not been reassuring. Owings insists that he is talking in modest terms but in the next breath he is outlining ideas that would involve that very expensive "modesty" that often appears in modern buildings. Steve, who knows Soriano, is bucking for him and I think he would also do a good building. Well, we will see. I don't think we'll be leaving the old store for at least another year, however.

We spent a good deal of time that spring and summer working out details of a pre-incorporation agreement between us and Steve, engineered by his father and drafted by an eminent and stuffy San Francisco law firm. The final accord provided that the building and land were to be sold to an investor with the proviso that Cody's Books have a twenty-year lease. During the first ten years of this lease we would manage the store; in 1975 management would be turned over to Steve. This suited us because we had in mind gradually easing out of the management responsibilities so that we could do other things; by 1975 Fred would be fifty-nine and I would be fifty-two.

One final note on the new store. Over the years, the myth has grown that Cody's in an excess of community spirit deliberately set the building back to allow a bit of urban space. The truth is that it was set back because of the city master plan. Berkeley hoped to get federal money to finance some of this plan, including traffic improvements on Telegraph.

The part of the plan affecting us was to make the last four blocks of Telegraph, from Dwight Way to the campus, a one-way street going north. Dwight Way to our south would become one-way going east and Haste on our immediate north, one-way going west. In order to allow motorists coming up Dwight to turn right on Telegraph, where it remained a two-way street from Dwight south, the plan called for taking off the southwest corner of Dwight so that a new lane curving south would peel off of the eastern-bound Dwight. Similarly, on Haste there would be a westward turn off from Telegraph, also with its own separate lane, which would be cut from the existing corner of Telegraph and Haste.

If we built in the ordinary way, using all the land right up to the sidewalk on both the Telegraph and the Haste St. sides of the lot, we would have had to shear off the corner of our building to comply with the plan. This is the reason Cody's is set back from the street in a mini-plaza where we planted twigs that now tower over the building. The city carried through this plan on Dwight, destroying the retail structures that had been there, but it never built the corresponding turn-off at Haste. So our corner plaza was left alone.

BEST-SELLERS FOR 1964
Mitford, *The American Way of Death*
Tawney, *Radical Tradition*
Pynchon, *V*
Marcuse, *One Dimensional Man*

CHAPTER SEVEN 1965 TO 1966

DESIGNING OUR WRAPPING PAPER   FRUSTRATING DELAYS
IN THE NEW STORE   POETRY FESTIVAL   MOVE INTO 2454,
EXPANSION AT ONCE   STEVE GOES TO FRANKFURT
ANTI-DRAFT PROTESTS

Remember that all the known world, excepting only savage nations, is governed by Books.

VOLTAIRE, 1694–1778

Fred's enthusiasm for books never flagged. A September letter:
The truth is that I have been working through the books we intend to feature this season and that has gobbled up most of my extra time. Chaplin's *My Autobiography* I've read and I anticipate that it will get not very good reviews because it is annoyingly reticent in some ways. But I liked it very much, possibly because it reveals so clearly that it is only in films that Chaplin can express himself and that it is by seeing them that you come close to him. Very little he says in the book, except rather a moronic passage about Shakespeare, and some other silly passages, does anything to destroy the image I have (and had before) of a man who is a stranger to the use of words as a means of expression, and also of a man who has practically no sense of the unique position he occupies in the history of the movies.

Sartre's *Words* are of another kind, however, and I must say that I think this first part of his autobiography is tremendous. It seems to me it speaks very directly to certain kinds of people, among whom I number myself. For others it will probably seem pretty much of a waste. The only book I could recommend without any reservations at all is the new version of the Ishi story that Mrs. Kroeber has done, *Ishi in Two Worlds*. If this book is not appreciated by a reader I would feel confident in saying that the lack isn't in the book but in the reader. I thought the first Ishi book was great but this new version, written for younger readers but completely convincing for others, is beyond praise. Anyway, this is a really extraordinary book year and we are having a wonderful time choosing from the fine plums hanging from the publishers' trees. I know that I have said they are an exasperating lot but the fact still remains that they do do a lot of very good stuff.

I've been busy gathering materials for reproduction on our wrapping paper. It occurred to me that it would be a good idea for a bookstore to originate its own very characteristic wrapping paper and what better than to feature great title pages, printers' emblems, and some tasty fleurons? At first I was satisfied with a selection of sixteenth century printing but then I began to lament that it was not possible to include a Dickens title page and also that I couldn't include something from our own time. So now I'm holding up on the project until I can gather a really outstanding selection. I've grown more and more interested in the history of printing so I think I have a fairly good idea of what should be included. The difficulty is in finding material which can be taken from out-of-copyright books since I don't want to get involved with publishers in making requests for permission to reproduce. However, I have most of what I need now and a little more ransacking should turn up the rest. I do have permission for the present-day title page that will be used—the very handsome and elegant title page for the aforementioned Ishi.

Meanwhile, I ache for the visit to New York which is to be during the first two weeks of October. This time I will stay at a cheap hotel in Manhattan so as to have the maximum freedom of movement and make the most of my time. I tend to go back in New York to the days when I saved every penny and borrowed a few more to come from West Virginia. In those far-off days I went to as many as two plays, a movie, and two museums in one day and night, finishing up at one of the late movie houses on 42nd street. I don't believe my old bones will endure that kind of punishment now but I do like to roam around New York at night and not have to worry about catching a late train out to somewhere.

All the legalities concerning the new store, the necessary incorporation and the pre-incorporation agreement seemed frustratingly slow, but they did move along. In October Fred wrote:

Our plans for the store proceed. There have been disappointments and frustrations along the way, of course. We had hoped that the building would be designed and the construction supervised by an architect friend of ours, Claude Stoller, a fine man. But a tangle ensued and our financing plans changed and Claude finally bowed out. So now we will have a strictly utilitarian building of rather nondescript appearance and will have to work on the interior as best we can to make it attractive. The lot on which we'll build has now been cleared of the filling station and it looks absolutely limitless. We are in the midst of an urban renewal plan for the area so that our design for the store has to take this into account but this is all right since a set-back demanded by the urban renewal plan fits into our design, as we never intended to fill the lot in the first place. As the design now stands we will go up twenty feet so that we can later put in a mezzanine when expansion of stock calls for it. For the first time we will actually have an office and adequate storage space and that will be a blessing of the first order.

Our foremost concern, though, is to have the stock we will need for the new store. Our stock of French and German books has expanded greatly but we must expand it further. We are also doing very well on art books and it seems apparent that we can do a great deal more there. Then we want to have all the basic works in such fields as philosophy, psychology, poli sci, anthro, lit and so on so that we will be that most useful and admirable bookshop, what the English call a "stock carrying" bookstore. In other words, we want to be the best bookstore in the area and, eventually, in the U.S. This seems a heady aim but going toward it gives us the sense of direction and purpose we need.

The wrapping-paper project, such a labor of love, involved going to the Rare Books section of the University library and then having photographs done by the library of the printers' marks Fred wanted to use. Finally the paper was printed, in sheets not rolls, and Fred put some into a tube and sent it off to an editor at Publishers Weekly. *This prompted a telegram asking what we had sent, so Fred let her know:*

I'm sorry that I have been the reason for provoking you to send a telegram inquiring about that mysterious roll of paper. You have been the victim of a failure of coordination at a low executive level. I meant to accompany the roll with a letter explaining just what it was but it went out into the world alone and mute.

So herewith the explanation. Yes, it is wrapping paper, and yes, it is mainly of printers' marks. These latter are mostly of famous printers of the sixteenth century. Some were reproduced from old books, others were photographed from the actual books through the cooperation of the Rare Book Room of the University of California Library, Berkeley. The other elements in the paper are illustrations, also mainly from sixteenth-century books and again the same sources were used.

Why such a wrapping paper? Well, we've looked for years for a really appropriate wrapping paper for books. For a couple of years we found a Swedish paper of excellent and dignified design that met the requirement but that design was discontinued and we could no longer obtain the paper. We went through numerous sample books looking for something else but with no success. So we were driven at last to think of producing something ourselves. During the past several years I have grown more and more interested in the history of printing so that it was natural that I would think of a paper that would suggest something of the rich heritage to which all of us are heirs. After that, it was merely a job of research in the material, arranging it in what I thought was a pleasing layout, and then having it printed by photo-offset.

How do people like it? Very much. In fact, numerous customers have asked for sheets to put in their offices or homes, while other people have purchased sheets to use for their gift wrapping. Of course, there is no color in the design, but we overcome this pretty well by using a red ribbon around the package. This, it seems to us, makes for a very elegant and attractive book wrapping. The cost per sheet is seven cents. Admittedly, the cost is high but we charge up part of it to promotion on the grounds that customers will be appreciative of the thought and effort that has gone into providing an appropriate wrapping paper.

The lack of letters for several months of late 1964 and early 1965 may reflect the 1984 flood in brother Bob's cellar, when one box of correspondence became a soggy pulp, but in any event there probably weren't many letters. We were busy with construction of the new building, with our four energetic children, and with an increasing measure of community involvement.

A comprehensive program for integration of the Berkeley schools began in 1963, and this led to a campaign against the School Board. We worked in October 1964 to defeat an effort to recall some of the Board; our success was in effect a mandate for educational changes.

Meanwhile, on the University campus the Free Speech Movement (FSM) stimulated another kind of change: freedom for advocacy on campus. The struggle reached its climax with the arrest of nearly eight hundred students sitting in at the administration building, Sproul Hall. Again, Berkeley was not in a vacuum; sit-ins were by now a familiar tactic.

The "establishment" was being defined, and an anti-establishment awareness was changing the consciousness of the young. The paperback editions of the books of the Marxist philosopher Herbert Marcuse could hardly be kept in stock on the store shelves. And the new consciousness was being expressed in other writing, in clothing, in theatre, and especially in the music of the young. The association of "dope" with the same consciousness now found its spokesman in, among others, Timothy Leary. South Campus began more and more to exult in a life-style that set it apart from most other parts of the city.

Spring of 1965 brought a diversion for us, a Poetry Festival in April created by our partner Steve. The Oakland Tribune *story commented,*

". . . there are precious few bookstores or book departments which offer a really good selection of poetry. . . . Poetry readers . . . know that paperback stores usually have the best selections. In this area, the reader . . . has probably already discovered Cody's Books . . . Cody's prides itself on one of the largest poetry stocks on the West Coast—a selection that runs to nearly 1,000 titles. . . .

"This year . . . Cody's plans a unique poetry festival . . . Stevens Van Strum, the man in charge of the affair, told me earlier this week about the really awesome task Cody's has set for itself.

" 'On opening day, we'll have what is possibly the largest collection of poetry ever seen in this area,' he said. 'We're attempting to get everything available together under one roof. These are books that are seldom if ever seen in other stores, and many of them have been out of print for years. They'll be on exhibit and for sale.' Among hundreds of rare and unusual volumes will be first editions of works by Wallace Stevens, Gertrude Stein and Robinson Jeffers, and by lesser known poets such as Leonie Adams, Elinor Wylie, Robert Creeley and Philip Lamantia.

" 'We'll have books of verse by some surprising poets, including Havelock Ellis, Helen Keller and Max Eastman, and a lot of items associated with poetry,' Van Strum went on. 'We want people to be able to get a real sense of modern American and British poetry.'

"He explained that as part of the festival Cody's will hold a drawing for a valuable collection of volumes by William Butler Yeats. It will include some of the poet's early works and several first editions. Tickets for the drawing will be free. In addition, visitors to the store during the festival will receive a 10 by 14 inch sheet on which are printed (handsomely) two poems about poetry by Dylan Thomas and Robinson Jeffers.

"All in all, the festival promises to be a rare and wonderful thing. . . ."

It was everything we had hoped for, drawing attention to the many Bay Area poets, and letting the small presses and self-publishers know that we wanted to carry their work and provide space for their readings.

Meanwhile, the store business was growing. As the months went by in 1965 and our new building became a reality, we could hardly wait to get inside. In August I wrote to Bob and Fi:

We haven't really felt the need for a vacation—the excitement of the new store has been stimulus and change enough. It is nearly completed and in fact the physical edifice will be ready before the legal one is so that it will stand empty for a week or so, since in order for the buyer to get full tax depreciation it must be an un-used structure when he buys it and it is considered used if we so much as go inside it to build our fixtures. This is all very aggravating, considering the pressure of time on us with registration at the University starting around the middle of September. We will send you photos—it really looks handsome.

We came closer and closer to actual possession of our new premises, but like the perils of Pauline, new troubles arose, as Fred described in a November letter:

We have been going through rather a trying series of difficulties during the past month or so involving the new store. To put the thing in elementary terms (and how grateful you should be that we do) our contractor has fouled us up very badly. He did this by taking the money that was paid to him for various parts of our building and paying some of said money to sub-contractors who had worked for him on previous jobs. This left some of the sub-contractors on our building holding unpaid bills. These sub-contractors thereupon filed what are known as liens on the contractor for their work and when he failed to come through these liens were then laid on us.

I use "us" in a very loose sense, meaning mostly Steve. Now that we look back we can see many sins of omission and commission but like most of these backward views they have only a cautionary value in an experience which I ardently pray we will never encounter again. The working spirit of all of us was badly battered and last week I realized that unless remedial measures were taken we would end up in the slough of despond. So I embarked on a program of action for action's sake—cleaning up the present store generally as much as I could, and trying to enlist everyone else in a frenetic round of activity. By and large it seemed to work. We also went very thoroughly into the matter with everyone, explaining just what we were up against and now I think we are prepared to weather the wait.

The wait may be quite prolonged, under the circumstances, since we may not get into the building because of all the legal tangle until around Thanksgiving. Meanwhile, there sits our new store, pristine and pure, waiting (even aching) for us to move into it and bring it to life. It has been exasperating but it has also forced me to look very sternly at just what is involved, or what we have at stake, in the store. Both Pat and I have put much agony and work into it and I think that is what bothers me most when I see it endangered. Also we have many plans for what we want to do with the store and it is hard to see that menaced or delayed.

Fortunately, we had insurance against mechanics' liens, so our new capital from Steve's share purchase could be spent on fixtures and stocking the store. Only three weeks later, we moved in, and I wrote:

At last we got possession of our scrumptious store, on Tuesday, November 23, at noon. We must be out of the old on November 30 at midnight since lease expires and it is re-leased. The shelves have been built and today the guys are moving the books in, for opening on Tuesday. So yesterday was the last day at the old stand. Fred said he felt sad yesterday afternoon; the old store was more "his" than the new one. But that is the story of most growing businesses that become too large and successful for one person to handle. In a way it's like the parent whose child grows up.

Christmas was more hectic than ever. In January Fred noted:

We are finally getting the store in some kind of order and I am carrying on, believe it or not, a vast campaign to make everything as neat and orderly as possible. This sounds improbable but I have finally realized the importance of doing it and we now have probably the neatest bookstore you've ever seen and our stock receiving room has a clinical look of an almost awe-inspiring nature.

That same month, Publishers Weekly *had a feature story on our new store:*

"Probably the largest store devoted to paperbacks in the United States. There is floor space of 6,500 square feet, including a selling area on the mezzanine, and a gallery which will be used mainly for the display and sale of art reproductions. . . . Cody's new store has some interesting features: a timbered ceiling twenty-two feet high which covers the entire area, including the gallery room; a ceiling of Douglas fir and fixtures and shelving, also of Douglas fir . . . there is a circular counter, made of laminated two-by-fours, which, Mr. Cody says, 'has been likened by some to the vast circle in the center of the British Museum Reading Room in London, and, by others, to a bar or a butcher's block.'

"There are floor-to-ceiling windows so that in the daytime the store is flooded with natural light; at night, the lights in the store illuminate surrounding areas. Skylights in the ceiling bring in even more light into the store. . . ."

Fred took time off in January for a visit to New York—museums, publishers, plays, other bookstores. He wrote about it:

My interview with the Great Jovanovich, of Harcourt, Brace, was a spectacle in itself. He is of the new breed of businessmen who are as restless and adventurous as a renaissance prince. He is full of ideas and very conscious of enjoying money and power but with something of a rueful sense of self-appraisement. As you may gather, he did most of the talking and I was so awed by the magnificence of his establishment that I sat quite still and drank it all in. But he does want some kind of a study group of booksellers and publishers set up in which each of us would do papers which would be circulated in advance and then meet, probably in Chicago next fall, to have two or three days of intensive discussion growing out of the papers. It sounds all right although I am a little dubious about people in the book trade taking that much trouble just for a silly project like finding ways to improve retail bookselling. Anyway, I will promise to participate and then see what happens.

We were hardly in the new building when we expanded. Here's what I wrote in March 1966:

Did I tell you about the great breakthrough? Our building was constructed in two retail units, we have lease of entire building, intending to sublease the other unit but have control so when we wanted to expand we could. We discovered that no one would take less than a ten-year lease, and at our growth rate we figure we will need the space in three years. So rather than face seven years' overcrowding, we decided to move into it now and absorb two or three non-profit years until the volume catches up with the additional expenses in rent ($28,000 a year now) and staff to man the extra space.

So, Sunday down came the non-structural wall, the new shelving was put in place and books moved in and voila—we are now certainly the largest paperback store in the U.S. (a position the *Publishers Weekly* already gave us in their article on the new store in the January 17 issue, page 126). We have 8,820 sq. ft. of which about 70% is sales area, the rest stock room and office. Now we can settle down and polish our jewel without worries about leaky roofs or rapacious landlords.

This breakthrough made possible our transition from a paperback store with a limited number of clothbound books to a general trade bookstore. As a mostly paperback store, we had been limited to those books that had generated enough sales in cloth to warrant a paperback edition. As a result, we lacked the excitement of the brand-new titles, including many good books that would never generate enough sales to warrant reprinting in paper.

Now, however, we had the resources that permitted us the satisfaction of ordering the new clothbounds. How Fred enjoyed those meetings with the salesmen, or "travelers." It was from this time on that Cody's built its present reputation, through the selections Fred and some of our staff made of what we considered the best of the new books. Best did not mean bestsellers. Fiction only made it if it had literary merit. The emphasis of the clothbound section was in new ideas on social concerns.

On the University campus, the free speech issue continued to be a struggle. "Outside agitators" were cited by an uncomprehending administration. When one of the first of the off-campus rallies took place, outside our bookstore, the police declared it "illegal" for not having a prior loudspeaker permit and seized the loudspeakers. It was aggravating for me to have so much time taken up with the mundane drudgery of day-to-day store matters when I would have preferred spending more time on antiwar work. My work for the store—the financial management—was still done at home. I had an office at the new store, but Celia was only two. Child care was hard to find and expensive, and I wanted to be at home with the children if I could. I felt fortunate to be able to do much of the work in my back room study, and in the evenings. Here is a typical small business owner's lament that May in my letter to Bob:

Long silence, punctuated by much activity here with the usual work load, at least half of which is created by a meddling government bureaucracy (you should just see the monthly payroll reports I have to make out, federal and state). I meant to write before, but didn't even get a birthday card to you, my dear, what with tax reports. Just so you will feel really sorry for me, in April alone I have to file: federal income tax, state income tax, county property assessment, city ditto, state unemployment compensation report for the first quarter, state disability tax report ditto, federal FICA quarterly report, federal withholding tax report, and three others I can't recall at the moment, I know there are eleven in all. And God forbid you should make an error, they hound you about it for years and your files bulge with memorandums and orders and IBM cards.

A look at those tax reports shows that, like most businesses (Fred once said, "We're not small business, we are teeny-tiny business"), we were building it with sweat equity. I was not on the payroll at all and Fred was getting around $10,000 a year, which was not much even then. My earnings from my economic reports were about $3,500 a year, and we had income of about $1,000 a year from an inheritance. We scraped by, driving an old car and economizing in every way we could, because we wanted to make Cody's a fine store. It was an uphill battle, because we were not working in isolation from a troubled society, as is reflected in this note I wrote in June 1966:

Fred has every intention of writing, but to tell you the truth, as soon as he gets home at 6:15 he doesn't even come in the house, he goes right to the garden. That is his release from tension, to work there, watering and weeding and making new plantings. And believe me, there is some tension in running a business with a staff of about twelve capricious people and all sorts of demanding customers and the whole "scene" on Telegraph Avenue, especially now that schools are out and the "instant" or "weekend" hippies, as they are variously termed—the young kids from straight families in Concord, Walnut Creek, etc.—come into the great mecca of Telegraph Avenue in Berkeley. Some of these kids are really sad sights, dissipated from drug use, lost souls. . . . And if anyone has sensitivity—which Fred certainly does—it is upsetting to see what could be creative people building a life, turning to nihilism in despair at the hypocrisies of the Great Society.

It was with real pride that Steve went to the greatest book trade show in the world, the Frankfurt Book Fair. Thousands of publishers from all over the world present their wares there in five or six huge exhibit halls every October. Fred wrote in September:

Talk of noble self-sacrifice! This morning Steve took off for Europe for three weeks to attend the Frankfurt Book Fair and then go on for a week each to Paris and London, with a visit also to Oxford to go through the extensive operations of the Oxford University Press. Our business with the latter has grown to the point that we could sell practically their entire list if we stocked it. Steve is of the younger generation that never, or almost never, allows any enthusiasm to show itself. But he was certainly bubbling last night on the eve of his departure and I imagine he will run himself ragged soaking up everything he can.

The great kick out of it for me is to see the store in a position that it is actually good business for us to send someone to Europe to buy and make contacts for us. Much of the credit for this goes to Steve because he has made the French and German books really go. The libraries far and near come flocking to us and our prices are so competitive that, without giving discounts, we still get the business which, I might add, we don't at all discourage although we do nothing to promote it. We are now doing Spanish books but are in a bad position with that stock because the libraries came in and took away everything except the dogs so that we are left with the shell of a collection to be filled in by orders not yet arrived.

Pat has just come back from Telegraph Avenue bringing loads of money from the store and also some croissants for breakfast. So you must imagine me on a misty morning typing away to you while munching. By the way, do you do anything about covering current graphic expression in your classes? If you do, I think you might be interested in some posters that we are now selling at the store that are done to advertise concerts by such groups as The Mothers, the Jefferson Airplane, and other such aggregations. These posters, some of which are so convoluted as to be almost indecipherable, owe much to the excesses of Art Nouveau but this only seems to have spurred interest in them. They are responsible for having created a collector class among the under twenties who won't let them stay on the walls if they can possibly get their hands on them. If you are interested, I will send you a choice sample of them. They should at least provide a bizarre note for the decoration of your office.

In November, I wrote a brief message:

We are snowed under with work right now—the Xmas rush started yesterday just as though someone had turned on a faucet, and much as we deplore the excesses, it is the time when we make up for about nine months of break-even business, and make a profit that carries us forward, and allows us to carry all those scholarly books that Fred and Steve love, but that do not have either the turnover or the margin to pay their own way.

It was not only the scholarly books on a low margin (20%) that did not pay. There were the hundreds upon hundreds of self-published books and small press books, all taken on consignment at 20%. Consignment meant that we did not pay unless they sold. But consignment books generally were slow-moving and took up valuable space that we could devote to books that would move out more quickly. Other low-margin books were those ordered in small volume, where the publisher required a minimum of ten or so to get the "usual trade discount" of 40%. And then there were the books that were slow-moving "back list" books: part of our cultural heritage. They had to be there if we were to hold up our heads, but at a sale rate of a copy or two a year, they too did not pay their way. They did pay in psychic income. We felt wonderful about having the Oxford Dictionary of the English Language *in all its volumes. Its enrichment of our store was worth the nine months it took to sell the set.*

Other people felt this enrichment, and this is how Cody's built its reputation. Most bookstores believe they cannot afford such luxuries as a substantial back list, and certainly small stores cannot. We had the space, and our desire for a great store was far stronger than any wish to make a lot of money.

Outside our windows, the demonstrations gathered momentum. In December when an anti-draft table was ordered off campus but the adjacent Navy recruiter left alone, student protesters were arrested, held a rally, and voted to strike the campus. Something new was added: a strike committee leaflet with a yellow submarine on it "as a symbol of our trust in the future and our longing for a place fit for all of us to live in."

Early in 1967 the Free University of Berkeley, an outgrowth of the student-run classes during earlier sit-ins and strikes, announced a list of thirty-four courses to be taught at various locations around Berkeley. City elections were scheduled for April, and the new left had candidates for mayor and city council. One of them was Ron Dellums, and he won. This was the start of a political career that took him to Congress in 1970 and has kept him there ever since.

Contrary to the myths of the national press, all Berkeley was not radical, nor was the majority of the student body radical. Many residents were upset about what they perceived as a constant uproar increasingly visible on the streets, no longer confined to the campus. The broad range of books we carried and our support for anti-war activities made us the target of anonymous threats. One came from the fascist Minutemen with the drawing of the cross-hairs of a rifle captioned: "This is on the back of your neck."

BEST-SELLERS FOR 1965
Sorensen, *Kennedy*
Berne, *Games People Play*
White, *The Making of the President, 1964*
Tolkien, *The Hobbit*

BEST-SELLERS FOR 1966
Greene, *The Comedians*
Capote, *In Cold Blood*
Lane, *Rush to Judgment*
Masters and Johnson, *Human Sexual Response*

CHAPTER EIGHT 1967

CENSORSHIP BILLS HIPPIES AND STREET PEOPLE
AN EVENING WITH ANAÏS NIN

Of the many worlds which man did not receive as a gift of nature, but which he created with his own spirit, the world of books is the greatest. . . . Without words, without writing and without books there would be no history, there could be no concept of humanity.

HERMANN HESSE, 1877–1962

Ronald Reagan was elected governor in November 1966, and one of the items on his agenda was legislation against "obscenity," which amounted to censorship. Several such bills were introduced into the state legislature and Fred took the trail to Sacramento in June.

Life has been full enough during these last several weeks. I have been mainly involved in (1) fighting obscenity bills and (2) what might be called hippie care. To take (1) first. During our last state election there was a proposition on the ballot which would have resulted, in the brief period before it became unconstitutional, in prosecution of every form of expression that could be construed as obscene by any primitive religionist. The voters in their sovereign wisdom rejected the proposition two to one. But Mr. Raygun and Attorney General Lynch (surviving Democrat in the present governor's official family) both, though opposing that measure, were certain "some form" of obscenity legislation was needed.

A number of bills went, therefore, into the hopper of the legislature, many of them so extreme that even their sponsors probably never meant them to be taken seriously. Two bills finally emerged with the backing of the governor and the A.G. These had to do with punishment for the purveyors of porn to what were referred to as "specially susceptible groups" and to the tender under the age of eighteen. The latter called for the production of either identity cards or parents when the little shavers were about to consummate the purchase of lewd girls like *Candy* and *Fanny Hill*. Our state Library Association early drew a bead on these bills and declared solidly against them. They were of course joined in their opposition by the ACLU whose northern California chapter is a model for the nation.

Where were the booksellers in all this? Belatedly, the president of our northern California association learned of the bills and called, about two weeks before the bills were to come up before an Assembly committee (they had already passed the Senate) a meeting of the Board, of which I happen to be a member. At the meeting we heard a lawyer whose heart is in the right place but who is given to the most inordinately long lecturing explain why we should be against them. With the help of another bookseller present, we planned an open meeting here in Berkeley for the booksellers of the area at which a Library Association representative, the ACLU legislative counsel, and yours truly would speak.

I then began calling around the state to see if we could possibly get a broader expression of opposition at Sacramento. Mr. Epstein who owns the largest chain of bookstores in the south (and a former president of the American Booksellers Association) said it was nice we were concerned but that he was so busy with opening two new stores that he couldn't be. He suggested I call the president of the Southern California booksellers and I did and he said he would have to study the matter because he wasn't at all sure that he didn't favor the bills. So then I called the president of the Association of College Bookstores but he had to be in Seattle, apparently to attend some kind of a fixture trade show, but he was interested and hoped vaguely that something could be done although time was certainly short and he couldn't possibly assemble his board at such short notice, etc.

We had our meeting in Berkeley and six stores were represented. But we did succeed in getting ten booksellers from the area to promise to go to Sacramento to appear before the Committee, or at least be present. I was chosen to express the sentiment of the group. Came the Committee hearing and our group was the only group to represent booksellers—none from the south, none from the college stores. The ACLU and the Library Association had done great work behind the scenes and due to their efforts the Committee split five to five on a party basis. This was enough to knock out the bill.

I spoke and was attacked by a right-winger on the committee who wanted me to say that booksellers had to read everything they sold before they could sell it. I said I thought I got through about fifty books a year and while this was considerably better than the national average it was nothing to brag about. We horsed around on this quite a bit and he finally impatiently waved me away when I refused to endorse his sentiment that the entire state was awash in a sea of filth. On the whole, this little foray into state politics was very interesting. I was surprised at the intelligence and sobriety of many of the legislators on the committee. Most of them are young and fairly brainy and pretty conscientious.

The main point of the experience was that it showed that the booksellers are so apathetic on the subject of intellectual freedom that it is frightening. We (a few of us) are trying to do something about remedying that situation but it is uphill work all the way. It makes you understand much of recent history, to some small degree. We are hopeful that we can organize a small group of concerned booksellers who will learn ways to reach the remainder. The Library Association will help out on this.

The hippies come into the picture because of a damned committee formed of ministers, interested lay people (what terms!), businessmen along the street who aren't Poujadists or worse. We meet every week and talk and talk and out of this we got five thousand bucks from the Presbyterians and finally hired an Episcopal minister, just graduating from seminary, who wears psychedelic neckties and is apparently with it and turned on and carrying a bag and doing his thing and all that. I am assured by everyone that I will have to take him as he is with a little of that old-time faith I thought I had foresworn.

We have now reached the awful stage of by-laws and forming a non-profit corporation and electing officers and a board comprising nine people. At this point I think I have served my usefulness and will now retire to the sidelines. There is something so inherently ludicrous to me in nine people directing the activities of one guy that I just can't get with it. Besides, you have no idea until you have been exposed to about twenty-four hours of it, how wearing it is to have to listen to the new theology. I find, also, that I have not developed a taste for the kind of interdenominational in-fighting characteristic of the clergy even though it gives one a new appreciation of the talents of the Good Pope John and what he was able to accomplish with the real pros in the field. But it has been interesting and may make a few pages when I come to write my sequel to the *Memoirs of a Bankrupt Bookseller.*

Your gripes over publishers are mild compared to what I feel about them. Except for a very few exceptions, I could cheerfully spend two weeks in New York inviting them out to lunch and administering fatal doses of arsenic to each in their martinis. For the most part the larger publishing houses are now the rather amusing tax dodges taken over as bijous by such large corporations as RCA and the *Los Angeles Times* crowd. Incidentally, we have not seen a Shorewood salesman in two years. Clark and Way, if that is their name, is owned by I forget what colossus now and has nothing but money. Like most publishers, though, their bookkeeping is probably involved in the electronic revolution and nothing can be learned until they find a way to untangle it.

I assume that you have read that Mr. Praeger has acquired (through the *Encyclopaedia Britannica*'s money which had earlier acquired him) Phaidon and that Time-Life International has acquired New York Graphic. World (the L.A. Chandlers) has distribution for Skira and bought Abrams. We now get showers of Abrams art books which no one has ordered and no one has ever thought of ordering and when we order books we do want we don't get them at all. I hope you will sue all of your publishers and if you need any money to prosecute them please let us know and we will scrape up all we can if we can have your promise that you will not desist until you have at least three of them behind bars. This is one thing on which booksellers are fairly united so perhaps we can get other funds released for other angry authors.

The committee of ministers and citizens that Fred referred to in discussing "hippie care" wanted to find ways to provide counseling, medical referrals, housing for transients, and other services for the thousands of young people drawn to Berkeley because of its reputation for anti-war and civil rights actions. From the Be-In in Golden Gate Park in January 1967 to the "summer of love" there was a steady stream of adventurers coming to California. Many of them settled in the old brown shingle houses of the South Campus area, often several to a room.

The University administration resented and feared these nonstudents, so it was not surprising when they announced that June their plans to buy three acres of land bounded by Dwight, Haste, Telegraph, and Bowditch. The Daily Californian *ran a picture of one of the decrepit buildings on the site, captioned, "Just one of the features of hippieland set for destruction." The plans were to use the land for playing fields, faculty offices, and parking. The University statement declared that the area "has been the scene of hippie concentration and rising crime." Thus what became People's Park two years later first appeared in the news.*

Changes in consciousness were not limited to youth. One of the qualities that makes Berkeley special is the presence of many lively minded adults who create and support adventures in all the arts, sciences, and philosophies, as this essay by Fred suggests:

People began showing up early in the afternoon even though Anaïs Nin wasn't scheduled to make her appearance at the store until eight in the evening. It was the autumn of 1966 and we were hosts to a publication party for the first volume of her memoirs. The early arrivals had just dropped in to check the action and make sure she was still coming. "We know her," they would say, "but we haven't seen her for a long time."

The anxious visitors were reluctantly moving into their middle years, most of them—bulging and sagging a little but still bravely flying the flag of their distinctive status as artists and non-conformists. It wasn't that their clothes were eccentric but they somehow managed to look sloppily casual and elegantly formal at the same time. The women had beads and lots of big rings and they wore long dresses that looked as though they had been designed in Paris and then put in a drawer for twenty years. The men wore the kind of shirts you get in expensive shops in Edinburgh or Aspen and tailored jackets that now appeared to have been grabbed off the rack in a free store (remember the free stores?).

They were in a state of suppressed excitement about seeing Anaïs as they stared around them at the young people in the store, who represented the one-third of Berkeley that was ill-fed, ill-clothed, and ill-disposed to those who, in a way, were the mothers and fathers of them all. We were close to the days when a popular magazine hardly dared to appear without a heavily sober piece on the generation gap but these young and these middle-aged people warily stalking each other were the prophetic symbols of what was to become perhaps the saddest breach between youth and age.

Not that it wasn't to be expected. It wasn't only those in their early youth who were defiantly seceding from the establishment during the late 1960's. People in their thirties and forties—some even approaching what we now call the "senior" years—had a way of appearing on the Avenue, taking a room or an apartment near the University campus, and making the scene, as the saying went. It must have taken real guts for some of them to outfit themselves for the experience. But even as middle-aged businessmen along the street, or some of them, were soon to let their hair grow longer and wear a string of beads around their necks, so an older drop-out soon managed to assemble the clothes and the trappings that advertised his or her rebellion. As time passed, some managed to assimilate completely to the scene with their own individual adaptations to the prevailing norm. It was tempting to speculate whether a man in his forties, wearing a handwoven peasant blouse and his hair tied up in leather thongs, had once been one of the more creative people on the Revlon account.

But the footing on the younger side of the generational abyss was uncertain, even for the audacious older people who dared to make the leap. Perhaps they were thought to be rather curious voyeurs, and certainly some of the older hippies had to contend against a completely unfounded suspicion that they were spies in the counter-culture ranks. No doubt some of the young women even had evidence to support their fear that among the males there were a considerable number of Dirty Old Men, and it was noticeable that the young men seldom emerged from their own ranks to mingle with the older men, even briefly.

I've always thought this was a chapter in the story of those years that never really got told. Perhaps it was Charles Reich in *The Greening of America* (1970) and later in *The Sorcerer of Bolinas Reef* (1976) who most accurately reflected this aching compulsion of those who were older to somehow erase the years and be young again. I feel that his writing about what could be called the rejected allies was valuable and true. And I know he was the voice of an aspiration and a yearning by many of those who were older—an urge that is not, after all, so exceptional, to see in the young the best that is in us.

Back to Anaïs Nin. On that evening when she walked into the store, there were few intimations of the effulgent presence she was later to become among feminists. Nevertheless, she was at a trembling moment in her life, balanced between her position as a cherished legend of the avant garde in the thirties and forties, and her transcendence into something approaching apotheosis as a goddess to young women who saw in her the fulfillment of what they aspired to become.

That night, though, it was the aura of the Paris of Henry Miller and the writers of the slim volumes published in small editions by the little presses that shone around her. And it was those who were remembering their youthful excitement and those long hours of good talk in the Left Bank cafés, the poring over the pages of the short-lived literary reviews, the nights of their joy and gladness, who were upstairs in the gallery with their Anaïs.

And Anaïs felt the waves of affection that flowed toward her in the crowded room. (There is a warmly written note on the evening in a later volume of her *Memoirs*.) She walked with a light step as she moved among them in her long ivory gown—a princess at her court. When she finally stationed herself in the center of the room to talk with a circle of people around her, it seemed entirely natural that Lawrence Ferlinghetti should advance with a bucket, raise it above the small figure, and shower down on her a cascade of red rose petals. She hardly glanced toward him as she went on talking, not bothering to brush away the stray petals that clung to her hair and lingered on her shoulder.

We had stocked gallons of wine for the party but by eleven o'clock the supply was running low. It was still an animated, noisy scene when I ran down the stairs, drove to the nearest liquor store, and then hurried back with some gallons of white wine in the car. But the store was silent when I returned and the gallery was empty. Scattered across the room was the litter of those who had gone, the only record of the hours just past.

I grabbed the broom and began to sweep the floor and hardly paused when I came, in the center of the gallery, to the circle of trampled rose petals.

BEST-SELLERS FOR 1967
Terkel, *Division Street: America*
Styron, *Confessions of Nat Turner*
Galbraith, *The New Industrial State*

CHAPTER NINE 1968

FIRST RALLY AND RIOT IN FRONT OF CODY'S   SUMMERTIME
OF TENSION   TELEGRAPH AVENUE CONCERNS
COMMITTEE   POLITICS   STEVE LEAVES

The process of reading is not a half-sleep, but in the highest sense, an exercise, a gymnast's struggle; that the reader is to do something for himself, must be on the alert, must himself or herself construct indeed the poem, argument, history, metaphysical essay—the text furnishing the hunts, the clue, the start or framework. Not the book needs so much to be the complete thing, but the reader of the book does. That were to make a nation of supple and athletic minds, well-trained, intuitive, used to depend on themselves, and not on a few coteries of writers.

WALT WHITMAN, 1819–1892

Through all this time in the late 1960's, as the U.S. intensified its war in Vietnam, the resistance at home intensified. Marches, teach-ins, full-page ads, Stop-the-Draft weeks, all across the nation, and nowhere more vigorous than in the Bay Area. In February 1968, the National Security Council had cancelled graduate student and occupational deferments. This would affect 2,000 Berkeley students that year, and the graduating class of 1968 was described as the first 1-A class in the U.S., with 60% of its male graduates to be drafted by September 1968. The first half of this eventful year saw the Fulbright hearings in the U.S. Senate on the war, Johnson's announcement that he would not run, the emergence of Eugene McCarthy and Robert Kennedy as presidential candidates, and the assassinations of Martin Luther King, Jr., and Kennedy.

Anti-establishment fervor was not limited to the U.S. French student strikes in May 1968 nearly paralyzed that country and energized the new left movement in the U.S. At the end of June, a group came and asked us if they could use the set-back space in front of the store as a site for a rally

*"in support of the French students." I wrote about it in a July letter to Bob,
who was on sabbatical in Paris:*

You probably had only sporadic accounts of what happened in
Berkeley the weekend before July 4th and it is hard to convey the
essence of events, since just to recite the facts doesn't get the spirit of
the matter.

It all began on Tuesday, June 25, when Peter Camejo, the head of
the Socialist Workers' Party and a twenty-eight-year-old former grad
student, went to the City Council to inform them of a street meeting
planned at the corner of Haste and Telegraph (our corner) on Friday
"in solidarity with the French students" and stating that the street
should be closed to traffic. He did not ask for a permit, and this is
where the thing began. He said he did not ask, first because there is
a constitutional right of assembly, second because asking for a permit
is just asking for a refusal and setting yourself up for arrest for an
illegal meeting (since you imply by asking for permit that it is legiti-
mate to have these things only on a permissory basis). The City
Council said no meeting could be held, and there matters stood at a
deadlock. The SWP had other groups in on their meeting, more as a
token of anti-establishmentarianism than anything else, a collection
of radical groups including Peace and Freedom party and Black
Panthers.

Well, they said they would go ahead anyhow, so all day Friday the
tension mounted. Fred and some other enlightened merchants plus
some of the church people who have been active in south campus
affairs went to the Mayor at 5 P.M., pleading with him to just ignore
the whole thing; pointing out that it was not a burning issue and
chances are the speakers would bore the hell out of people and any
crowd would soon drift away; that on Friday nights there are always
about 1,000 young people in that one block so it was foolish for the
authorities to seek a confrontation. However, iron resistance met
their pleas, the Mayor (an opportunistic Republican) and the police
in particular were just itching for an excuse to break some heads.

The meeting went on, using a flatbed truck with the red and black
flags of the anarchists flying, truck parked in bus-stop right in front

of the store. There were about 300 or so people, all of them on the plaza in front of the store and traffic was moving through all right, when by accident or design, some kid on a motorcycle parked it square in the middle of the intersection a block south, which stopped traffic. Cops had been on the roofs of buildings on both sides of the 2400 block all evening and now they sprang into action. First they said it was an illegal assembly and should disperse. They spoke through bullhorns and about 3/4 did not hear them. Then they said "chemical means" would be used and still most did not hear.

In the meantime, a phalanx of Berkeley and Oakland cops had been brought up on one of the side streets and they now started throwing tear gas freely, and while people were incapacitated by it and could not run, they would beat up on them with truncheons. There were no arrests and no shots fired. They just went delirious with the joy of gassing and beating people. You had to see it to believe it. They would throw the canister at someone's feet, then as the person staggered back four of the cops would jump on him and beat the hell out of him (or her; they seemed to enjoy hitting the girls). Fred had, in collaboration with the Free Church, set up a first-aid station in the back of the store. The store was closed but the plate glass windows provided observation posts. The guys at the store would open the doors, let in victims, and close the doors again. The cops spread out throughout that area and used their cars to chase people down. They really rioted, the cops that is, screeching to a halt beside any moving person and getting out and clubbing them whether the victim was a young person or a middle-aged lawyer walking his dog.

Finally things quieted down about 3 A.M. and Fred came home. The next night, Saturday, cops were heavy in the area and when some of the kids spilled into the street from the crowded sidewalks the same thing happened again, only worse. This time they had Oakland cops, California Highway Patrol, Alameda County sheriff's office cops, all of whom hate "Berkeley" with a vengeance. The gassing and clubbing as before, and this was when one of our windows was broken by a cop—not by accident but intentionally out of what looked to us like frustration at the refuge and surveillance provided by the store. Then Sunday, the police put a curfew on a fifty-six-block area of the south campus. Some of the activist kids held a meeting Sunday afternoon and at 6:30 (curfew to start at seven) voted to move their meeting downtown outside the curfew area. They did, and went down by City Hall. They then started marching along one of the main streets and a few windows—mostly in banks—got broken so curfew was clamped over the whole city. More beatings and clubbings all over Berkeley and cops as thick as flies—some at every intersection. It was like Nazi Germany and as though we were all under house arrest.

I forgot to mention that again Fred did not get home until three A.M. and on Monday he was up at eight and down on the avenue to see what could be done to cool a situation that was getting desperate. He spent the day down there and in the afternoon when he called to tell me he didn't know when he'd be getting home, there were Highway Patrolmen on the roof of the store with tear gas grenades and rifles, and he could hear their walkie-talkies down the ventilators. This time, they had 900 cops altogether, so of course there was no mass rally or anything else, and Fred got home relatively early, after having his car stopped by the cops to ask him why he was out during the curfew.

The next day, more meetings by the kids, and KPFA came in the afternoon and taped an interview with Fred. They broadcast it that night at 7:30 just before the tapes they had of the kids' meeting that day. I was just amazed. Here Fred was under such strain for several days, little sleep, etc., and he sounded as cool as a cucumber, with very sensible suggestions about what was wrong. He got many phone calls at the store complimenting him, including one from the mother of Richard Dyer-Bennett.

Anyhow, Tuesday was the City Council meeting and for seven hours they heard one person after another get up and talk about the beatings they had had at the hands of the cops. KPFA taped all this and rushed the tapes to the studio so they were almost simultaneously broadcast and this had an important effect on how people reacted and felt about the whole thing (thus underscoring the importance to real democracy of having the public informed). The kids had made a new request, to have the street closed on July 4th for a party, and after seven hours of testimony, that dumb council voted 4–3 to REFUSE it. That night, the activists met again and after a session— likewise taped—that was so democratic it was almost ludicrous, they voted to go ahead with their party anyhow, on the issue of constitutional freedom to assemble.

Meanwhile, the phones of the "liberal" councilmen must have been burning that night, because Wednesday A.M. the Council met again and on a face-saving new motion, sponsored by twenty-two ministers who said they would be the sponsors, this time voted to let the street be closed on Thursday for the party. I did not get this news until Wed. noon and it made me realize how tense I had been about the matter, because you could tell from the tone of the kids' voices that this time if the cops had come in there would have been retaliation with guns in self-defense and I believe there would just have been a blood bath since the cops would kill twenty for every one of them that was winged. So then Fred was occupied in planning the party, and down there at 9 A.M. on Thursday and stayed until 1 A.M.

The street was jammed, there must have been 15,000, there were rock bands and speeches and we put up $250 to buy ice cream and soft drinks to give away to people, from a stand right in front of the store (which was of course closed). The ministers plus some of the activists had a monitoring system to keep order and keep the cars out and there wasn't a cop in sight (except plain-clothesmen, we assume). About 11 P.M., when Fred and the others were gently suggesting it was going-home time now (since the permit to close the street expired at twelve), a far-out group who had been organized as a splinter group from the rest because the rest weren't militant enough, calling itself the Delaware Affinities, got in the middle of the street and sat down.

They just planted themselves there and told the monitors they were not going to leave, the streets belong to the people all the time, not just by permit. Fred says he thinks they were just being mischievous but it did cause some anxious moments, since crowd psychology is such that they might have gotten a bunch with them who didn't realize it was a joke. So Fred and another guy went up to the U. C. Folk Festival, which was having an outdoor concert on campus, and asked them if they would let people in free, and having gotten their consent, came back and in a Pied-Piper way made such an announcement. This siphoned off a few hundred and then when the monitors started cleaning up the streets, the rest, who didn't want to be bothered helping, left, and everything quieted down.

Since then the local rag, which is only slightly to the left of the John Birch Society, has been having hysterics about the "capitulation" of the Council, about the need to "clean up" the avenue, etc., etc., so we are not out of the woods yet. Much ado about little: if we can get the Council to realize that the kids are right—that people do have priority over automobiles and that closing Telegraph on Saturday night when there is no traffic to the campus would not inconvenience anyone. But you realize how deeply corrupting the values of this society are, and how foreign to most people is the idea that once in a while you can close down a street: A STREET? So CARS can't pass? They look at you like you're out of your mind.

Just as I feared, in re-reading this it doesn't convey the sense of crisis that we lived with for about five days. I have a feeling it was something like the way people must have felt in France in May, only on a smaller scale of course. That is, a real sense of tension, conflict, and people acting with a clear sense of community, this last the strongest and most important feeling.

Fred also felt this spirit, as he noted in writing to the Herberts about these events:

It has all been rather healthy in a way for me. I feel that I am doing something and being completely open and honest about all that I do and I have discovered, particularly in the ministers, a good many friends. I also feel that there are many, many people of good will but that they find few ways to exert any real influence. The most dismal thing about America, I think, is that the political process is really in a terribly atrophied state at the local level. People talk and talk and talk and most of what they say is unexceptionable but they find that only in a crisis can they rouse themselves to more than that. If this is true in so politicized a place as Berkeley, think what it is in the rest of the country. Still, that is not to be ungrateful for the fact that, when the police bore down here, it did produce a day's outpouring of protest before the City Council that had its effect in their later decision and that did reinforce the respect we have for this city and its people. In many ways, it is something unique in this country. I now feel very strongly that there is no other city in the country that compares with it in a number of important ways.

Somehow in the midst of the tension that all of the country is experiencing in this summer we felt it would be a good idea to try and see if there was enough interest and enthusiasm for us to have a block party on our street. The kids of course couldn't have been more enthusiastic, and they busied themselves making up invitations and announcements and signs and the first thing we knew it was apparent that we were going to have quite an affair. So last Saturday evening between two of the houses next to us the party came off. We have grad students from Biafra and they came, Japanese families, Chinese families, hippies from across the street, and all the rest. Each family brought a dish and we had a gourmet smorgasbord spread on the tables with good red wine to wash it down. The party was to last only from six to nine but didn't break up until about 11 for a number of the people. We had rock music on tape, a folk song session in a garage, and children's games in a backyard. About 100 people of all ages showed up and there was a unanimous demand for a Harvest party in October.

The store goes along well. Mario Savio [*the electrifying speaker at the 1964/65 rallies of the FSM*] has applied for a part-time job, and we think we want to have him and that he will be fine for the store. The job interview with him was the most enjoyable I have ever had. Savio has a great deal of what can only be called charm and a kind of openness about him that is very impressive. We already have what I'm sure is the most brilliant staff of any bookstore in America (pardonable exaggeration to be permitted, I hope, in the interest of fond charity) and working with them gives me a lot of satisfaction. We had a new-book-buying session the other morning when we went over the winter announcements of the new books and made up some orders. It was a great session full of humor and just plain animal spirits.

That summer was to bring a spectacle of another kind in Chicago when the television cameras recorded the violence and brutality at the Democratic National Convention, from those moments when Mayor Daley hurled an anti-Semitic invective at a United States Senator to the harrowing scenes of police literally running amuck. In the wake of such a vast explosion, the nomination of Hubert Humphrey, a Vietnam hawk, someone said, transparently disguised as a garrulous parrot, seemed almost beyond contempt. In Berkeley, a street rally was of course announced to attack the nominee and to protest the Crimes of Chicago.

In September, Fred wrote a long letter to brother Bob, dealing not only with the June fracas but also with the riots and curfew of late August following the riots at the Democratic Convention in Chicago:

The kind of writing I'm doing these days will never make the printed page, although I did get a long feature story in the *Oakland Tribune* quoting from one of my "proposal" papers. They happen to have a very intelligent and able reporter and he picked up a copy of this thing down at City Hall, came to talk with me for a couple of hours, and then did a very sympathetic story that ran about a column and a half and got a fine position on the front page, second section. I got a kick out of this because there is evidently an imperial order posted in the offices of the *Berkeley Gazette* that forbids them from mentioning my name unless driven either to the utmost necessity or in a damaging context.

I won't bore you with a long account of what has been going on here this summer. Suffice it to say that I found the store in the very center of one of the damndest exhibitions of crazy politics anyone ever saw. It built up and built up and with the cooperation of a City Council that often acts on the best intentions but is as dense as it can be, they finally arrived at the long-hoped-for (by the activists) confrontation. We had two nights of glorious struggle outside the door in which gas was flung to the winds with the wildest abandon and heads, shoulders, buttocks and legs were bruised and bashed by the gendarmerie that had finally found a perfect excuse to relieve itself of its antagonism to the hippies and the protestors.

There was a little rueful humor in the fact that perhaps the most irate complaints to the city and the ACLU (which gathered material for a special report) came from nice middle-class burghers who had come downtown for a quiet little dinner at one of the restaurants in the area and who ventured out on to the streets, there to be met by a cop who proceeded to treat them as though they amounted to something politically. One would have thought the victims might have responded with a little more pride in being taken for what they weren't but the human beast is innately ungrateful, after all, so all they did was yell like they never yelled before.

The above is deceptively frivolous. The truth is that we had rather a serious situation and it probably isn't over yet. We had a first-aid station operated by the Free Church on both nights of the actions. This seemed to irritate the police and they lobbed gas very freely all around the building and particularly at a back corridor. It happened that I was performing one of those duties no one else may do for us when a veritable barrage was launched next to the facility and, although I hurried through the ritual, I still got enough to leave me reeling. Shortly after that the gas got so bad on the lower floor we had to go up to the second floor and close ourselves off in a room there.

All this took place at the end of June. A group of the ministers in the area stuck their necks way out and tried to act as peacemakers and mediators and you know what an ungrateful task that is. I finally decided I would join the clerical party and I worked with them might and main. We finally got the Council to agree to give a permit for a July 4th party in which the street would be closed off. (I've been so close to this that I neglected to say much of the whole mess was caused by demands by the young people that the street be closed off for political meetings.) The idea of the party was that we were trying to show that the world would not inevitably cave in if permission for the avenue closing was given and people assembled for a be-in. The Council gave permission.

So there we were with the party and the full responsibility for what happened while various and sundry helpful city officials went about spreading the word that July 4 was the day when the anarchists were planning a series of sabotage and wrecking operations throughout the country with Berkeley as such a key city that they would not be satisfied until they established themselves in the city hall surrounded by the liberated criminals from the municipal hoosegow as they planned the march up the hill to liberate the Lawrence Radiation Lab. It was a chilling thought but not as frightening as the fear that there was always the chance that some advanced element in the radical ranks would feel that he could make a small but striking contribution to the revolutionary struggle by hurling a fire bomb from the roof of one of the surrounding buildings.

It seemed to me in my simple-minded way that serving free refreshments in front of the store might be interpreted as a friendly gesture from one of the capitalist enemies so I put up $250 and the Free Church begged, borrowed and stole all the soft drink, ice cream and cookies we could get for it. And you would really be suprised at the large quantities of such things you can obtain—there seemed to be a ton of it—when we began dishing it out at about noon on the Glorious (if suspenseful) Fourth.

A plentiful crowd was there all right. Even the most hostile papers estimated at least 15,000. They packed the street for two solid blocks. The ministerial monitors circulated continually among the crowd murmuring soothing incantations, and I was prevailed upon to take a bull-horn and go up and down the street pleading with people to come down off the tops of buildings. The Mime Troupe came over and performed and there were a number of other attractions including some rock bands and a speech by Eldridge Cleaver. The sound permit for the party was to expire at ten o'clock and it was thought that, considering the way the police had waded in before, we should not tempt them with another oppportunity and that the street ought to be cleared off by midnight. So we went among the throng expressing this simple sentiment.

But the anarchists were disappointed at such a tame day and they established themselves in the center of the avenue where they beguiled all our hearts with a snake dance while chanting "Ho Chi Minh is going to win." This went on for about a half an hour but there are limits to everything and perhaps they had had too many free cookies and were bloated; anyway, they finally offed and the cars started to come through and the party was over with nothing more untoward than the visit during the afternoon of a young couple who sat down for about an hour quite unaffectedly in the middle of the street and who would have hardly occasioned any comment at all except for the fact that they was nekkid as the day they was mistakenly born.

In the weeks that followed there was restlessness. City Council meetings were marked by bitter vituperation. Then about two weeks ago confrontation began to loom again. Again a meeting on the avenue, again the question of whether the street would be closed by the crowd, again the question of whether the police would then move in, as they had before, and disperse the crowd . . . All this, I should point out, was of more than academic interest to me because they have a habit of holding these meetings precisely in front of Cody's Books. But this time the Council held back and the police maintained a distant reserve, if one may use so quaint an expression.

The meeting, which was on the subject of Mayor Daley's manner of providing security for a national political convention, went on its rather loud way and ended at ten when the sound permit was up. The crowd could then have quietly gone home and about half of it did. There remained, however, a somewhat disgruntled remnant which ranged up and down the street while rumors flew of marches on Berkeley City Hall, or to liberate Huey Newton, or to catch the mayor and imprison him in the Campanile. None of these rather laudable projects having won any substantial following, everyone had to be content with provoking a break in the windows of our local Bank of America branch. The police then came and moved the crowd down the street and did it with a minimum of force. The crowd fled and then re-formed and again attacked the Bank. Now the police brought in the gas and used it freely. The crowd again dispersed but this time as it went some in the crowd smashed perhaps thirty more store windows.

On the following evening, no meeting, but crowds on the street again. Police called out in large numbers and in the midst of the hullabaloo on that night there was one hell of an explosion that blew up the water mains in a building under construction in the area. Meanwhile, the rumors flew thick and heavy that the anarchists were preparing to bomb everything from the headquarters of the local Trots to the equally loathed buildings of the University.

At this point a state of civil disaster was proclaimed by the city manager—no loitering, no public meetings, no lots of things. It was during the ensuing period of relative peace that, such is the peculiar nature of things, we had seven windows broken, not by mob action but by people, I'm convinced, who had been so stimulated by the general tension that they had to relieve their feelings by socking rocks through our nice big windows. (We had had one window broken in the June revels but this was done by a policeman who didn't like us watching the action from inside the store.)

A few days ago the state of disaster was lifted and since then we have had an uneasy quiet punctuated by rumors that the anarchists have now taken their movement completely underground from where they shall emerge in their own good time and give us all some lessons on what the struggle is really all about, baby.

These anarchists (and I know how curiously dated that word sounds) are indeed a woolly lot from my sheltered point of view. I have had occasion to exchange a few words with them and it is certainly a strange experience because there are just no common points of reference, and I find myself feeling so much at a loss that all I can do is stand and stare. I really believe that some of them are convinced that the country is ready to be toppled over by a series of actions modeled after some of those fantastically successful campaigns waged by the late Che Guevara. All other approaches to reform or even revolution are viewed by these people as sell-outs to the enemy and puerile concessions to outmoded concepts. Nor are they at all hamstrung by any thought about whether one action has any relation to another since the chemistry of revolution is such a random brew that it distills its essence as it boils and is utterly unpredictable. Nor can they be bothered with thoughts leading to the conclusion that it is barely possible that their capers may have such effects as building more support for George Wallace and, in general, polarizing people to the point that nothing like a civilized political life can be carried on in the country. It amuses them rather that there are still people so childish as to harbor such antiquated thoughts.

Well, now, in the midst of all this I have found it essential to my mental health to feel that I was "doing something about it." It seemed to me that I would get nowhere trying to work out any kind of consistent pattern from the attitudes and actions of the anarchists as embodied in the communes and affinity groups through which they express themselves. It did seem to me that we were perhaps seeing something rather new in the country and that what was at hand was a manifestation of the rapidly growing feeling of dis-association of young people, or a sizable number of them, from the society. Talking to many of them I heard again and again phrases and usages which had a close resemblance to the way that blacks talk.

I took cognizance, too, of the fact that drug use and abuse had somehow gotten almost inextricably woven into the situation and that we were experiencing a queer mixture of narcotics with politics. I also observed a strong tendency on the part of people who oppose all forms of political action that take conviction into the streets to associate the young rebels (hippieness and drug use) with the dissenting left. You may have observed that Senator Eugene McCarthy is not immune from such attacks.

It will come as no news to you that I sympathize pretty strongly with young people and it never occurred to me that I should not act on that feeling. The problem was how to do it given the circumstances. It did seem to me as I talked with some of them in various "rapping" sessions we've had that there were certain basic needs that underlay much of the violent rhetoric and abuse. They are rather simple, really. A conviction on their part that the society is alienated from human relationships of any really satisfactory kind; a belief that they ought to be allowed to find their own way in their own time toward what they call their own "life style"; a marked feeling of weariness with the old posturing and pretending; a determination to experiment on their own, to make mistakes that have been made before but to do it in their own way.

But I suppose the greatest factor is that they feel estranged from the world they knew as they grew up and now are trying to find some way of relating to one another that is of another kind entirely. Strangely enough, I think, the society's alienation from them is the cause of it all. And it is beautiful that they who are so often called alienated are suffused with the idea that they must find their potential as human beings by finding ways to express what amounts to a feeling of brotherhood.

Anyway, in this rather confused way I see it and I have acted on it by attending scores of committee meetings, by talking with anyone I can talk to, by writing out proposals and submitting them to anybody that would even promise to glance at them, and so on. I suppose the most effective work I've done is as a member of a city-manager-inspired ad-hoc committee (Telegraph Avenue Concerns Committee) which meets once a week at City Hall and works out specific projects for the area. We are apparently about to get a free clinic off the ground and we have hopes for an art center soon. We have much more ambitious hopes for a community center.

It is hard to know whether this is or is not simply whistling in the wind. We most certainly are a badly fragmented society in which fear, suspicion and antagonism raise all kinds of hell with any idea of people coming together. Who knows? Yet I do find many people of good will who will spend time and effort to try to work through to, not solutions, but possibilities.

One of our correspondents in London complained that our letters were too full of politics. Fred answered that September:

I'm afraid it is very difficult to separate "politics" from our lives because it does impinge quite a bit. In fact, sometimes it comes whizzing through the windows so often that we lose our insurance on them, as we just did. But I will try to obey your injunction to avoid it although you will have to be charitable enough to forgive if once in a while it insists on breaking in. I will only say at this point that I found that it is far better for my mental well-being, in my present circumstances, to involve myself in my own way in what is happening, or what I think might be happening, than to seclude myself with the sulks in the back room. But I take no particular credit for this, if any might be due, because history collided with me. I either had to run away from it or try to face it head on. Doing the latter has been a kind of marvelous experience and I have learned a lot that is awful and some things that are beautiful about all kinds of people and institutions.

Our kids seem very happy although I feel that I am not as close to them as I should be because of preoccupation with many other things. Still, I think they are learning to share a little in understanding that and we do try to do things together and then the love comes back around us and all is well. Each is a fragile wonder in his own way.

I am suffering now from not having been able to get away, as I used to, for such visits as those I used to inflict on you when you were in our very own New York City. And in a way I am of a divided mind now about the whole business of "losing yourself" in a great city. I'm almost afraid to try it again for fear it won't work. I went in January to New England and was going on to New York but when I looked down the Hudson from Bear Mountain and saw the towers of Manhattan something told me to stay away and I didn't go into it at all. Now I think if I do go it will have to be for a "purpose," in this case a pre-arranged tour (through friends in social planning—I can hear your ugh—in City Hall) of projects that attempt to do something constructive about our sullen and intransigent youth.

Meanwhile, I think of going to Pacific Grove for three or four days and walking a lot and spending time at Lobos counting sea lions. Most recently, Pat and I went over to S.F. for a cocktail party and then dined out in the Fisherman's Wharf area but there is something now about the whole establishment scene in a big city that jolts me so much that I can hardly wait to be away from it. Perhaps the kids have made me into rather an unsettled old man.

We see the Keplers now and again and I did a KPFA broadcast with

Roy. We sat and ruminated in rather a middle-aged way about the nature of violence. People who heard it were fairly nice about it. The best compliment was from someone who said I sounded as though I was trying to come to grips with it and that of course was just where I was with it. I continue to serve in a kind of addled way on the KPFA board where my main contribution is to ward off all offers from the Montgomery Streeters who want to "help" the station and themselves with the most marvelous schemes for raising money. I kind of enjoy KPFA and its problems—they remind me of the early days of the UN on a miniature scale.

I wrote to our London friends about how the Avenue was changing:

In between and round about there has been a variety of leaflets distributed and a lot of tension. The avenue has changed considerably from what it was a year ago when there were lots of "flower children" around—there seems to be a larger group of permanent dropouts, greater use and abuse of drugs: it's not just pot anymore, but a lot of other things, featuring "speed" (amphetamines), more drug dealers. More health problems, more alienation than ever, more paranoia.

The Hell's Angels—a *lumpen* motorcycle gang—is reputedly moving into dope dealing; at any rate they are on the avenue all the time; likewise drug dealers, who have a bad reputation for burning their customers. I look back with nostalgia on the days when all we had to worry about was shoplifters.

Fred is increasingly being approached by people to run (or be drafted) for City Council or Mayor, but he feels (and I agree 100%) that if nominated he will not run, if elected he will not serve. No thanks: we have eighteen-hour days as it is.

We had a major loss at the store in 1968 when our partner Steve decided that he wanted to move with his family to the country, far from urban tensions. He had always been interested in gardening, and in fact had worked as a landscaper before coming to Cody's. We understood how the peace and quiet of Mendocino County contrasted with the tensions of trying to do bookstore work in the midst of the unstable world we had. Of course we were sorry to see him go, depriving us of a dedicated colleague with great skills. His departure left us with the entire responsibility for management of the store.

BEST-SELLERS FOR 1968
Whole Earth Catalog
Castaneda, *Teachings of Don Juan*
Malraux, *Anti-Memoirs*
Solzhenitsyn, *The First Circle*

CHAPTER TEN 1968 TO 1969

For I bless God in the libraries of the learned and for all the booksellers in the world.

CHRISTOPHER SMART, 1722–1771

That fall (1968) the controversy over whether credit would be given for a course featuring Eldridge Cleaver as chief lecturer embroiled the entire campus, with the Academic Senate supporting the students. Sit-ins, conferences, rallies, suspensions. The emergence of the Third World Liberation Front calling for a strike in January led to weeks of leaflets, pickets, blockades of the campus, and sit-ins by protesters in campus buildings. Early in February 1969 Reagan declared a state of emergency on the campus so that the Highway Patrol could be brought in.

At one point late in February, an afternoon confrontation spilled over onto Telegraph Avenue and tear gas was again in plentiful supply. We had learned the hard way that when riots occurred the prudent course was to close the store and go home. By five o'clock, the streets were deserted, most shops closed. A small group of people were standing outside of Cody's, using water from the outside faucet (installed for care of the trees) to wash the gas from their eyes. Halfway up the block to the north was a policeman with one last gas canister in his Vietnam-era grenade launcher. Perhaps in a spirit of not wasting it by bringing it back to headquarters, for certainly that little group threatened no one, he lobbed the tear gas toward them. It missed and crashed through the plate glass by our front door.

An hour or so later, a repairman from a glass company came along putting up plywood over broken windows. By now this was a routine: the glass company was the first on the scene and the next day would call to ask if you wanted them to replace the broken window. He stepped through our shattered glass, took the smoking canister, and put it outside. Just then a policeman came by and ordered him to put it back inside. He waited to see that this was done and the plywood in place so no one could relieve our problem by removing the canister.

When we arrived the next morning, the poisonous gas was so heavy none of us could stay there. We tried everything to clear the gas. We got the fire department to come down with blowers. Someone suggested trays of charcoal to absorb it. Every book we picked up reeked. What finally worked was a suggestion from the Doubleday salesman, Bruce de-Garmeaux. His brother worked for a chemical company and one of their products was a vapor used to clean the smoke-laden air of nightclubs and hotel meeting rooms.

In the meantime, we lost days of business. In retailing it is not possible to recover such losses, but of course our expenses remained. We had to keep the payroll going—it was not the staff's fault that they could not work—and of course the rent also went right along. Fortunately, the books were not permanently harmed—that would have meant bankruptcy. Fred wrote:

In the course of time the fumes lessened and the books, though still rather pungent to the nose, proved saleable as we lengthened our hours and began to resume a normal schedule. Indeed, visitors to the area seemed almost regretful that only a few pockets of tear gas were still to be sniffed at in odd parts of the store space, and they seemed pleased that the books still retained a tearful aura as a souvenir of what we often referred to as the "Telegraph troubles."

But business had suffered. The decreasing volume of sales and the mounting accumulation of unpaid bills from publishers were no joke. We explained to publishers in some detail that we were on a "survival trip" and asked that they be patient until we could fight our way back. In the succeeding weeks, a steady stream of credit executives from publishing houses "happened" to be in the area and dropped in for a casual visit. They could not fail to see the gas mask hanging above the order desk. Many publishers went on filling orders even though we were in arrears, and only a few made threats of legal action.

So we limped along. My sales records for 1969 show repeated laconic notations: "Closed for riots 1 P.M." We reduced the "proprietor's draw" for Fred.

We had barely recovered from the gassing of the store when the central event for Berkeley in 1969 started: People's Park. We were only half a block from this muddy acreage, which the University had more or less abandoned after tearing down the old rooming houses. The Regents could not find money to do the building that was the excuse for moving the hippies out, nor even for bringing it into a modest social usefulness as a parking lot. Gradually it became an unofficial parking lot, no one in charge, no fees collected.

The waste of this land, in a densely populated district with no parks, became an opportunity for a visionary group of young people to build their own park. That year on an April weekend the first shovels and sod appeared, and the counter-culture weekly the Berkeley Barb *invited everyone to come and share the work.*

There was a great need among young people—and some not so young—for positive events in life. Frustration abounded. The long student strike at San Francisco State University had ended with repression, not victory. Minority students on the UC campus met with a molasses-like bureaucracy. City elections early in April brought a right-wing majority, although Ron Dellums did keep his place. There was a G. I.–Civilian Easter Peace March to the Presidio in San Francisco—and still the war ground on, overshadowing our lives.

Accordingly, the invitation to help create a "Power to the People Park" was joyfully accepted by hundreds. There was a proclamation that the Park was a protest against the University's effort to destroy the Telegraph Avenue community. Art Goldberg, one of the student activists, told the Daily Californian *that "This is the beginning of resistance. After a couple of weeks, the kids won't let anybody take away their park." There was a note that "contributions for grass and shrubs can be brought to Cody's and to the Telegraph Avenue Liberation Front."*

From a letter I wrote on May 4, 1969:

We have a desperate need for parks in the area, and about three weeks ago the kids took things into their own hands. They took up a collection, bought some sod, hired a bulldozer to level the site, and hundreds of kids went to work building a park. They brought in plants, they put the sod down, and each day since then more have been working on it, with a Sunday turnout of hundreds of people. One section is a "People's Revolutionary Corn Garden," in another a place for carrots, lettuce and radishes. There are flower beds, and pews from an abandoned church were brought in for benches. Someone donated some used play equipment for children. Week by week the park gets bigger, and the parking lot shrinks to the edges of the vacant land. It is one of the most poignant things I have ever seen, the way these kids are so enthusiastically trying to do something about making the kind of world they want.

Of course, officialdom rears its ugly head. That's state property! You can't do that! That's anarchism! Fred is on a hastily improvised committee trying to find a compromise, but with Reagan as governor and member of the Board of Regents, you can appreciate the possibilities for confrontation here. And—if they bulldoze over the People's Park, there is going to be so much anger and frustration that I don't want to predict what the kids might do to the adjacent campus.

Meanwhile, back at the ranch . . . the store goes along, it makes us a living, it gives lots of problems, so much so that we are no longer open nights because there was too much tension for our staff anticipating what might come next from the gangs that congregate there. Young people from all over the U.S. are drawn to Berkeley and they are a mixed bag of idealists, draft dodgers, drug pushers, hedonists, runaways, etc. Our regular customers, the intellectual community, don't come around at night anymore, so although our volume has gone down we are just about breaking even or a little more. It isn't too bad—we never intended to get rich running a bookstore, there must be easier ways.

The University's response to the park was an announcement that it planned to start work on the first of July on playing fields at this site. More grass and plants were the answer from the community. And then the meetings began—sometimes two and three a day—between University officials and the park committee, the Telegraph Avenue Concerns Committee, and other ad hoc groups.

It all came to naught. The University representatives had no authority to do more than listen and try to put their views across.

On May 14 "No Trespassing" signs were posted and the Daily Californian *carried a statement from Chancellor Heyns. He said that "The University is now prepared to proceed with site development" and that "First we will have to put up a fence to re-establish the conveniently forgotten fact that the field is indeed the University's, and to exclude unauthorized persons from the site. That's a hard way to make a point, but that's the way it has to be."*

We were awakened at 4 A.M. on May 15 by a phone call telling us that a chain link fence was being erected. Before dawn a crowd had gathered, and after a rally on campus, students streamed down Telegraph. They were met at the park with massive police force, and for the first time in our experience they had guns. Within two hours, fifty-eight people were sent to the hospital with buckshot injuries, onlookers James Rector was mortally wounded and Alan Blanchard blinded, and the entire area saturated with tear gas. The Daily Californian *reported that 500 police from nine different jurisdictions were in Berkeley, and the National Guard began to move in. Governor Reagan ordered a 10 P.M.–6 A.M. curfew.*

From a letter I sent at that time:

We had a police riot with tear-gas and buckshot used freely against a bunch of the students, followed by the death of one of the kids, blinding of another, hundreds injured, the National Guard occupying the city, curfew, etc., all to the greater honor and glory of our governor in pursuit of political gain elsewhere in the state from the red-necks who think all the students should be stood up against the wall and shot. One of the things the National Guard did was to hem in one group holding a rally and then gas them from the air with blister gas. Nice, huh? They were firing pepper gas from police cars roaring up and down the streets indiscriminately aiming at anything that moved, even old ladies in tennis shoes. Some of it got into Martha's school and the children had to be sent home early. She said she was so scared that her hand shook when she tried to do the combination on her locker. Well, one thing they achieved was to make radicals out of about 50,000 middle-class parents and kids in Berkeley.

The next days were a blur of meetings, rallies, marches, tear gas, meetings. Fred describes this in a July letter:

I soaked in the bath for about two hours last night and then hit the sack and went to sleep before my head hit the pillow, I think. As a result, I woke just before six this morning and am writing this in the cluttered old back room looking out on an urban Corot backyard scene.

I have never been quite so emotionally tired in my life, I think, as I am now although, physically, I guess I am in fairly good shape. I suppose that during the past two or three months I must have attended at least one hundred meetings and conferences of various kinds and the involvement has been so intense at times that I have tended to lose all perspective and go back and forth between quite foolish peaks of joy at some (mostly imagined) triumph and low points of despair and anguish at some (disproportionately measured) defeat. On the whole, I've been able to do a few creditable things but I have also had to learn an enormous lot in a very short time.

The store being where it is, we had either to get very much involved or act, as most of my neighbor merchants have done, as though we were somewhere else. People's Park is on our street just a hundred or so feet up the way. I made it a habit to go there regularly and spend a good deal of time talking to the people there from the time that it began. I have rather mixed feelings about some of the subsequent developments but, so far as the spirit that went into the park, I haven't any doubt at all. It was magnificent. It was also a frightening condemnation of the society.

It was also, in a way, a kind of personal vindication because the city committee I have worked on for a year had recommended in 1968 the use of the exact area for a park–youth center and we got absolutely no response from either the University or the City and, indeed, got a negative vote on a pocket park proposal that we submitted that was adjoining the People's Park area and, in fact, would have used a small amount of that precious parcel of land. You can imagine our dismay to find that the recommendations of our committee for action were now being interpreted by city officials during the park crisis as proof of their concern.

The occupation of the city by thousands of National Guardsmen was harrowing. Each day that passed gave us more and more of a sense of utter desperation that we had become the victims of a state administration that was determined, once and for all, to do us in as a political entity in this city.

For over a year something called a Communications Council had been meeting downtown once a week. I had refused to attend because I detest so much the idea of merely talky-talk. As the dowager chairlady always insisted at every meeting, this was decidedly not an "action" group, uttering the word as though it had connotations too fearful even to think of. Nevertheless, she was so insistent that I come and talk about the Avenue that, against my better judgment, I went.

When I got there, it soon became evident that under the strain of events, the concept of non-action was rapidly being altered. There was much talk on the Communications Council of forming some kind of ad-hoc group to come up with a statement demanding that Park people, University and City, sit down and negotiate an end to the struggle that would get the troops out of the city and restore some measure of local control. I took to the first meeting of this broadly representative group—ranging from the retiring president of the local Chamber of Commerce to a left-wing Black politician—a one-page statement as a draft to work on. For three days in five-hour sessions each day we hammered away at this thing. I was set on not signing it unless we could emphasize clearly that we recognized the Park people as having legitimacy as a negotiating partner. We had to state very clearly the issue of local government as basic in the matter.

Probably events themselves helped us to arrive at decisions. When the campus was gassed by helicopter and even the most uninvolved faculty wives and their children felt its effects as they were relaxing at the nearby faculty recreation facility, indignation began to expand beyond normal limits. We finally came out with a fairly good statement considering the fact that we had only lost a few prospective signers along the way. In the end, I think the statement by our ad-hoc group had some influence on the University administration and helped Heyns stiffen his stand before the Regents. It also helped the City Council finally get to the point where it made good proposals for leasing the park and working on a user-developed concept. But of course nothing could shake the Governor or the Regents and the damnable fence is still there and is still the subject of endless provocation.

The days wore on, the tension increased. Here is a statement Fred wrote that was read on KPFA and appeared on the evening television news on May 23:

Even at a time when this city struggles to regain its integrity and that issue trembles in the balance, I feel there is room for hope.

I think something is happening in this country. Something is happening that has been a long time in the making but it is happening nevertheless. There is being forged a community of interest among people who have been, to a large extent, disenfranchised. Among them are the poor, the black and other minority peoples, the old and the young. They are asserting their right and their determination to be a functioning part of our society, and, it seems to me, they will never rest until they have achieved it.

Far from being a demand that might strike fear in our hearts, it seems to me that this movement is probably the main hope for the survival and growth of our society as a living organism. For what is being sought is an extension of participatory democracy to a degree of which we have had, until now, only the faintest glimmer. The consequences of such an extension will and must penetrate and permeate every institution, public and private, of our society at every level. As it transpires, it must come to affect each of our lives.

I think it is not only the young who are finding a way to fling down this challenge, but I think they perhaps bring to the striving an energy, spirit, and a fresh enthusiasm that youth peculiarly possesses.

Yet in doing so they are coming to know that they are not alone in presenting the opportunity and the promise to all of American society in a way that is most strikingly appealing and compelling. And I think the consciousness grows among them with every passing day that they have found a common ground with millions upon millions of other Americans.

The hope that I nourish today is that the society will take up the challenge and enter into a process that will, as it goes on, enable us to transform our country by bringing to life the millions of the frustrated, the discarded, and the unused. I think that some part of that aspiration found expression in the spirit that went into People's Park. I think it may well be that in digging there they somehow uncovered the conscience of a city.

To return to Fred's letter:

As the days passed, a new crisis began to develop. The Park people announced a Memorial Day demonstration calling on students and the public generally to come from all over the state to protest the decisions on the park. Somehow or other the figure of 50,000 got established as the number of people who were expected to participate. Since Berkeley is a city of 120,000 such an addition would be rather a lot of people and there were very substantial—and from a later conversation with the police chief—very accurate fears that federal troops might well be called in if something went awry during the demonstration. So it had to be peaceful, or so it seemed to me, although among the Park people that feeling was not so well established.

The demonstration itself was strange. The strain the city had been under somehow relaxed during it. People were very emotional, very close to each other, always very close to tears or laughter. It was hot and at times the streets were so packed that it was impossible to keep moving. Residents along the march route got out garden hoses and sprayed us and everyone raised their arms and opened their mouths and were quite grateful for the relief. The tensest moments came when we first approached the campus and saw it rimmed with the unhappy National Guardsmen staring straight before them and again, when we came near the park and saw on the roof-

tops the dread blue meanies—the shotgun users, the killers and the blinders from the Oakland Sheriff's department—staring down at us from above.

Anyhow, it had been peaceful. Fred noted a cooling in feeling toward him from a good many of the Park people who felt he had played the establishment game. But there wasn't too much time to think about this because other things were happening or about to happen. We worked on organizing a Telegraph Avenue Summer Program, using some old school buildings next to Cody's that were no longer in use. The School Board and some of the churches donated money for supplies, and we also held a benefit fair. There were art and sports programs, a child-care center, free store, free library, free food. Many people from the community donated their time for the myriad tasks of the program, which ran from June through August.

From a second July letter Fred wrote:

A group of communes undertook to organize this celebration. They came to me with their plans and asked me to present them to the various people and I did. I learned later that they really represented a group called the Berkeley Liberation Program which has produced a lengthy document of a somewhat utopian nature one of whose points is "We will protect and expand the Drug Culture." Just before the fourth they came with the official leaflet for the celebration and the main part of it was a quotation from their document and which identified the celebration as having their sponsorship. This in the face of the fact that they had emphasized repeatedly to me and others that this was a "general" community event. Being very much involved in the People's Pad thing at that moment I felt that the whole world was engaged in a plot to betray me and I reacted accordingly. But when I talked with the organizers I could not for the life of me determine whether or not they understood at all that they had acted dishonorably. They honestly seemed puzzled at my indignation and unable to understand what I was objecting to. So I finally pulled up short, said to hell with it, and walked out of the meeting.

July 4th was peculiar. The organizers had settled for a large amount of space, including the Summer Program grounds off Telegraph, so that the program was spread over two blocks on school grounds and parking lots. There were art projects, rock bands, a child-care center, and god knows what else and everyone who was in the area had a fine time. But up on Telegraph the politicos of the new left were busy taking over the street, blocking traffic, turning on fire hydrants, and so on. The tension grew during the afternoon and there was great fear that the police would clear the area with gas and clubs. They came to me and demanded to know where the monitors that had been promised by the organizers were located. I said I didn't know but I would look for the organizers and tell them the police were interested in this. I found them and gave them the word. Now a strange situation came about. The commune people took over the responsibility to somehow keep the day peaceful and of course the new left reacted by calling them people's pigs so we had another fragmenting of the movement and a considerable degree of bitterness developing on each side.

This was the background for Bastille Day. This was a mystery action mainly promoted by leaflets of a highly suggestive kind which drew a parallel between the storming of the Bastille and possibly (?) the destruction of the fence around the People's Park. The day before the day, it was announced that there would be some kind of action around the fence and on Bastille Day there was the story that a large quantity of loaves of bread had been baked and that in the loaves there were wire snippers. So it turned out, and on the day, about 1,000 people, most of whom had no more to do with the People's Park than you have, showed up and began to cluster around the fence while the new left people marched up and down before it exhorting them to various actions.

At last the inevitable incident occurred that brought out the beast in us all and the batons began to come down and the gas began to be launched and in the space of half an hour the whole area around the store was turned into a battleground. Wearily, we closed the store at 3 o'clock for the twelfth time within two months and went home to follow it on the radio. Worst of all, in the early evening the police wantonly moved in on the clinic and fired three gas canisters through the windows creating havoc and such indignation among some of the doctors that they wanted to go down to the city hall and personally gas the Chief. The next day we spent going over the situation and organizing an effective protest on this and now we are looking forward to another "action" on the fence tomorrow.

I suppose this must be almost as exhausting to read about as it is to experience. I have only given you a brief outline of it so you can understand just what things are like for us. It has been a time of great anguish but much happiness too. I think I've learned a good deal but am a long way from coming up with any very specific conclusions about it all. I have to be very wary about doing that because of being so much involved that, at times, I get that old martyr syndrome going and then I get very gloomy and negative.

Unless things come down too heavy, we will be able to leave this weekend for a week in the Sierra in the restful atmosphere of the Co-op camp where the most pressing problems that are considered are the exploitation of the consumer in a shameful manner by Campbell's Soup. As you say, it is very difficult to get away from this but very necessary. I am very anxious to get a small acreage within an hour's driving distance. If we can find this, we will grab it, because Pat and I both feel that we simply must have a weekend place we can take the kids to and where she can relax and I can get out and work hard on a garden. I really don't see how it is possible not to remain very much involved in what is happening here, and I don't know that I can do anything else but hang in. But we must have the chance to get away and unwind. Meanwhile, we have finally acquired a Volks bus and this should be very useful for our plans for the future, as well as for the immediate vacation week.

Telegraph is now being haunted by the media vultures who are making a thoroughly exhaustive coverage of all its most repellent and bizarre features. I actually feel murder in my heart as I watch them going about their trade. There is a pathos and an anguish on the street this summer that is very painful but I doubt that any of this is going to come through. The faces of some of the kids really frighten me and perhaps unreasonably. There seems, in some of them, such an unreflective absorption in self-destruction.

I certainly anticipate that Cal will be in for it this fall. I finally got a chance to sit down with Chancellor Heyns. He is so weary he can hardly manage to nod his head as he listens. The fact is that the University is utterly demoralized. The faculty has almost given up doing anything but reacting when an emergency comes and their strongest tendency now is to sit in their offices and brood over the inadequacies of the administration and to condemn it in a defeatist way. I talked to someone who is in environmental studies at UC the other night and was utterly flabbergasted at the way he set himself up as judge and jury with no sense that it might be remotely possible for him to involve himself in the decision-making process itself. Rather, the attitude was that this was for other, more vulgar, minds to consider. Meanwhile, he could issue his decisions from the sidelines.

We certainly did get involved. Fred was asked to speak to a church forum about "the Avenue" and to express his thoughts on our responsibilities to the young:

I was raised in a home where Franklin D. Roosevelt was one of the household gods to whom my father, in particular, rendered the warmest possible homage. I early became imbued with the idea that the world would be a very dreary place indeed if it had reached such a state of perfection that all that remained to do was to run a polishing cloth over it every now and then just to make it shine. So I have not been without basic sympathies for those who strive for a better world. . . .

Of one thing I am fairly certain and I take cheer from it. And that is that the young are as they always were—dreamers and seekers, as Carl Sandburg once called us, very bravely, I think, as a people. It wasn't so long ago in America that they struck out in answer to the westering urge and who does not know, from his own experience, of those years in life when all kinds of yearnings and strivings seethed within and seemed almost too much to bear. The impatience felt then is still felt now. All these qualities take somewhat different forms now but we can never doubt for a moment that they remain as a constant of the young heart and mind.

So it is really offering an insult to our own human-ness to say that young people are not as we were. It is also a most terrible indictment of what we as a people are and have been since young people come from us and are of us.

Accepting that, perhaps we begin to see a little light. It is to be expected of the young that they will make a blanket condemnation of the establishment or of the older generation generally. Young people have always done that and I can recall some pieces that I wrote for a college newspaper that had that same passionate note back in the late thirties when the world wasn't all that cheerful either. But I think it is a little dense for us to take that blanket indictment at its face value. In one sense, it is true that we who are older are responsible for the world we live in now and I am willing to accept that. What I am not willing to accept is the idea that at my age, having acknowledged my inadequacies and my guilt, I can't have another try at it. Despite the failures I would like to keep going even if it is only as a way of trying to make amends.

Now this I take to be a position somewhat differing from that usually assumed by the young. Not having a record they don't have to come to terms with it. Reasoning from our own experience of life we are certain that they, too, in their time will finally have to discard the arrogant mantle of the self-righteous. They are right, however, in one respect: they have the potential for making their dreams come true, and the energy, and for that we must have the deepest reverence, and we must cherish and nourish it in every way that we can.

You will have observed from what I have said that I am not unsympathetic to young people. I am not and for a very personal reason— I draw a great deal of strength from the young and I happen to believe that most of us do, in some degree. I am not at all satisfied that I could not find much more comfort and hope in them and so I arrive at the idea, by extension, that one of our highest priorities ought to be given to finding some way of building not bridges but a society which is a meeting ground of the generations and not an anguished field of battle.

It may just be a crucial task. Crucial, most of all, for the older generation. When I was "rapping" during the summer with young people, at first I was appalled by the seeming intransigence and the determined rejection of hard reality in much of what was said. But as time passed and I listened, not to the words, but to what was behind them, I began to marvel all over again at that quality in youth that refuses to accept the world as it is and as it probably is going to be, and insists on what ought to be.

It was after one such session when I expressed to a couple of the young men my mild alarm at the free-swinging nature of some of the fantasies that had walked during the night that I got a certain amount of insight into the matter. They both looked at me with some surprise and then laughed and said, "Well, you know we like to spin it out and see where it goes. It's a trip, you know, and you hit all the highs you can while you're up there." I don't pretend for a moment that that is all there is to understanding what happens with young people in the realm of ideas these days but I still think it was an instructive nudge toward the beginning of a comprehension of them.

Some young people are unwilling to tie themselves down to what they consider a routine job. They have the audacity to want to work only enough to make a subsistence at jobs they enjoy doing. They want, if they can, to find work out of doors—gardening, say—or even hard manual labor. They would like, if they could, to work in our forests, for the feeling that man has alienated himself from the sustaining strengths that can be drawn from the wilderness is very strong among many young people. I cannot say that I do not share a good many of these feelings, and I can at least understand that a young man might want to turn away from our decaying cities toward the open fields, the forests, and the mountains.

We have been very generous with our young people in the material sense but we have been grudging about granting them the only thing that really counts—an identity. An identity means a personal force, a power to extend one's potential to the fullest.

I am a partisan of the young and cheerfully acknowledge it. I am prepared to search endlessly to find ways to work with them for the future of my country and the companions during the coming years of my own children. I will always give such the benefit of my every doubt, and in defending them I defend the hope that is in my own flesh.

BEST-SELLERS FOR 1969
Hesse, *Glass Bead Game*
Roszak, *The Making of a Counter Culture*
McGinniss, *The Selling of the President, 1968*
Roth, *Portnoy's Complaint*

TOP *Fred in the doorway of the tiny Euclid Avenue store. Photograph taken in 1958.* BOTTOM *C. P. Snow signing copies of his books for Fred, 1960, in the courtyard of the Euclid Avenue store.*

TOP *Fred holding Martha, Pat holding Anthony, about 1959. Photo by Harvey Richards.* BOTTOM *The first Telegraph Avenue store at 2476, across the street and south of the present store.*

TOP *The present Cody's Books under construction, in 1965.* BOTTOM
Inside the new store, looking out, later that same year.

Memorial Day, 1969: TOP *National Guardsmen block Telegraph Avenue at the corner of Haste. Cody's entrance visible in background. Photograph by Richard Sammons.* BOTTOM *Troops block the street at Dwight, the next corner south.* Berkeley Barb *photograph.*

Almost everyone used Cody's Plaza (in front of the new store): TOP *Hare Krishnas in 1968, photo by John Jekabson.* BOTTOM *Flute maker, photograph taken in 1983 by Michael Russell.*

Fred with novelist Tom Robbins during a book-signing at the store, 1976.

Hollywood comes to Cody's. Director Karel Reisz and Fred during the filming of Who'll Stop the Rain? *which used the store as a location, 1977. Photograph by Bruce McBroom.*

TOP *Fred at the lectern upstairs in the new store, 1976.* BOTTOM *Pat downstairs at Cody's, 1991. Both photographs by Richard Bermack.*

Books are the treasured wealth of the world and the fit inheritance of generations and nations. . . . Their authors are a natural and irresistible aristocracy in every society, and, more than kings or emperors, exert an influence on mankind. How many a man has dated a new era in his life from the reading of a book.

HENRY DAVID THOREAU, 1817–1862

As in many university towns, the start of the new school year that September (1969) brought renewed vigor and activities. They were sparked by a Disorientation forum designed by campus activists to give freshmen a history of the kind of place they were now in. Then the organizing began for anti-war actions. A Vietnam Moratorium on October 15 was a big success despite rain. In a November moratorium with the theme of "Bring the G. I.s Home Now," 150,000 marched in San Francisco.

People's Park remained unsettled. Fraternities voted in October 1969 to boycott any playing fields that would be built there. When a parking lot opened there in January, leased by the University to the Parking Corporation of America, pickets showed up with signs saying "Only Pigs Park Here."

In February 1970, responding to the sentences given in the trial of the Chicago Seven on conspiracy charges connected with riots at the August 1968 Democratic convention, scattered "guerrilla" groups ran through Berkeley breaking windows and looting a Safeway supermarket. April saw anti-war rallies on campus, tear gas, and demonstrations against the ROTC presence on campus. The May attacks on Cambodia set off a firestorm of protest in campuses across the nation and a state of emergency was declared on the UC campus. Three hundred sixty colleges closed and students were killed at Jackson State and Kent State. In Berkeley, ads in *the* Daily Californian *headed "Leaflet, Write, Liberate" appeared over lists of the departments, times, and places for meetings. A march on the first anniversary of People's Park was combined with protests against the war.*

In the midst of this year of tension, we faced the anxieties of keeping our business going. Our customers always included many people who were not students at UC. We had a general store and did not carry texts.

We were a "trade" store with paperbacks predominating. We had started the store with paperbacks only, and we grew with the growth of the paperback industry. There were bookstores then that prided themselves on keeping paperbacks out, as though their presence would cheapen the clothbound books. All the more for us, we used to think, that kind of dinosaur attitude has done many a business in. We took pleasure in the expanding variety we could offer, and as time went on we began to add clothbound. By the time we moved to the corner of Telegraph and Haste in 1965, we had a considerable selection of cloth books, mainly in new titles. It takes about a year from publication as a new clothbound before a book, if sales warrant it, comes out in paper. We were in this business because of our enthusiasm for books, so it was natural that we would want to have the latest titles in the social sciences, in fiction, and in art, and that meant expansion into more cloth. Choosing the new books was one of the chief pleasures for Fred. He loved to meet with the sales reps, hear their presentations—and their gossip—take a chance with something that excited him.

Here is an essay, written years later, about the "travelers":

I remember the first sales representative of a major publisher who came to Cody's. I should—it was perhaps the most exciting thing that had happened since we opened the store. The "rep" who walked in on me early one afternoon in July 1957 was William Ashworth, who later became trade sales manager for Harper and Row.

The visit was totally unexpected. It was not only that the store was "committed," by principal and by necessity, to paperbacks, but no traveler for a publisher could expect to carry away an order large enough to make a call pay. So when Bill introduced himself I was torn by a hundred conflicting thoughts and emotions. Strict logic, I knew, would have required me to thank him for being so kind, but thanks, no thanks. The idea that Cody's—a Mom and Pop shop of the most modest dimensions—should be initiating relations with a publisher of Harper's magnitude was clearly ridiculous.

But there's a curiously provocative thing that happens in even the smallest bookstore, at least for the owner who, as I did, absorbs every bit of information I could get about books, both new and forthcoming. Such a bookseller suffers from what you could call, paradoxically, a grandiose solipsism. Knowing very well that specializing in paperbacks was the only proper policy for Cody's, I still speculated, every time I read about a new or soon-to-be-published book, whether or not it should be added to our stock. The fact was that I tired of confining my thoughts to trying to guess when or if it was ever going to appear in paperback. It was childish and absurd but I couldn't help it: I wanted it now.

There was another factor that caused me to waver. That was the undoubted fact that, from time to time, someone came to the store and asked for a hardbound book. I was very divided about such people. At times I was paranoid enough to believe that they only inquired for such books as a way of letting me know that the store was really not a bookstore at all. But at other times I took their request at its face value and the pain and suffering I experienced in having to mumble the perfunctory reply that "I could order it for you" was almost more than I could bear. The fact was that, given the physical dimensions of the store, not to mention our financial incapacity, the idea of doing something substantial with anything but paperbacks was ludicrous.

Beside that, paperbacks were then a holy crusade for us. There was a lot of very loose talk going the rounds in those sweetly naive days that the paperback was *the* book of the future and that what was happening was a revolution in the book trade. As one of the first paperback stores in Northern California we had, as they say, a sense of mission and dedication. We were on the barricades, valiant partisans of the paperback defiantly flaunting our banner. When my paperback fervor was flowing at its crest I was given to wholesale onslaughts on publishers as predatory profiteers who were the crass Canutes of the book trade resisting the paperback tide for their own mean and self-ish ends. Some of this, given our own necessities, was sheer opportunism but there was some genuine conviction mixed in. I liked the idea of being on the cutting edge of publishing and bookselling, as I was pleased to see it. It brought a sense of excitement and stimulation into the day's work. There was a kind of Quixote-like quality to my feeling, but then I've always been a sucker for lost causes.

So when Bill Ashworth called I wavered. I knew a bit of Harper's history and that also gave me pause. Bill was heir to a lot of literary lustre for me. I thought of the glorious history of *Harper's Monthly,* of the place in American cultural history reserved for the *Illustrated Weekly* with its ties to Winslow Homer and Thomas Nast. I remembered, too, some of the Harper authors: Mark Twain, Aldous Huxley, Ignacio Silone. . . . I recalled that I had often debated with myself—when in the course of time I should write a book of my own—whether I should bestow the honor of publication on Harper or Alfred A. Knopf. Perhaps some of this came through to Bill. I'm sure I must have seemed in an excited state.

But he settled down calmly enough beside the funny old cash register, because there was no other place where we could sit down together in the customary way. And between the customers who interrupted the session only too infreqently, he began to "present" the fall books just as, I imagined, he would do at Paul Elder's or Sather Gate. It really stunned me. There wasn't a book I could resist—every one of them seemed, in its way, a book I had to buy. What's more, it seemed to me in the euphoria of the moment that we could actually sell them. So I was doing my ones and my twos and threes and sometimes hopping up to five and even taking a plunge on a ten as we went along, until I looked up to observe that Bill was getting a little disturbed. At the next especially outlandish buy, he spoke.

"Do you really think you can sell that book?" He said it very gently, with an innate kindness natural to him. But it jolted me and I came crashing down to earth.

My first impulse was to be angry and offended. But I knew damned well that my ordering any of the books at all was plainly absurd.

"Well," I said embarrassedly, "perhaps I ought to think about it."

"Maybe," Bill said, "you ought to ease into selling hardbounds."

"That's true," I said lamely. "After all, we're mainly a paperback store."

I was ashamed of myself for betraying the revolution. The prestige and glamor of Harper and the hardbound had made me forget my loyalty to the paperback at the first real test. The thought of not having all those brand-new books to put into my window was almost enough, nevertheless, to make me weep. But Bill's questions had given me time for some faint forebodings to take form. Among them was the thought of what Pat would say when she saw the order amounting, probably, to more than my "open to buy" for a month or more. She had already, after prolonged and agonizing experience, made me agree to submit all orders for her review. There would be hell to pay when her eyes lit on this supremely idiotic outlay.

"Well," I said, "maybe I ought to go over the order and send it on to you later."

"Maybe we ought to forget about the new books," Bill said, "and talk about the Blue-Ribbon Plan."

It was a grievous come-down but I patiently listened while Bill went over the details of a stocking arrangement of back list titles Harper then offered. They were books—reference books, juveniles, gift books and so on—that had had a steady sale over the years—market-tested books, as Bill explained. As I remember, the books were put in, stock was checked after a certain time, upon which books that hadn't sold were returned for credit and other tried-and-true titles then replaced them. It wasn't exciting, God knows, but it seemed eminently sensible. And the money and commitment required was not anything as large as the sum that would have been needed for the dangerous venture in stocking the new books. So I signed for it.

I don't think we were particularly successful with the Blue-Ribbon plan. The fact was that most people who came into the store simply didn't expect to buy hardbacks there. A good many of them didn't seem to come in for much of anything except some company and a little conversation. Even when I stocked the rare hardbound the people who brought them up to the register almost invariably asked if they were on sale. They seemed, when they learned they were not, a little resentful that I should have added them to the stock. What they were telling me, I suppose, was that it was the lesser cost of the paperback that had brought them into the store so that prices of all books ought to be lowered to the soft-bound scale. It was fair enough. Cody's was quite evidently destined to rise or fall with the paperback. Harper or no, it was a case of being driven to put into practice what I so loudly preached.

Despite the fact that Bill had done no more than give me a glimpse of the tempting world of hardbound publishing and bookselling, I always remember him with the warmest affection. Later on, when a larger store made the visits of the sales reps almost a daily occurrence, I came to respect and like them even more. The story of the book reps has never really been told and it probably never will be because they've all been so busy at their exhausting trade that they've never had the time or the energy to write it. Perhaps some part of it could be pieced together by painstaking research in publishers' files but, if it were done that way, most of the real flavor and meaning would be lost.

It's rather difficult now, I suspect, for the travelers to have the same kind of relation to their publishers and their stores that they had in a less depersonalized time. The older book reps seemed to have a very clear understanding of their relation with the houses they worked for. They really believed—and I think it was true—that they were respected participants in the publishing process. Most of the houses were small enough for the reps to have a personal relationship with the publisher and the editors, as well as the head of the sales division. Yet because of the intimate relationship that developed over the years with "their" stores, they were also the booksellers' defenders and friends who could be relied upon to argue their case from minor issues such as an error in an invoice to the major decision on the part

of the publisher to wait a little longer for payment during a lean period for the bookseller. So strong was their advocacy of the booksellers' cause on occasion that they sometimes ran the risk of incurring
the anger of their employers. But most of them stubbornly maintained their position even when they did so.

I only wish now that I'd had the good sense to take notes on some
of my conversations with these veterans of a hundred publishing seasons. It was a part of their approach to their work that they resolutely
refused to be hurried. The person in the store who did the buying
usually had to wait while they roamed about the store talking to the
people working on the floor. I was impatient with what seemed to be
their waste of time until I realized that the appearance of casual daw-
dling was not so purposeless as it seemed. Studying their behavior a
little more intently I saw that their seemingly casual glances were
really shrewd appraisals of the "state of the store." They were checking on the attention to good display of the stock and to the standard
of housekeeping maintained generally. They were also taking a reading, I'm sure, on the spirit and feel of the place—because there's no
doubt a store in the doldrums usually can't help but give off the sour
smell of failure. And no doubt they were looking at the stock carefully
so as to learn as much as they could about what kind of a store it really
was—its strengths and its weaknesses—the "character," if you can
put it that way, of the store as reflected by the books it stocked and
featured.

Even when they finally sat down on the other side of the buyer's
table they were still not ready to present their books. The travelers
are really the main communication link in the book trade as a trade.
An enormous amount of detailed information was accumulated as
they traveled, some of them, down from Seattle to northern California with trips through the Rocky Mountain states. Some of them even
covered the bookstores scattered over the Southwest in Arizona, New
Mexico, and part of Texas. Few of them, I suspect, kept anything like
a set of carefully annotated file cards in which they entered information concerning the stores, the buyers and their idiosyncrasies, and
other such details. All that—and much else—was lodged quite nat-

urally and firmly in their heads. You had only to call the name of a store to mind, no matter how small or obscure, to release a flood of information from them.

Sometimes when time was short, I tried to hurry them a little to get on with the job. It was usually without effect. They worked at their own speed and in their own way and nothing would budge them from their usual practice. For the most part, though, I was an eager listener and I know there were times when Pat would look in on me spending the third or fourth hour with a rep who had not yet even opened his case.

Listening to some of the reps half the day as they talked of their work it seemed to me that a few of them had been selling books forever. I remember one curiously ageless man who had started out sometime in the early 1920's, so far as I could determine. His memories went back to the time of his first trip out when he was a mere nineteen or twenty. He had been assigned eight or nine southern states and after his sales conference he was to leave from Penn Station of glorious memory in New York. In those days the rep sold the list by establishing himself at a hotel in the town or city along the way. He had apprised the booksellers of his impending arrival by means of a postcard. The traveler held court in a two-room "suite" at the hostelry, one of the rooms being used to lay out the completed copies of the books, mainly forthcoming titles, he was selling. Sam—which must do for his name—said that most of the books were merely dummies, however; inside the book's cover there were only blank pages. By the time he had collected all the books he was to sell on the trip they filled a large trunk. The thought of laboriously lugging this millstone over half the country made his heart sink but he heaved the trunk into a taxi and proceeded to the railway terminal.

The redcap who helped him unload the trunk from the cab was quick to engage him in conversation as he wheeled the trunk through the station.

"What's in there?" he asked.

"Books," said Sam morosely.

"You a book traveler?" the redcap persisted.

Sam said that he was, and at that point the redcap put the trunk down.

"Now look here," he said, "I tell you what you want to do. You want to go to the drugstore and you want to get yourself some single-edge razor blades. Then you want to go get yourself a plain suitcase from the luggage store. Then you want to bring them blades and that suitcase back here. I'll wait for you and when you get back I'll show you what to do."

The redcap spoke with such authority that Sam said it never occurred to him not to follow his orders. He lost no time in making the purchases and returning to the redcap and his trunk.

"Now," said the porter when he returned, "I'll show you what to do after you open the trunk."

After the trunk was opened, the redcap grabbed one of the books from it, seized a razor blade from Sam's hand, and with a couple of swift swipes cut the blank pages out of it. The waste paper he discarded in a nearby trash can, the book he deposited in the new suitcase. In a moment, Sam was at work performing the same operation and, within a few minutes, they had emptied the trunk and transferred the gutted books into the suitcase where they fit perfectly and did no more than ballast it properly.

"Ain't nobody wants to bother with those blank pages," the porter said.

A kiss, Sam said, would have been misunderstood but he did tip and tip generously.

Sam was warmly approving of the old way of selling books on the road. It had been very pleasant to host "the trade" in the hotels. There was a pot of coffee and often something a little stronger on hand; the booksellers relaxed in the ambiance; the orders were done at the close of their visits, almost as an afterthought. Nowadays, Sam still went back to New York for his sales conferences by train but he had long since succumbed to the convenience and speed of covering his stores by car.

With Sam and some of the other older reps, though, I often felt that they had managed to revive in their visits something of the atmosphere of the decades past. They worked very much at their own pace. Their cases were never opened until they had expansively unburdened themselves with a string of anecdotes and gossip of the trade. They were, in their own persons, a walking news-letter of accounts of other stores and of the trade generally. They could be quite candid in their reports of stores they felt to be mismanaged or incompetently run but I always had the feeling there was little malice in their talk—they were mainly concerned over opportunities missed. As I became familiar with the reps and their sales technique it became a game to try to figure out when they judged me ready for business. But I often was proved wrong in my expectation. It was better simply to wait until, at last, the hand slipped down to release the catch on the case and then emerged with the first sheaf of covers and advance material on the books to be presented.

The sessions could be quite exhausting. Most of the older travelers were "commission reps" who represented as many as ten or more publishers, receiving from their houses ten per cent on the books sold in their territories. For the reps, these were their "lines." There was a code of honor among the travelers that condemned to shabby disgrace any rep so reprehensible as to go behind their backs to "steal a line" from another salesman. Most of the reps tried of course to get lines that were as saleable as possible but sometimes sheer necessity caused them to take on publishers whose books were, for various reasons, not much in demand. Even so, no matter how mediocre the line, the rep made a brave attempt to "place" the books, struggling with the buyer to sell enough copies to make up an order for the smaller houses. Ten was the magic number required. And if, after a half-hour of sifting over new books and back list, the total still fell short, the rep would sigh, tear up the order sheet and go on to the next line. It was to be noted that on the next call, in such instances, the rep would no longer be "carrying" that line.

There were legends that circulated among the booksellers about the huge fortunes accumulated by some of the older reps. Some of them were reputed to have made vast piles of money from their commissions and were now thought to continue making their seasonal trips only because of their love of the trade, greed, or a combination of the two. I doubted that more than a few had become wealthy—it's best to inherit money in the book business—but there was no doubt they had an almost pathological attachment to their work. They knew all the places to stay on their travels where the beds and food were good and the staffs were pleasant. And they never gave the impression of having become jaded about their calling, no matter how many years they had been on the road. "Now this," they'd say, as they dove into their case, "is a good line. There are some good books here for you from these people."

There was, of course, always the painful subject of returns—the difficult moment when the rep went with the buyer over to the shelf where the books that hadn't made it after six months or more of display in the store had to be packed and sent back to the publisher for credit. The reps, who were usually authorized by the publisher to issue return labels, tended to take care of their sad duty as rapidly as possible, glancing over the spines, shaking their heads, and then ruefully scribbling their names on the shipping labels.

There were few of the reps who ever tried to "load" a store with their books. They had little respect for the publisher who insisted that they put in books by overselling the bookseller. They knew from experience that the certain result of such a practice was to generate a flood of returns. But if a publisher was determined to go after big sales and promised to take heavy returns if the books didn't move, then the rep would sell them that way. "You can go heavy on it," they'd say, "if you don't sell them, you can send them back." In such cases when, sure enough, the books did not sell, the reps made out the return labels on their next visits with a vengeful satisfaction.

The reps were, in their way, remarkably independent. They had no patience with a publisher of esoteric or specialized books who expected them to sell like more popular material. They felt themselves equipped by their experience—as they usually were—to determine if the publisher was taking a realistic view of a book's sales potential. Shrewdly, they made certain that they maintained the respect of the bookseller by not loading them with books that had little chance of selling. Seeing a buyer pause at a particularly unlikely candidate for even a one, the rep would turn the page and remark with a smile, "A skip, I'd say. A decided skip."

Part of the reps' sense of independence came, no doubt, from the fact that they were laying out their own money for their seasonal tours. Commissions were not paid until well after the sales had been made in the stores so that months elapsed before the publisher had completed the accounting needed to produce the total figure owed to the rep. Publishers were often suspected of "cooking" these totals and there was no doubt that, in some cases, they delayed as long as possible in issuing the checks.

One rep told of a New York publisher—of some prestige so far as the books he published were concerned—who was especially delinquent in paying his commission travelers. Returning to New York after a long trip financed mainly from loans, the rep went to the offices of the publisher high in a Manhattan skyscraper to collect the long-due commissions he had earned from an exhausting series of forays, covering the eleven Western states and Alaska. The treasurer of the firm, when the rep inquired if he had the check, stared at him coldly and said he had not been authorized to issue it. The rep then stormed past the publisher's secretary and burst into his office to demand his money. After a prolonged argument, the publisher finally pulled a check book out of a drawer, opened it, and picked up his pen. "Jesus," said the publisher, glancing out of the window high above the city, "I know I owe you the money but I swear to God I'd rather jump out that window than write this check." "Write the check," said the rep, "and then jump out the window."

Most of the older reps made no pretense to being widely read or having a great interest in reading. Certainly few of them were what could be called bibliophiles. It was the trade they loved, not books. The books they were familiar with were almost exclusively those from the publishers they were representing or had sold for in the past. "Ah," they would say if a book happened to be mentioned in the conversation, "I sold that book. Pickwick started with two hundred."

What counted with them was their experience in selling the book in the stores; often they had never bothered to read it themselves.

With some of the reps I sometimes glimpsed a darker side in their personal lives. Something would happen as we sat in the back of the store that was deeply distressing. The mask would fall away and an agony would be disclosed. An older man who had never married— who had in effect married the trade—would suddenly begin to release some part of the feeling of anger and despair at the endless round of calls, the lonely nights in the motels, the mass of detail that cluttered their lives. The fascination of traveling widely had perhaps drawn them to becoming book reps but, after so many years of making the rounds, it had no doubt begun to pall. It was seldom they spoke of friends and, for some of them, the death of their mothers had left them ravaged and permanently bereaved.

Some of them were extraordinarily puritanical and stiffly conventional about the ways of the world—especially in sexual matters— considering how much they had seen over the years. There were flashes of pruriency—a glimpse of the hidden life of lurid fantasy that lay just beneath the bluff facade. What they saw along Telegraph Avenue on their way to the store often was a matter of extended comment. In reality most of what they saw had far more of the pathetic and tortured in it than the glamorous. Yet for the older reps the long hair, the beads, the exhibitionism, the fantastic clothes, seemed the costuming of a revel and an orgy rather than a grimly compulsive and destructive pursuit of a desolate lifestyle.

Their snickering reaction to the street people was understandable enough when I reflected that, for most of these men, any sort of hedonism was very remote from their own experience. Most of them had had to go to work early in their lives, often before or just after finishing high school. Superficially they seemed to enjoy a romantic, almost gypsy-like kind of existence but the facts were quite otherwise. The hard reality was that they kept to a schedule requiring that they visit hundreds of stores. There was no revelry for them in the hotels because, on most nights, they were making up the orders to send to their publishers. Their lives had been, in a sense, a series of arrivals and departures.

There were a few of the reps—whether grimly or with spirited enthusiasm—who literally never gave up until the end. The story came back months after it had happened. A traveler in his seventies had worked through the day in Montana and then gone to his motel, had his dinner, and returned to his room. He was found dead the next morning slumped in his chair. On the table near him, neatly stacked, were the day's orders ready to be mailed to his publishers. I remembered him then, a weathered figure trudging through the store, his arms stretched taut with the weight of his heavy cases. The pride and pluck of him was curiously moving. How many entrances into how many stores had he made in the long procession of the seasons and the years? Yet the shoulders had been kept square and the head was held high. And the smile of recognition was ready to appear. A soldier, I suppose you'd say, of "the trade."

CHAPTER TWELVE 1970

STAFF PROBLEMS THOUGHTS ON SELLING THE STORE

SUMMER CHANGES CRAFTS VENDORS ON "CODY'S PLAZA"

*Far more seemely were it for thee to have thy Studie full of bookes, than
thy Purse full of Mony.*

JOHN LYLY, c.1554–1606

In the parlous months of 1970, it was hard for us to recall the rewards
of the book trade. Riots and demonstrations, over civil rights, over the Vietnam War, over People's Park, were having a devastating effect on business.
Our nonstudent customers continued to stay away from the Avenue, so
that sales fell even on the days when my ledger did not show "Riots—
gas—closed at 1 P.M." To make matters worse, there was a recession.

Another way the turmoil affected us was in Fred's frequent absences
from the store. He was on permanent emergency call, it seemed, to go to
meetings where peaceful resolution of conflicts might possibly be forged; or
meetings working out the issues of setting up, for example, the free clinic.
Some of the staff at the store could not fathom his preoccupation with outside matters, so without his full attention, and the support and understanding of our staff, we were drifting as a business.

Neither of us had the skills needed to be expert managers of a retail
business. We tried to share decision-making with the staff and hope that
those we hired were self-starters. Some of them were not, but Fred found
it hard to fire anyone. My role had always been to manage the financial
side of the enterprise, not the staff deployment and activities. As the store
had grown, our staff had increased. By 1970, we had about 18 employees
and a manager for administration of schedules and work assignments. We
were beset with worries over our dire situation. Those customers who did
come ran the risk of being asked to leave because we had to close to avoid
tear gas. Losses from shrinkage were greater than the usual bookstore rate.

The Avenue was not an easy place in which to make a living, and staff morale suffered. Here, then, is my letter to Bob and Fi from April 1970:

I have been telling myself daily that I must write to you. You recall from your visit here, and Fred's talks with you in the spring, that we have been thrashing about intermittently with the idea of whether we should give the store up or not. We have been like timid swimmers approaching the water, finally dipping a toe in, retreating, then approaching again. It seems we just can't make a decision and we don't know whether our failure to decide is because it is such a complex thing, for us, to decide, or whether we are just failing to recognize necessity out of a dis-inclination to make such a drastic change in our lives. We have not been under the gun to make such a decision—life has been relatively quiet here in the revolutionary capital, ever since last May as a matter of fact, so there is no crisis atmosphere. Sales have been down, but I think that may be more the general recession than anything peculiar to Telegraph Avenue, and we have countered that by returning to our former evening-open hours, so that we are meeting our bills and doing moderately better than breaking even.

What has pushed us toward a decision is the fact that the fellow who was acting manager left us in December and at the suggestion of the three senior staff people, we more or less divided his work among them, that is, created three separate functions with one of them in sole charge of shipping and receiving, another the daily managing, a third the ordering. However it soon became apparent that a stronger hand at the helm was needed and things were slowly going downhill, from the standpoint of efficiency and morale. . . . A series of small, nagging things at the store just seemed to be the final straw. We either had to, both of us, put hard and dedicated work into the store or give it up. Our experience has taught us that a personal bookstore cannot be delegated to others. Does Fred in fact want to make that kind of commitment? We finally decided that we do not want to spend the rest of our productive lives this way.

Now, we just reached this decision about two weeks ago, and I called the real estate broker to whom we had assigned the task last October of trying to find a buyer (at our price of course) and from

whom we had heard little, save of his earnestly trying, and not succeeding; by mutual agreement the affair was in limbo, as it were. I
told him that we were now prepared to take little or nothing for our
lease, if we could just get out from under the bloody thing—it has
until 1985 to run! We figure that some speculator or other might
want to take over the building, divide it into a number of shops, etc.
The broker told us that the man to whom the building had been sold
in 1965 would probably not let us off the lease—why should he?—
and our best outlet would be to try to persuade him to sell the building which, since he is a timid coupon-clipper insulated from life by
his money, might be possible. So that is the approach we are using.

Among the strands in this rich tapestry is the fact that about three
weeks ago our insurance agent called to say that his company is can-
celling all our policies because they don't like the risks involved. Our
lease requires us to carry insurance on the building, and of course we
have fire insurance on our stock. Further, the landlord's mortgage
requires him to have insurance on the building. We have found another carrier, but this is just one more instance of the constant anxiety
to which one is prey.

Well, weekend before last, on a Friday night, when Fred went
down to the store, he was presented with this:

"We, the working staff of Cody's Books, have decided that certain
structural changes should be made in the corporation. The condition
of Telegraph Avenue creates a situation, where in a standard retail
store operation, high personnel turnover and constant discontent
among the employees will be inevitable. We wish to eliminate this
condition by structural change within the store. We offer these
changes in order to create a situation where a healthy business can be
operated by dedicated and involved employees.

"In order to implement these goals and provide a strong and co-
hesive staff, we have organized ourselves into the Union of Cody's
Employees. As a union, we present the following demands.

"1. The immediate creation of the post of Executive Manager. This
person will have the authority to hire and fire personnel, change sal-
aries, and generally administer the employees within the store.

"2. The managerial staff must have free and ready access to the financial records. This will require that the books and records be kept in the store. We feel that this access is absolutely necessary, as the store managers must have a full understanding of the exact financial condition of the store at all times, if they are to be able to properly manage the store.

"3. The implementation of a share-ownership plan. At the end of the calendar year, employees who have worked at the book store for one year or more would receive shares computed on the basis of yearly salary. Before any person could be admitted to the corporation through receipt of shares, the corporation members would have to ratify his admission. A majority affirmative vote would be necessary for ratification. The plan should be instituted immediately by giving one share each to the staff members who have been working at the store for more than one year.

"4. All shareholders will be presented with a complete statement of the financial condition of the corporation, such a statement to be made monthly. Shareholders will also be presented with a statement of the corporate by-laws and terms of the lease.

"5. Upon receiving shares, members of the corporation will be entitled to participate in all corporate decisions.

"6. If any employee leaves the store, the corporation must buy his shares. No one who is not a working member of the staff can retain his shares.

"Our representatives will be glad to meet with you on Monday, April 6, to discuss our demands."

Since you don't know the people involved, and it isn't your store anyhow, you will have to project your sympathies to imagine how we felt. In the first place, only three of the people in the store (the aforementioned senior staff) have been working there longer than last September. So how they can claim such a deep share in the business is a wonder. Second, only one of them has any claim to seriousness at all, since she is a professional book person, but she has only worked at the store 2½ years, and at wages higher, and conditions better, than her past jobs—we helped to cure her of her ulcer. Of the other two "senior" people, one is twenty-three, has worked for us for four years, and is juggling his schedule now to allow him to pick up his schooling again. The other—twenty-seven or so—told us a month ago he wants to go on half-time, or quit, in June so he can polish his guitar playing.

This document made us deeply depressed, and actually made me, literally, sick. We were so upset we called in our wise friend and lawyer Henry Elson, who said we should realize that Fred's judgment on it was correct—i.e., this was a rather pathetic attempt on their part to get into the mainstream of what was going on about them. None of them are serious politicos—the most they do is sign a petition now and then—Fred is far more involved in the community than any of them. I think they resent that, and his absence from the store—like children who don't like it when their parents go out.

A good deal of my anger comes from the fact that I know only too well how hard we have both worked, for nearly fourteen years. To be told that we should just hand it over to them is ridiculous. And it isn't that I'm such a bony-headed capitalist. We only got where we are with the store because I worked unpaid for eight years. I'm still paid less than any of them. Fred worked at low wages for fourteen years, so technically the corporation owes us about $100,000 in back pay, for starters. To me, their asking, rather I should say demanding, that we GIVE them shares is the same as if I were to ask Tom to give me his guitar, or Diana to give me her weaving loom.

We met with them last week, and Fred told them—on the advice of our lawyer, but against the advice of our canny businessman friend down the street—that we were trying to sell the business and for this reason we could not give out shares because we could not have any limitations on our freedom to dispose of the business. Most of the meeting then settled down to their dissatisfaction with the way the store is run. It would seem to me that if the senior staff do not like the troika arrangement, it would have been best for them to meet with us and discuss it, rather than drag in everyone right down to the cashiers for what is essentially a managerial problem.

The staff then proposed that we should just turn the store over to them—if not in the present location, in another—and they would pay us over the long term for the stock they need to open it. Fred said he would think it over and let them know. Needless to say I would have kicked him had it been possible to do so invisibly because I knew damn well such a thing was not possible. What would we pay our bills with if we sold off half the existing stock and gave them the other half on a long-term loan? I don't think we'd ever see a penny if we did because I have little confidence in their ability to run a store.

Well, we set a meeting date for a few days later, but it was not to be. There were demonstrations against the war and the ROTC, riots, tear-gas, window-breaking, and we had a couple more days of living on the edge of the precipice, some of us got sick from the gas being used, etc.

Meanwhile, I was completing my semi-annual financial statement which involves tabulating the entire inventory that had been taken by the staff on March 1 (and which I hadn't got to finish sooner because I was doing other things), going through all the accounts payable, the ledger of running inventory we keep, and so on. I finally completed it last Thursday, and discovered that the rate of "shrinkage" (errors by staff, employee and customer theft) has TRIPLED from previous six-month periods, and far from the usual (which is bad enough) $10,000 or so—retail—it was almost $33,000 from last September 1 to this February 28. That is nearly 12% of our sales. If it weren't for the fact that Christmas came during this period, we would have run a deficit; as it was we had such a skinny profit that a good wind would have blown it away. Should this rate continue unchecked, we will run a $12,000 deficit during the March–August period.

I was glad that we had already decided to get out, before we discovered this, so that our decision was reached by facing up to basic issues about ourselves and our society, rather than a panic decision because of the theft. However, you can see that if we hadn't decided to quit, this would be hard to refuse to do now. There is really not much we can do about it—the theft, that is. It makes us realize the degree to which this society has become a jungle when one's friends prey on one. I think you know how deeply Fred has been involved in issues on the street, and how hard he has worked. Of course, we can tie our losses in stock to the general desperation and frustration that young people—and not only young, but the young are our customers—feel about this society. In other words, the solution, or the answer, is far beyond our individual efforts, as far as staying in business is concerned. If we called in the cops—a real exercise in futility—we'd probably get all the windows broken, the theft would triple, and we'd be worse off than we are now.

I also think that the theft would not be as great if the staff were more alert and spent less time socializing—doesn't that sound like the typical boss?—but it is a scandal. They have taken advantage of Fred not being in the store, when he is at meetings, and we must be the easiest mark in town. We finally had our postponed meeting with some of them last night, and gave them these figures. After some talk, they said, "Well, but we want to hear your answer to our idea of taking over the store, and of your lending us the stock to have our own store." Now, can you imagine how dim-witted that is, after we have just gotten through giving them the financial figures? And at an enlarged staff meeting this morning, called specifically to discuss measures we can take on the theft, again they brought it up, and Fred was in despair to try to get it through their heads that we simply could not go on, we had to get out of the lease, sell off the stock, pay our bills, and get out.

Our broker has talked with the landlord, and gotten him to agree to sell the building—that is the only way we can get out. There is, remarkably enough, still retailing interest in the street, the fast-buck people are still around, so we are hoping that it won't be too long on the market. We certainly don't look forward to all the harassments of closing down a business. As soon as word gets back to the publishers we will be hounded about our bills, and there is just the physical labor of running a gigantic sale, returning the books that we can return for credit, and so on. I have no idea whether we will come out ahead or not. Nominally we should but what I know of stores going out of business doesn't make me too optimistic.

However, we are not really worried about that. For one thing, I will write to the London office of the Economist Intelligence Unit and can probably get more reports to do, thus increasing my earnings from that source to about $300 a month. So we have a cushion of sorts, and as we have never lived high, we don't have so far to fall. In truth, we will have one of the highest standards of living possible—we will be free. Fred doesn't have anything specific in mind, first he wants to unwind, somehow, if that can be done without leaving Berkeley.

It was not to be. A few days after I concluded that letter, the national uproar over the invasion of Cambodia and the deaths at Jackson State and Kent State threw our community into another agitated time of protests. Then, the long delayed "improvements" to the Avenue began in May. The street was literally torn up to the edges of the buildings—sidewalks included—so that it was like walking through an old west town to pick your way over the brown dirt. Dust and grit seeped into the store and lack of access meant another reason for people to stay away. This lasted for months, and the bills piled up. The Avenue had long been a place to buy marijuana and LSD; now dealers in hard drugs were moving in. For a time Cody's was used as a drug drop. We learned this when in checking stock in the philosophy section, one of our staff found behind a volume of Wittgenstein a plastic bag with a white powder in it. He flushed it down the toilet, and this became our way of discouraging dealers.

Fred wrote about the Telegraph atmosphere in a September letter:

The summer here has been peculiar. Tension is still much in the air. We began with a $50,000 trashing on the Avenue on the evening of July 4th. That alone did quite a lot to poison the air for the summer. A petition for a referendum to vote community control of the police got enough signatures to qualify for the ballot in November and that has added quite a bit of tension. Police actions earlier in which the minister of the Free Church and people at the Clinic were beaten have added their bit to the air of continual controversy. The ACLU has just issued a long report on a whole series of grievances unsatisfactorily disposed of by the police. The city itself faces law suits for civil damages involving police complaints totaling about $23 million. A city councilman, black, beat out the Democratic incumbent for the district's Congressional seat. The Council, itself, is split pretty evenly between liberals and conservatives and the result is that it delays and quibbles rather than taking any decisive action. And over it all hangs the question of what will happen when the University resumes in the fall. The fear of what could happen is very pervasive. I have heard very serious people talk of the danger of some kind of brutal confrontation that could lead to a massacre.

I taught for a week at the Unitarian school for the ministry here— a special seminar on social change. For the first time, I was paid for teaching—$150—which I contributed to the clinic, along with a $35 fee I got for speaking at the Unitarian church service. The course was pretty demanding and exhausting. Three hours every morning for five mornings. We used the Telegraph area as our lab and I drew people over from it for the discussions. I think the morning that was the most satisfactory was when the medics from the clinic came and talked about their work. One of the ministers who was attending said that it had puzzled him in listening until it occurred to him that the clinic people were really talking about a kind of mystic passion and that what we had heard had really been a view of religious service and devotion.

There were about twenty-five people, fifteen of them under twenty, who went through the week. I was most moved when, on Thursday, the talk had become so dismal—God, how the young can be dismal—that I had to assert some kind of hope, no matter how desperate. So I talked about my own compulsion to do something for the something's sake and not for goals or any kind of political objective. I had thought I had fumbled around and made a total mess of it but later on three of the kids sought me out and embraced me and thanked me with tears in their eyes and one of them mumbled, "that was very heavy, man." And higher praise in more eloquent language you can not expect than that.

I've gone on working on our community Council on Drugs and Society, and I think we have finally worked toward doing something constructive after a long period of months of casting around for some sense of direction. The drug thing in this country really assumes tremendous proportions. Heroin is now making big inroads and yesterday our manager found four stashes of the stuff hidden behind books at the store. He removed it and flushed it down the toilet. The dealing all along the Avenue is very intense. We have even put up a sign on the door warning that dealing is not permitted inside.

It's hard to describe the kind of tension and ugly atmosphere that results when you are in the middle of this kind of thing. I have been pushing very hard for the Council to make itself into the information and educational force in the community to stimulate it to really come to grips with the problem. One of the things that is so dismaying is that the present process takes someone on heroin, dries him out at a state institution, puts him back on the street with no follow-up and no alternative offered, and then when he goes back on the drug, puts him through the same process again. There are many people who, at the age of twenty or twenty-one, have already gone through this process four or five times. At the clinic we get people who have taken weird combinations of drugs. Recently, there were four people who had taken hog—one of these concoctions that resulted in a series of highs running in a succession for forty-eight hours.

At the store, changes have taken place. All of the old guard of our staff have now either departed or are just finishing up. In some cases this was better for all concerned. I can't help but feel a little impatient with people who found the store a fine place to work in when things were rosier but who now complain so bitterly about the street and the changes we have had to make.

I have been buying the new fall books as the salesmen have come in and it has been a kind of strange experience. In the midst of such uncertainty it's been very hard to sit there and listen to people describing a piece of complete crap and then try to make up your mind whether to take one or none. We are re-doing sections in the store and getting better display. Pat is juggling the accounts and doing her best to satisfy our hungry creditors. I think I am getting down to harder work at the store, partly because the new staff we have hired take a more serious and cooperative attitude to their work.

On the outside of the store, some of the street people along the Avenue turned to crafts to support themselves. In November of 1970 the New York Times *headlined a story "The System's Dropouts Are Turning to Handicrafts in Search of New Values." Describing Berkeley as "bellwether of the moods of the nation's young," the story on a renaissance in handicrafts referred to marketing that ranged from "the counters of expensive boutiques to the bare sidewalk in front of Cody's bookstore on Telegraph Avenue, a spot many feel more conducive to honest trade than the merchant's stall."*

The *"bare sidewalk in front of Cody's" was no longer bare. In 1967, Hassan and Barbara Erfani asked us if they could set up a flower stand at the southern end of our sidewalk space. They were the only enterprise there until 1970; free-form rap groups and ad hoc political discussions took the space, and there was Haji's commune with their rugs and samovar. But then some craft workers came to us in early December and asked if they could set up a display on our sidewalk.*

At *this time Berkeley had the typical "peddlers' law" requiring street sellers to move every five minutes. Our space was private property up to the city sidewalk. One by one they came: leather worker Bill Anderson, carvers of redwood burls, makers of candles. In the cold of December they would camp out all night so that no one would take their spot. The Erfanis volunteered to oversee this free market, making sure no one "crashed" a regular vendor, that only hand-made-by-the-vendor articles were sold, and that everyone had both a city permit and a state sales tax license (otherwise, the tax collector who showed up one morning told me, "Cody's will be responsible for the sales tax on all the goods we estimate are being sold here").*

Our *space was bursting with crafts, requiring that I chalk-mark a path to be kept clear for our customers. More and more young people wanted to make a living from handicrafts, opting out of what they perceived as a soulless industrial machine. They began to occupy other space on the street, often to the irritation of established stores. After many a clash over this issue, some of the vendors came to Fred and asked for his help in getting the peddling ordinance changed. As people who had also started our independent business life in a small way, we felt sympathy for them. And, after months of meetings with city officials, a new ordinance was passed.*

Ever since then, for nearly twenty years now, Telegraph Avenue has a daily street market that comes to a climax every December. Merchants have learned to live with it and some of them will even concede that it is an attraction that brings thousands of visitors to the area.

Fred wrote in November of that year:

No, the store is not sold, and I don't know when it will be. I have the feeling that if there were a considerable economic revival it would be much more marketable. Berkeley being what it is, it may be that what we are experiencing here is something that is going to become much more general among young people—namely, a determination not to consume in such dimensions as have marked the past. Sympathizing with that, I can hardly blame them if they extend the practice to books, since many of them aren't worth buying anyway.

We are on the borderline between being a going and losing business and I suspect that we are finally coming into a period where we will be a going one, partly because the born losers and grousers who were working at the store are gone. I take part of the blame for their presence myself but I think a share of it has to go to a former employee, a person given to being attracted to such types. Yesterday I took a grim kind of pleasure in finally firing the last of this breed. I can truthfully say that we do not have working in the store a single high powered intellectual of the peculiarly dismal kind but simply a group of people who work in the store as a job and who do not believe in making everyone around them miserable in the process.

Over the twenty-one years we had the store, while we had employees who stole time, money, and merchandise from us—as any retail establishment has—we had a lot of wonderful people. We had those who shared our love of books, who brought special knowledge about a particular subject and made it their task to build a good section. Fred and I had many gaps in our education, most conspicuously in the hard sciences. We had part-time employees who were grad students in the new computer sciences and made an impressive special section. Who were we to know that a telephone-sized paperback called Gravitation, *weighing in at about three pounds, would become a steady seller month after month? We had students of French culture, of physics, especially of philosophy; we had ex-*

perts in linguistics, semiotics, and the deconstructionists. Cody's owes much of its reputation to the staff that, despite all our problems, worked hard to make the store successful.

Sometimes books or periodicals came to us because the authors chose us. We arrived at work one morning in the early 1970's to find a note under the door: "Look behind the bushes on the Bowditch side of the Christian Science church." Curious, Fred walked a block east and there found a bundle of the magazine Osawatomie, published by the Prairie Fire Distribution Committee and featuring the writings of the underground radical left Weathermen.

Many books also came to us because of suggestions from customers. It is essential for a store like Cody's to have a constant dialogue with readers, and we were well placed to get ideas from teachers and students of a great university. Our customers truly helped create Cody's, not only by their purchases, but also because they assisted us in selecting stock.

Writers were part of that process. Obviously there could be no bookstore without writers; my reference is to local writers and their help in two ways. One was in their expertise in suggesting books we should carry. Nonfiction authors know their field and could tell us about important new work. The second way they helped was in their presence in our midst and the reality this brings to the bookseller to meet, talk, and sponsor readings with people who have the talent and energy to get their ideas on paper. We especially treasured writers published by small presses. They gave a unique flavor and excitement to the store. People often praised us for the attention we gave to small press work. We explained that the gratitude was on our side for the contributions these presses and their authors made to the mix at the store.

BEST-SELLERS FOR 1970
Clark, *Civilization*
Speer, *Inside the Third Reich*
Segal, *Love Story*
Toffler, *Future Shock*

If I read a book and it makes my whole body so cold no fire can ever warm me, I know that is poetry. If I feel physically as if the top of my head were taken off, I know that is poetry. These are the only ways I know it. Is there any other way?

EMILY DICKINSON, 1830–1886

Three hundred years ago, printing and bookselling were one occupation. Many of us who are drawn to the bookselling profession share an interest in this ancient craft: the yen to create and print something of our own, on however modest a scale. Fred's interest in nineteenth-century illustrations had led him to create a line of notecards that we sold for 5¢. In December 1969 the first of our Thoreau calendars appeared—an 18 × 24-inch sheet combining old woodcuts and quotations from Thoreau with a twelve-month calendar. We printed one thousand and gave one away with every purchase, until Fred walked down the street and saw one in the gutter. He came back to the store and put up a sign "1970 Calendars—10¢."

There were ten of these Thoreau calendars, from 1970 to 1979. Fred had a deep interest in Thoreau, a fellow spirit reaching across more than a century. The identification went beyond Thoreau's absorption in his natural environment to encompass his engagement in the great issues of his time, just as we were citizens of a broader world than the one within the four walls of the bookstore.

Since the mid-1960's, Fred had designed the wrapping paper we used, and in the spring of each year, what we called a broadside: a poster that we gave away with each purchase. Our former partner Steve had contrib-

uted his ideas and one of the best of the broadsides was a combination of medieval German woodcuts on spring, and poems on the subject. In the spring of 1971, Fred did a broadside "In Praise of Gardening" as well as a 10¢ pamphlet "An Aid to the Digger and Planter in Berkeley: Seed, Nurseries, Tools, Vegetables and Herbs, the Organic Necessity."

Shortly after the gardening broadside was published, Fred wrote of it and of the Thoreau calendar:

I was afraid the broadside was not going to sell but it has picked up now. I think we will have no trouble in selling the 2,000 we had printed and perhaps go on to sell another 2,000 of a reprint. The Thoreau calendar has now sold close to 9,000 copies and we will do 4,000 more to be taken east by a guy who has already tried selling them to other stores in the Northwest. He found that college bookstores were, by and large, so hidebound and enmeshed in red tape that he could sell only a few to them. But the organic food stores, the head shops, and the stores run by young people were very enthusiastic even though they had to buy in small quantities. Anyway, he had no trouble in selling 500 at 50¢ each within a week in Washington, Oregon and northern California.

We are also getting orders from stores now for the cards as they circulate more and more. Most recently was an order from a bookstore in Honolulu. So perhaps we will end up as publishers yet. I have all kinds of ideas for doing more cards and large sheets and perhaps even a book or two. So far, I feel we have been very lucky because all of the projects have paid their way and even made some profit as well as being very good promotion for the store. Even an astronomy sheet I did using plates from an old school book is now selling fairly well and should sell out in a couple of weeks. The low price in these days of galloping price rises usually surprises people and seems to make the sheets almost irresistible.

We could do these projects because they were self-supporting. The wrapping paper and calendars cost 4.6¢ per sheet, the cards with envelopes 1.3¢. Other bookstores that saw Fred's work wanted to buy in bulk from us, but we finally concluded that we did not want to put our energies into wholesaling what was a specialty unique to Cody's Books. Fred's further thoughts on this are in an essay he wrote in 1976 on "Publishing on Your Own."

So far as books are concerned, I was very hesitant to risk what seemed to us a large amount of money. But, in small hand-made editions, we did issue a selection of fables illustrated by Grandville and a hand-calligraphed anthology of poetry and prose entitled *Spring*. These were given out free to customers as a good-will bonus for coming regularly to the store.

The small press movement has gained considerable momentum during the past ten years and Berkeley has been one of the centers for this development which is so valuable to young writers and publishers. When Julia Vinograd brought in a sheaf of poems I yielded to temptation and joined the ranks of the small presses by editing and designing a small collection of her work called *The Berkeley Bead Game*. Later on, after this had gone into a second printing of a thousand copies, we published a collection of her poems which were principally a reflection of the impact of the Viet Nam war. This volume, *Uniform Opinion,* was also reprinted.

Julia is a publisher's dream because she is an authentic street poet, drawing most of her themes for her work from the public places and restaurants along Telegraph Avenue. Dressed in a long black gown crowned with a worn yellow cap, she patrols the area daily and, during the past ten years, has sold thousands of copies of her own work.

Since I could not give an author anything approaching the kind of promotion, sales, and distribution promised by a large press, I made arrangements accordingly. There was no advance paid but Julia received a royalty of thirty percent on copies sold. And of course the best display at the store, usually near the register, was guaranteed. In Julia's case, this privilege was always enforced by her. She checked the store on a daily basis to see that the book was in its usual prominent place. A special species of hell broke out if it was not.

Tommy Roberts, a street puppeteer, was next to join the highly selective Cody's list. Like Julia he was anxious to have a book of his own to sell at the conclusion of his appearances in Sproul Plaza and elsewhere as he made his itinerant tours. Together we selected poems and some autobiographical material and these, together with some photographs of Tommy in performance, made a small book he called *I Gotta Hunger, I Gotta Need*.

It is very difficult for a playwright to get a play published, especially a one-act play. So I debated soberly and long before agreeing to publish a play with a male sexuality theme by Daniel Rudman called *Hold Me Until Morning*. What is being held during this drama is the male sex organ and, indeed, the play consists of a dialogue between a man and his penis. Dan had already given performances of the play and, when the printer delivered the books, it was performed before an audience of about fifty people at the store. Later, the play had a short run at one of the theatres in the Bay Area, the Berkeley Stage Company, and it has been performed—with and without permission—in many American cities, in Canada, and in England, France and Germany.

Since only 500 copies of an offset typescript were done and the price was only $1.00, neither Dan nor myself anticipated that we would make any money from the play. My hope was that it would come to the attention of someone who was doing an anthology of writing on male sexual themes and that he would then be paid a permission fee. Although this did not occur exactly as planned, a nonprofit organization did write for permission to include it in an anthology.

Nevertheless, the publishing of *Hold Me Until Morning* was proof that even the issuing of a book in such a small edition may provoke a surprising response. Orders were received from all over the United States, Canada, and Europe. It was reviewed in a number of publications and chosen on booklists.

Finally, I have to admit that I have published books of my own at the store. The first was a book called *A Guide to the Real Berkeley* in which nineteenth-century engravings from books and magazines were accompanied by captions of a satiric intent. The first thousand of the two-thousand copies printed sold very quickly at $1.45 a copy and then we seemed to have exhausted the market. It was the first book to which I was forced to have recourse to remaindering and at nineteen cents it vanished in a few weeks.

More recently, I wrote verses, somewhat in the style of Hilaire Belloc, to go with engravings selected from children's books and annuals of the 1870's and 1880's and put them together in a book called *Haunted Homes*. When Fred Schmaltz-Riedt, the Doubleday sales representative, happened to see the book, he sent a copy to New York. In a few weeks came word that Doubleday wanted the book to be published as a Dolphin paperback.

We had always thought of the store as a kind of community center, so it pleased us to have opportunities for events like the one I described in a letter in March 1971:

Did I send you a copy of the little poster advertising the concert we had in the store on February 21? The same group of fifteen musicians, augmented by singers, is going to present the St. John Passion by Bach at the store on April 4. It is so great, the acoustics are good because of the wooden ceiling and all the bookshelves, and the public is enchanted with the idea of the musicians on the mezzanine. We don't pay them, we couldn't afford it, they just have this idea of moving music out of the concert hall and into the lives of the audience, and they take up a collection—which is meagre, of course. They all have other jobs to live by.

Nineteen seventy-one also marked the beginning of Fred's association with what is now The Berkeley Monthly, *an unusual shopping give-away that has become a model of its kind for the quality and range of its editorial articles. It started as* The Telegraph Monthly *at very few pages, and the youthful proprietors talked with Fred about ideas for its contents and focus. He contributed an article for their July 1971 issue on "Architectural Pleasures of the South Campus Area: A Possible Walking Tour" that the city later reprinted to give out at conventions. It was at this time that Fred published,* I Gotta Hunger, I Gotta Need. *Fred wrote about that in this letter just after the 4th of July 1971.*

I just bought from a desperate student an IBM Selectric for $175 and this letter is the first production from the instrument. I bought it so I could use it for photo-offset reproduction because as you will note from the enclosed we have now done our first book. Publishing it has been quite an experience. The author is an original, I think, and the writing, although it has no pretensions to literary quality, has an honest ring to it that I think makes it worth having in print. Tommy has been selling it himself and we have been selling it at the store. So far, in only two weeks, we have sold 200 copies of the 1,000 printed.

I did a piece on publishing it which will come out in the Sunday book section of the *Chronicle* during the latter part of this month and the Glide People's Art Center is doing an autograph party for the book on the eleventh. I am sending you a copy of the flier we did for that which Anth and I took over to the Glide Memorial Church in San Francisco yesterday morning.

This weekend the collectives and the political groups have been having a Lifestyles Festival in a park about four blocks from the store. I got involved when they applied for a permit to close one of the streets bordering the park. The plans for the affair were very elaborate but, as it turned out, no one took them very seriously and by the middle of the second day the thing degenerated into hundreds of people sitting around having a good time. One of the more pleasant things was the almost continuous street theatre and music that popped up all over the park. There are now at least five quite good satiric theatre bands and of course there are all kinds of balladeers and small musical groups who set up and play and sing. These people did the most to make the affair really festive.

I enclose a leaflet—nothing is really in operation in Berkeley until you issue one—on our new enterprise, Cody's Supplies. This has now been going for about two weeks and is already making out very well. The contact with the young people backpacking across the country is very interesting and I spend as much time as I can in the place. The resilience and toughness of these kids has to be seen to be believed. One guy came in who had simply worn out his backpack on his travels getting here from the east coast. So he came in, bought another, gave the old one away, and went on to the next stage of his journey. We are having a lot of fun and people seem to like the place. I wouldn't be surprised if eventually it is much imitated in college stores and the bookstore chains that operate close to campuses.

But despite our enthusiasm, Cody's Supplies turned out to be ill-fated. Some of our staff had persuaded us that we could augment our meager book sales by setting up a sideline that would sell equipment to hikers and climbers. We took the southeast section of the store which had its own door and installed the kind of merchandise our volunteer consultants told us would go. Never was there a truer proverb than "Shoemaker, stick to your last." The enterprise was too small to really work, even though this was in the days before other such stores came into existence, and we gave it up after several months. Back to what we knew—books.

Conflict and turmoil continued to be the order of the day. Anti-war rallies and demonstrations continued, intensified by the U.S. invasion of Laos in February 1971. In May, there was another fruitless attempt by the youth to seize People's Park, a symbol by now of past dreams and present betrayal.

The tensions of our life in Berkeley made us long for relief. Our next-door neighbors, Clare and Joe Fischer, had been talking about getting some country property for weekends and vacations. Several times Joe and Fred went out exploring in Sonoma County in response to ads for "country property." Then on a Sunday in October, Joe went off alone to look at what seemed too good to be true: 160 acres in Mendocino County on an all-year trout stream, with cabins to stay in, for only $16,500. He came back with a thirty-day option and a chance we couldn't refuse. We got a third family, June and Abe Brumer, our accountant, involved, so each of us shared the $8,250 down payment. Our part came from a small inheritance. What we dubbed "the property" is located 1½ miles up a hand-made road that is off the county road, about twelve miles east of Willits. It was our summer vacation site after that, and most important to Fred as a place to unwind on long walks in the woods.

That December we had a personal crisis: Fred was in an accident on December 21 when he was driving our VW bus and was hit broadside by a sixteen-year-old trying out the new family car. Fred suffered a concus-

sion, punctured lung, and broke two bones in his left leg. After ten days in the hospital he came home in a cast and was unable to work until the end of July 1972.

This enforced idleness for him and double duty for me made us mostly spectators of the continuing tensions over the war. In 1972 there were rallies and student strikes. The police began to use an Army jeep with metal screens that poured out a mixture of tear gas and smoke along Telegraph to move the crowds along. At the People's Park Memorial demonstration on May 15, once again asphalt was replaced with flowers and the City Council voted to try to lease it from the University.

There was another change in the street that year: the old building at 2476 Telegraph that had been our first southside location was condemned by the city and razed. Successive enterprises, each one seedier than the one before, had replaced us there. The landlord was unwilling to bring the building with its upstairs apartments up to code. At the end, it had become a hangout for drug users.

A third change on the Avenue was the closing of Sather Gate Books, a trade store that had been there since 1915. When we first came on Telegraph in late 1960, Sather Gate was in the first block below the campus, a traditional bookstore with faculty charge accounts and a management that refused to stock paperbacks and did not deal in text or technical books. Their attempts to keep afloat consisted mostly of a wholesaling business they set up specializing in school and library accounts. But competition from larger wholesalers doomed their hopes of keeping the store alive, and they closed in October 1972. The liquidator who managed the final burial sold us some of the fixtures, including the lectern still in use during readings upstairs at Cody's.

A significant business change for us, and later for all bookstores, came with a break in the barriers to having direct accounts with the mass-market paperback publishers. This ended our dependence on a local distributor, who usually did not carry an important part of our stock, the back list of steady sellers, and who did not give us enough discount to do more than break even. It had been sixteen years since we started our store, sixteen years of slow progress and repeated frustration. Finally the pub-

lishers would open direct accounts. Probably this was a business decision with them, a need to get the higher wholesale price from bookstores than they could get from wholesalers.

BEST-SELLERS FOR 1971
Brown, *Bury My Heart at Wounded Knee*
Revel, *Without Marx or Jesus*
Bach, *Jonathan Livingston Seagull*

BEST-SELLERS FOR 1972
Wigginton, *The Foxfire Books*
Comfort, *The Joy of Sex*
Halberstam, *The Best and the Brightest*
Jenkins, *Semi-Tough*
Roszak, *Where the Wasteland Ends*

BEST-SELLERS FOR 1973
Alistair Cooke's America
Thompson, *Fear and Loathing on the Campaign Trail '72*
Jong, *Fear of Flying*
Misner, Thorne, Wheeler, *Gravitation*
Piercy, *Small Changes*
Boericke, *Handmade Houses*

I would rather be a poor man in a garret with plenty of books, than a king who did not love reading.

T. B. MACAULAY, 1800–1859

All the restlessness of these years meant a decline in sales. Suburbanites were unwilling to come into Berkeley. Since our former partner had left, we could not look forward to moving out of a managerial role in 1975 as our pre-incorporation agreement had provided. The lease ran until 1985. By that time, Fred would be sixty-nine and I would be sixty-two. We did not want to spend the next twelve years working under what we felt would be duress. It had been a great challenge to build the business. Now it was more of a maintenance job and less a time for the excitement of innovation. We were just plain tired.

When Fred went to the American Booksellers annual trade show on Memorial Day weekend in 1974, he mentioned to some of the sales reps that we were interested in selling the store. That word of mouth eventually led to negotiations with three separate groups in the autumn of 1974, but none resulted in the sale of the store.

The first group were some people from the Boston area who lost no time in telling us that one of the first things they would do would be to set up a chain or franchise. No statement could be more guaranteed to turn us off. We were horror-struck at the thought of capitalizing on the good name we had so long and painfully achieved. It was apparent that their interest was a fast profit, not running a fine bookstore. Fortunately we did not have to make any difficult decisions because they did not have the money we required. In talks with our accountant and our lawyer we had concluded that we would only sell to buyers with enough financial resources to convince

*the owner of the building to transfer the lease. We were not willing to re-
main on the lease, in effect having a buyer as our sub-tenant.*

*The second group were people we were more comfortable with. They
shared our ideas on what a good store is, and the importance of relating to
the community. But again, they were undercapitalized, so weeks of discussions led nowhere.*

*The third prospect was Kepler's Books from Menlo Park. When Roy
heard we were interested in selling he said that our price seemed "very
reasonable" and wanted to talk with us about it. We did, but he concluded
that he did not want such a big commitment.*

*In notes I made at the time, I wrote of the conflict we both felt about the
prospects of selling the store:*

Many times I've passionately wanted to be rid of the hassles and
responsibility. But on the other hand, being so fully involved with the
engaging parts of the business has been a good part of our lives. Re-
calling now the high hopes that attended our negotiations ten years
ago for the new store building—had I been writing this journal then
I'm sure it would have been filled with as much positive outlook on
our decision to build the store as we feel now in deciding to sell it—
but life is chance and changes. Fred says there are risks either way—
risks if we keep the store as great as those we will take if we are able
to sell it. And I am TIRED of the daily grind, the minutiae, the coping.

Business was very good in December but somehow it seemed like
a strange Christmas, perhaps because of the heavy uncertainties of
world economies and tensions. I think that after all this time the realities of world shortages, an end to limitless affluence, are sinking into
the general consciousness.

*The talks we had with our accountant Abe Brumer during the negotia-
tions with potential buyers brought home to us that we would be in a much
stronger position if the store were more successful. In order to increase
sales, we needed a better inventory control system than the laborious hand
checking of stock against publishers' order forms. Computers were just
coming into retailing, and I researched trade magazines for descriptions of
what such systems involved. We talked with the Keplers and visited their
store to see the card system they used. This was a step toward computers:*

individual cards in the books that were collected as books sold, and once a week hand-sorted for orders to publishers. It was a step we could take; we did not have the money or the training to go into a full-fledged system that would track inventory and send out orders.

At that time, such programs were just being developed for bookstores. We were concerned about the costs of getting computerized—and the trauma. We had been on the receiving end as publishers computerized. The snarls were monumental: bills for shipments never sent, credit for returns never made. There was a time when one of the largest publishers did not bill us for nine months. We could not afford to let ourselves backslide by such an amount so I paid them according to my records of books received. It was a lesson I did not forget. We installed the card system.

In its primitive way the system did help us keep books in stock, and this improvement, together with the calming of political tensions, made for gradual increases in our sales. Early in February 1975, Fred wrote about this and other matters:

Been busy doing reading and choosing for three radio programs of a half-hour each I will do on KPFA at the end of the month. I decided I would, for purposes of comparison, do an anthology of stuff on the depression of the thirties. So I have been going through second-hand bookshops assembling material and then going through it for pieces that will reflect and portray the period. Been re-reading the short stories of William Saroyan and marveling all over again at how fine and fresh they seem even now. Also poring through Studs Terkel's *Hard Times*. What a great talent he has for drawing people out. Anyway, it's more a job of trying to select out of a great treasure of material. Strangely enough, it was an enormously stimulating and productive time and the writing about it is very rich.

I enclose a prospectus we've gotten out for a Bookmakers' Fair we're trying to get organized. The leaflet is intended to find out whether or not there is enough enthusiasm and interest to do a good job with it. So far, the response has been very good but we are still in the testing stage.

Somehow, although we still have hopes of selling the store, neither Pat nor I ever really became convinced that it was going to happen.

So it wasn't such a trauma to readjust to the idea that we would have to go on. In many ways I get a lot of pleasure and stimulation out of the store. It's true there is a hell of a lot of detail that is troublesome but there are also good things like dealing with the whole challenge of how to take books and present them to people and somehow create a genuine sense of excitement about them. Also the opportunity to work with people in publishing who are fascinating in their own right.

The store is holding up. We are busy as hell making it, we hope, much more efficient and attractive. We hope the street is quiet enough that we can open up the windows again so the science fiction shelves will be moved upstairs and we can have big display tables by the windows. It will let in much more light, create a good air of spaciousness, and make it possible to do some window displays.

We are running a test project with a science publisher out here, W. H. Freeman, which is owned by *Scientific American*. They will be doing special fixtures, ads and promotions with us, on new ways to present science books to the general reader and that is something I've long wanted to work on. Our poetry readings and other activities in the Gallery are going great guns with two or three events each week—fifty or so people showing up on average for each of the evening presentations. So all in all I think the store is coming to again have a community feeling to it with a continuous chain of happenings to keep it lively.

I see that in other stores too. At a booksellers' dinner I met two very interesting people. One was a woman in her fifties who runs a shop in Novato. In about three years she has got her volume up to beyond $70,000 and would be making a little money if she weren't so devoted to stocking good children's books that she has knocked down her turnover rate by over-buying. But she puts an enormous amount of energy into the store and it is a continuous stimulation to her.

The other bookseller was from a small city further north. This man, about thirty-five I would judge, has a store that grosses about $170,000. He early learned, he said, that he should just about ignore what was selling in the cities and the suburbs, and stock what the people in the town and the rural region around him really wanted. That meant that he concentrated very heavily on how-to and crafts books. He can sell books on quilting at just about ten times our rate although he can't do a thing with "literary" stuff or up-to-date books on politics or sociology or history. He sells, he says, a very large number of books on guns and his idea of a best-seller is to get in a really good book on cheese-making.

What has happened is that he has a store that is serving the needs of all the people, young and otherwise, who have established themselves in the country. Many of them are, of course, literate and very much interested in acquiring books that really help them learn the things they need to know in their everyday lives. It's interesting that the rural towns have been rather transformed and enlivened by the influx of people who have gone "back to the land."

Many writers came to the store over the years, both visitors from afar and those who lived in the Bay Area. In the 1970's, the "author tour" was on its way to becoming the fixture it now is. Here is Fred's reminiscence about one such visitor who stopped by in 1975:

Joseph Heller seemed not surprised to learn that when you sell the paperback rights to a novel for $350,000, there's a catch. The catch is that, the writing of the novel apart, something extra is expected, or at least implied. The catch and the extra in the case of such an author is a tour.

Author tours are of course nothing new in the history of popular literature. Perhaps the first author literally to kill himself with exhausting labors on behalf of his works was Charles Dickens in the middle part of the nineteenth century. And though Dickens was an especially remarkable example of the breed, he was hardly less assiduous in his determination to leave no ear unexposed to his words than that other traveler on the expanding railroad network, Ralph Waldo Emerson. Even Emerson's woodsy Concord neighbor, Henry David Thoreau, allured for a time by the siren seductions of the lecture trail, essayed a short series of forays on the podium before he retired in chagrin and disgust to the home ground.

But perhaps the most elaborately contrived nineteenth-century promotional tours, for authors of whom the public never tired, were the tented version of public television, the Chautauqua. William Ellery Channing, Robert Ingersoll, William Jennings Bryan, and a host of other figures toured year after year before hundreds of audiences, and there is no recorded objection from the publishers of the time that they ought to stop promoting and resume writing.

What often happens to the present-day writer on the national tour is that by the time he or she arrives at the rolling surf of our Pacific shore they are ready to leap into the waters and pull the billows over them. So it was with Joseph Heller. And when the Ballantine sales rep called, she made it clear that he would be glad to visit the store but that was all—no gallery appearance with the grad students from the English Department asking soberly analytical questions, no long line of people, book in hand, dictating detailed inscriptions, no fuss, in short, of any kind. Just Joseph Heller in the store for an hour or so.

It turned out to be one of the best author appearances we'd ever had. There are some authors who exhibit practically no curiosity whatsoever about the mechanics of the marketplace. When they come to a bookstore, they require that they be placed immediately at some vantage point to which a stream of book purchasers are expected to direct themselves for a word from the author and a dashed-off signature in the book. Once the supply of purchasers and books are exhausted they are ready to be moved to the next store. But Heller headed straight for the back room where the books are received and immediately demanded to know if Pat Cody was around.

Pat hurried downstairs from her rookery and Heller thanked her for a review in a feminist publication, *Plexus,* which had already been the subject of an exchange of letters between them. The people who worked in the store then crowded around, some of them with paperbacks of *Something Happened* and *Catch-22* which he signed. We asked questions but got nothing very surprising as answers because the answers had become a standard response. He offered to sign other copies and we pulled twenty-five or thirty paperbacks out of a box and stacked them on a table. He signed them while he talked about author tours.

"Doesn't mean much to sign them," he said, "when you think of how a book like this has to sell. It's a thing to do, though, so you do it."

Heller didn't say as much explicitly but, when someone suggested that he might better be at home writing, he shrugged his shoulders and said that sometimes you had to play the game of author and promotion. He said it casually and he had done the tour casually. It had all been done, it was evident, like the British Empire, in a fit of absent-mindedness. And perhaps that, for a writer of sensitivity and integrity, is the only way to do it.

BEST-SELLERS FOR 1974
Heller, *Something Happened*
Adams, *Watership Down*
Herriot, *All Things Bright and Beautiful*
Castaneda, *Tales of Power*

BEST-SELLERS FOR 1975
Doctorow, *Ragtime*
Trudeau, *Doonesbury Chronicles*
Bronowski, *The Ascent of Man*
Child, *From Julia Child's Kitchen*

CHAPTER FIFTEEN 1976 TO 1977

HAUNTED HOMES PROMOTING TOM ROBBINS HOLLYWOOD

AT CODY'S WE SELL THE STORE

THOUGHTS ON LEAVING

Once invent Printing, you metamorphosed all Universities, or superseded them! The Teacher needed not now to gather men personally round him, that he might speak to them what he knew; print it in a Book, and all learners, far and wide, for a trifle, had it each at his own fireside, much more effectually to learn it!

THOMAS CARLYLE, 1795–1881

The Bookmakers' Fair that Fred referred to in February 1975 became the Inkslingers' Fair held in May 1976. On his days off, he had been doing what the Inkslingers' Fair had preached—making his own book. Here he writes about that and his broadcasts in a September 1976 letter:

Well, there is no rest for the saintly and we have been busy as hell these last several days. I have been finishing up getting a book through the printers as well as doing no less than four broadcasts this week on the local radio outlet. At a meeting of seven people all of them were very enthusiastic about doing a series of programs on children's literature. But when the time came for the programs none of these people could be found except me and the guy in charge of the program. So I took it on and had a hell of a good time with it. I read some of the great fairy tales and then used Bruno Bettelheim's new book to spoil them for everybody by interpreting them. I also did some of the recent picture books, and I dug up some of the grisliest fables, ancient and modern, that can be found. Then I ended by having an expert on sexism in children's books come on and she did a fine job of reading some good and bad examples of the way some of the books treat the matter.

The book we are having printed isn't really a book—it's a pamphlet, practically, about thirty pages. As you know, that back room at our house is full of old books including quite a few children's annuals from the nineteenth century. I took a bunch of pictures from these and wrote rhymes that show the sinister things that are really happening under the surface in the pictures. Pat suggested the title *Haunted Homes* and was very enthusiastic about the book. . . . We will have it in several days and it will sell for $1.00. We had 1,000 printed, I had them use a fine grade of paper so if it doesn't sell we can find some other use for it here at the house. We are offering it to publishers: Doubleday, Bantam, and a small local press called Niche and Hitch are all in the running. We may hold out, though, until it's sold to the movies. I don't want much—just enough to buy Mendocino county. We saw several people when we went up there on vacation and it was very annoying.

Fred had a constant concern about bringing the original book to the attention of the public. In an interview with Publishers Weekly *in their issue of September 27, he was quoted:*

I know that people think Berkeley is a special case, but even here I notice a consistent tendency to underrate the intelligence of people who read books. I think there are many communities in the U.S. that would be much more receptive to the non-promoted book if they had a chance to look at it, and if booksellers were willing to spend a little time promoting it. The problem is that most publishers are not very receptive to the idea that booksellers may want to go out and do their own job on a particular book. We have promoted and done well with the whole range of intelligent books on science for the lay reader, for example. And poetry by Jack Spicer is a strong seller at Cody's.

When Houghton Mifflin published Tom Robbins' *Even Cowgirls Get the Blues* I bought high, 1,000 copies initially, because I felt very strongly that this was "our book." We had sold hundreds of Robbins' earlier book, even helped to get it reprinted in paperback after it had gone out of print. Besides that, I felt *Cowgirls* was a spring-summer book, light reading, no masterpiece but a really entertaining book. So Houghton Mifflin worked with us on advertising money, helped us get him down here—he's not your usual "promotable" author—but we had seventy-five or eighty people attend his reading one night and sold a lot of books in only a few hours. To date, we've sold 700 copies. For me, finding the type of book that is peculiarly suited for your store and lifting it up to another level—that's the real reward of bookselling.

I remember that 1,000-copy order. Bill McCullough, the sales rep for Houghton Mifflin, had visited us with the order forms for the 1976 season. After he left, Fred came to my office. "There goes a happy man. They're doing the new Robbins in both cloth and a trade paperback. I just gave him an order for 1,000 copies." I must have looked surprised because he went on, "Don't worry, we'll sell them. I love to give a big start to an author when I can."

Fred's comments about getting a national publisher for Haunted Homes *came true. Fred Schmaltz-Riedt, then a Doubleday salesman, liked the book so much he took it to New York and as simply as that, they bought it and brought it out in 1977 as* Haunted Homes: A Victorian Album *on their Doubleday Dolphin list.*

It was around this time that television and Hollywood came into our world. In an October 1976 letter I wrote:

We—the store—got some more good publicity recently when one of the Monty Python actors, Eric Idle, came to the store to sign copies of his new book, *The Rutland Dirty Weekend Book.* The local CBS station sent a camera crew and it will be on a magazine-type program that immediately follows the news at 7:30 on November 3. Wish it would be national so you could see it.

Speaking of TV, a couple of weeks ago Fred got a call from NBC studios in beautiful downtown Burbank asking him if he would come down to be interviewed to go on one of their programs as a panelist. He had been recommended, they said, as a literary expert. There was a ticket in his name at the airport and a chauffered limousine met him. At NBC—his first visit to one of the big studios—he said it was like San Quentin, guards carrying guns all over the place, badges required, etc. Well, it turns out this is a new program called "The $50,000 Question," and they were screening him to be a contestant in the "Great Lovers in Literature" field. They gave him a blue book and asked him to write brief essays on ten of the great lovers. Then they said they would get in touch with him, and he got a plane back the same day. He came home sadder and wiser, and said that since he was a little flippant (including Bonnie and Clyde) he doubted he would hear from them. But! Last week they called and said they want him for the program, and were perplexed when he turned them down. I think that he thought the program was to be something like the old "Information Please," not one of these crass quiz shows. Celia was disappointed.

Then early in January, Hollywood came to us:

We had some pleasant excitement this past week. It seems that Karel Reisz, the famous director (one of his pictures was "Morgan" about five years ago) is going to make a movie based on a novel called *Dog Soldiers* which won the National Book Award in 1974 (now in paperback). It is a seamy story about a writer in Vietnam who decides to try to smuggle three kilos of heroin into the U.S. and then runs into the bad guys. The script has changed this guy's wife from being a cashier at a porno movie house to being an employee in a bookstore run by her father and guess where they want to film those scenes? We will have to be closed for two days because with all that equipment you can see it could not be business as usual. They will bring in a set to make an office on the ground floor. The scenes are: girl gets phone call from husband John. She then goes in office to talk to her father about it. Scene of John arriving at store via taxi. Scene of his talking with her at our center desk. Scene of his going out the back door of the store, where—he meets up with the heavies. The stars are going to be Nick Nolte, Michael Moriarty, and the female lead will be Diane Keaton, Valerie Perrine, or Tuesday Weld.

You can imagine how agog Celia and Nora are. I asked the movie people if the kids could be there to watch and they said—putting on the Hollywood charm—"I'm sure that any daughters of yours would be so well-behaved that there would be no problem with them watching all they want. They can also be 'extras' as browsing customers in the scenes; also, they can go out to lunch with us."

Hollywood, here I come. They said they would rather have our staff be the "extras" as customers. We are charging them what it would cost us to stay closed for two days, and knowing how expensive it is to build sets in Hollywood, we are cheap at the price. I asked them why they didn't pick any L.A. bookstore and they said that since these scenes are set in Berkeley they want authenticity. The story is set in 1971 so we are to dig through our archives and see if we have any anti-war posters we can put up as background around the center desk. It will probably be April 5 and 6 although we won't know for certain for a couple of months. . . . They were in the store later this week taking measurements (art director, set designer, etc.).

They did come, in April, and filmed for two days. Tuesday Weld was the female lead for what became "Who'll Stop the Rain."

That same January of 1977, Fred wrote about the Haunted Homes *contract and about our ad in* Publishers Weekly:

Last week I went book hunting in L.A. This may seem odd. L.A. is not ordinarily regarded as a place where anyone would expect to find bookshops with interesting material. But on a previous visit I had been surprised to find three second-hand antiquarian stores with very interesting stocks, from my viewpoint. So when another bookseller said he was going down to do some buying, I begged a ride with him.

I'm afraid I went rather wild and spent quite a lot but I think I got some very good books. We also stopped at San Luis Obispo and Santa Barbara, both places with some interesting stores. Of course the booksellers themselves are always interesting and I think they speak with a candor and openness to someone else in the same field.

Tiring of the bookchase after two and a half days I decided to desert John—he planned more visits to shops in L.A. and San Diego—and come back on Amtrak.

The trip was in the nature of a celebration. Doubleday has decided to take the *Haunted Homes* book and will bring it out in a $2.95 paperback in the fall. The sales rep took it to them on a trip east and after it was sent out to the salespeople for their reaction it was taken before the Great Editorial Meeting and voted upon unanimously as being worthy of joining the company of Leon Uris, Velikovsky, and the rest. The advance will be $5,000. I have done five more to add to it and there will be repairs made to some of the verses and their faulty metric structure, greatly to their improvement, no doubt. I see stretching before me an endless vista of such projects and only pray that the public will be so grateful for my genius that these efforts can become financially worthwhile. I long to embark on a national tour and give interviews to the press across the country concerning the Nature of Humor. I have, as you might suspect, a vast fund of ideas for promotion, none of which will happen.

We have again put the store up for sale and an ad in the current *Publishers Weekly* testifies to the truth of the statement. We have only the vaguest hopes of finding a buyer but the sale seems at least as probable as someone publishing a book like *Haunted Homes* so we will see if our streak of luck holds for a space. So light a candle for us in the old farm chapel. Somehow, just thinking about it has cheered both of us very much. I get a charge out of thinking of all the Freedom out there and so does Pat.

Lawrence Ferlinghetti dropped by the store today so we had lunch together. He went over the book and laughed uproariously at the right places. Why, hell, he said, if you could sell that store you could do a lot of these. We passed on from this happy thought to satiric chatter about the gold mine he has discovered in the UC Library which is buying all his "papers." He used to throw everything away and now, Nancy, his partner in City Lights, says that he won't throw *anything* out.

I added to this letter:

Our ad for sale of the store appeared in *Publishers Weekly* of January 24 and January 31—we've had a few replies, only one of which looks serious. Also, as the sales reps move from store to store with their cargo of gossip, we've had inquiries from people who've heard in that way. We surely hope we can get free—it's been long enough.

The serious inquiry turned out to be Andy Ross, who did buy Cody's that June. The date for his assumption of ownership turned out to be July 9, 1977—just twenty-one years to the day since we had opened it. That fit with my answer when people would ask us how we could bear to part

with this wonderful store. I told them that creating, nurturing, and build-
ing the business was in some ways like having a child, and now, just as
with children, after a certain age you want them to go out in the world and
leave you free of the constant care and concern, able to do other things.

Fred's thoughts on leaving the store are expressed in these notes:

Did you ever have a feeling that you wanted to go, still you had a
feeling that you wanted to stay—that old Jimmy Durante song pretty
much expresses what I feel in selling Cody's. I suppose it's a matter
of putting a great deal of yourself into a store during the course of
twenty-one years. You know that you are leaving a large part of your
life behind you. We have all kinds of ideas of what we intend to do
with our lives once we leave the store. Still we are brought up short
with a realization that the pattern of a large part of our lives is about
to undergo a radical change. I guess there's always a question in the
back of my mind; I can't help wondering if I am going to miss it much
more than I think I will, and be lost and bewildered in dealing with
a relative degree of freedom.

Pat and I started with a very small store and worked very hard over
a period of years to build a good bookstore. Our energy level was
certainly higher in the years when we were younger and we were concentrating all the abilities we had on the store. Perhaps it's simply that
we explored a good many of the possibilities of what can be done in
creating the kind of store we wanted. It isn't that we feel smug about
what has been accomplished: we know there are all kinds of things
still to be done but I think we had doubts about how much enthusiasm and vigor we would be willing to expend on working on these
ideas in the future.

I believe that a bookstore is one of the primary institutions of a
good society. I will never lose the sense of excitement I feel in going
through a publisher's catalog for the Spring or the Fall seasons. I always make mental notes on reading ten times the number of new
books that I finally get time for. I wait eagerly for the book I think is
a book that is peculiarly "our" book—the book I feel will be a real
event at Cody's. I know I will miss the pleasure I got out of looking
at books in this special way. I will also miss looking at a book and

trying to work out in my own mind how it will be possible for us to do a good job in presenting it and selling it at the store.

I love old books myself and I spend quite a lot of time in antiquarian and second-hand bookstores but what attracted me to bookselling—aside from the necessity to make a living—was my conviction that there is nothing in the world more exciting than the birth of a new book. It's in new books that you can feel the crackle of excitement as ideas get expressed and begin to circulate in a widening orbit. It's in new books that you can participate in the process of seeing a great creative talent or genius coming into print.

There is talk now that the reps will become an anachronism in the book world. People in publishing have been heard to say that they would like to "just publish" and have the sales and distribution "farmed out" as a non-house function. And I do suspect that many publishers now are so fascinated with other aspects of the business— like the exciting game of subsidiary rights, and so on—that the sale of books to the general public becomes almost secondary. It seems to mean, in these cases, that a book is viewed almost exclusively in terms of what money it will bring in from the sale of rights for television, movies, paperback, and foreign publication. When a book does not show that potential, it gets a secondary effort on the part of the publisher, or no effort is made at all. Booksellers now tell stories of ordering a hardbound book and being told by the publisher's sales people that the publisher couldn't care less about shipping it because it has already been sold for paperback. The attitude seems to be contemptuous of the bookstore's interest in promoting the sale of the hardbound. Some publishers seem to think that booksellers simply don't understand what publishing is now about.

There also seems to be an over-emphasis on a very few books on a publisher's list that have "block-buster" potential as vehicles for the exploitation of subsidiary rights. In fact, you wonder how long the term "subsidiary rights" will continue to be used. In the case of numerous books these days the publishing of the book or property is so "coordinated" or "integrated" into the process of its use in other media that what happens to it in the bookstores—aside from a brief period when it is pumped up into best-seller status—becomes unimportant. With some exceptions, most of the larger publishing houses and the people in the top positions in them put most of their talents and energies into what amounts to managing or promoting books as "packages" or "properties." The other new books on their lists are left to make their way with a minimum of support. And the back list is either retired to oblivion or maintained as a perfunctory adornment. In such cases the sales rep functions mainly as an adjunct to the publisher's grand scheme for selected titles, and a hostile view is taken of booksellers who insist that a good bookstore is more than a way-station in the promotional campaign for books with exploitation potential.

To a large extent this is no doubt a "natural" development. Although the sums bandied about in the paperback, film, and TV industries are relatively small when compared with the massive entries in heavy industrial circles, still they are dazzling to publishing executives. And of course there are now many publishing houses that have become parts of conglomerate corporations whose feet are firmly planted in an inter-acting network of enterprises which can be utilized to march a literary work through its paces in each of the media under their control.

As I say, all this is what is dictated by an entertainment industry gluttonous for material for its mill. When, however, a publishing house becomes merely a secondary agent and functions mostly as a suppliant servant for the marketing of books by the various branches of the entertainment industry, those books that do not have a potential in that respect get shoved into the background.

Is it valid to say that publishing is still about ideas? Don't books still have a vital function to perform in the society beyond being the basis for exploitation in other media? Aren't we seeing already that the influence of the "big" media is tending toward the film or TV show where any idea of the complexity and subtlety of life and thought is subsidiary to a mindless array of technological wizardry? Are bookstores to become simply outlets for the spin-offs of other media, becoming increasingly dependent on what comes through the pipeline? Doesn't this mean that the audience for books that explore the complex diversity of thought and experience gets increasingly narrowed? What happens to the concept that in a healthy and vigorous society there is a large general audience for the serious study, consideration, and discussion of ideas, for books that grapple with them and whose appeal lies in their acceptance of the fact that there is a certain subtlety and beauty in thinking about the world?

To come back, after all this, to the sales reps may seem absurd but perhaps it is not quite that silly. Even in the case of publishers whose lists of new books are weighted heavily in favor of the big promotion, there are still books that are more ambitious in their scale and more far-reaching in their scope. The rep covers these books and at least offers them to the bookseller. The possibility thus remains that they will achieve some measure of "general" distribution. Specialized publishing directed as accurately as possible performs a necessary function in many professions and for many interests, but a good bookstore should at least offer a sampling of as much as it can of what is happening in as varied as possible a range of subject matter.

In the selection it offers the browser, the bookstore should always be suggesting the astonishing vitality in the proliferation of thought and ideas, in the myriad explorations of the human experience. And it should be avidly receptive to those who seek to break new grounds in whatever area, keenly attuned to the questioner of received values and convictions, an eager purveyor of innovative thought, a bookstore at the cutting edge of the creative mind.

BEST-SELLERS FOR 1976
Haley, *Roots*
García Márquez, *The Autumn of the Patriarch*
Boston Women's Health Collective, *Our Bodies, Our Selves*
Dean, *Blind Ambition*

CHAPTER SIXTEEN 1977

FRED'S TALK TO WRITERS ON RUNNING A BOOKSTORE
LOOKING BACK AT THE 1960'S

For not only a man's actions are effaced and vanish with him; his virtues and generous qualities die with him also; his intellect only is immortal and bequeathed to posterity. Words are the only things that last forever.
WILLIAM HAZLITT, 1778–1830

I would like to close our story of Cody's with two musings by Fred on those twenty-one years: what and why a bookstore can be, and the place it can have in the larger community. First, a talk he gave to a writers' group not many years after we opened our store:

I am a bookseller—the owner and operator of a personal bookstore. We are, I'm afraid, members of a fast-vanishing tribe. I agree with those who say that the small personal bookstore is a somewhat picturesque carry-over from the beginning of the nineteenth century. Yet there are still people who are so badly adjusted to reality that they insist on either writing books or selling them. As a bookseller, I must confess that I look at writers with something approaching awe—and as they look at me, I can only hope that they will have the grace to reciprocate in kind.

Writers, no doubt, could give me reasons why they chose to take up the precarious pursuit of devoting at least part of their time to writing. It will surely not come as a shock to them to reflect that there are any one of a thousand different things they might be doing which would provide better pay for the effort expended. But still they keep on writing. People who go into bookselling in a small store of their own are only a different kind of fool. They serve, if nothing else, to round out the lunatic picture of the life of letters.

I speak as a very small potato in the book retailing business. I do not presume to act as spokesman for the big chains, nor of the gilded palaces at the choice downtown locations, nor of the dividend-burdened ranks of the book clubs. These are the fat cats of the retail book business—they see things perhaps from a very different perspective. For my part, I can only stand from a distance and stare.

Bookselling and writing have in common the fact that they are generally regarded as things that can be done with ease. Among intellectuals or people with aspirations to being intellectual, there is only one thing, perhaps, that looks easier than writing a book, and that is, selling it. I have long ago given up trying to disillusion anyone on the latter score: it seems to me, indeed, that it would be criminal in any case to destroy an idea that seems to provide so much comfort—no matter how false the assumptions underlying it. It would be like a writer telling someone: No, dear sir or lady, your life would *not* make a good book.

But since we are on an intimate and confiding footing here, I am going to let you in on some of the more annoying secrets of the book trade, give a few details on what makes bookselling rather a demanding trade, and then try to suggest why, after all, it may be worth doing.

As an example of the kind of annoyance likely to occur I will adduce the case of the sandaled young lady who came in the other night, planted herself on a pile of books, and then dug into her purse for pen and paper. All this was merely a preparation for copying out her choice of recipes from a brand-new cookbook. And not only the ingredients, mind you, but also the directions. This seemed rather unfair, I told her, both to the author and to me and, after half an hour's work, she quit.

But what do you say to the man who steals in at least twice a week and leaves a trail of peanut shells behind him as he browses his way around the store? Or to the crunching apple eaters whose paradise seems to consist in poring over the art books? Or to other browsers who bring in ice-cream cones or Popsicles? Or to the leaners or the sitters?

Especially the sitters. I had no idea that so many people felt it was perfectly proper to take a book in a bookstore and plant their posteriors in the middle of an aisle, there to sit for as long as left undisturbed, not by other browsers, but by an imperious order from the management to assume a standing position.

Another terror and havoc-wreaker in a bookstore is the loud talker who moves from book to book delivering a commentary in argumentative or declamatory tones. A more insidious kind of torture comes from the chronic whistler who repeats a tune over and over.

These, however, are passing annoyances. More important is the fact that the owner of a small bookstore must gird himself for a variety of labors that demand the expenditure of a great deal of time, effort, and ingenuity. He must, for instance, be fairly adept with a broom and a feather duster and a talent for window washing certainly does not come amiss. Heaven help the bookseller who fears to climb on ladders for he will find it expensive to hire someone to adjust ceiling lights or put up wall posters. Some talent in writing advertising copy is certainly helpful—so is the ability to do sign lettering. Hefting heavy boxes of books requires a good strong back and the ability to make a neat wrapping comes in handy, particularly at the end of the year. And behind the scenes are all the things that have to be done to keep any retail business going—the keeping of records, the ordering, the checking, the paying of bills and all the rest of it. It is here that a partner willing and able to shoulder some of the responsibility comes into the picture. When a single person tells me he is interested in starting a bookstore and I learn of his marital status, I feel like saying, "Go, find yourself a partner, and then we can talk about it."

Beyond these aggravations and responsibilities, I have to warn any prospective bookstore owner to harden himself to hearing at least once daily that dread question delivered in a coyly accusatory tone, "Don't tell me that you actually *read* all the books in here?"

Or that other remark so often made, "Boy, do you have the life! Nothing to do all day but sit around and read books!"

That's another thing, by the way, that surprised me a good deal when I first began as a bookseller. I had thought that I was almost unique in wanting to run a bookstore. I have since learned that there are a vast number of people for whom it appears to be their most cherished dream.

Why? Well, I have thought about it a good deal and it seems to me that, in our poor world as it is now, being a free-lance writer or running a bookstore seems to many people just about as adventurous a way of life as anything they can think of. Individualism, whether rugged or not, has not died in America—it only tends now to take different forms.

Time was, I suppose, when the adventurous or unadjusted types simply downed tools and struck out for America, or, if already here, packed up and went West, or if they were out West, took ship for the islands of the Pacific. But as we all know, the ocean and air lines now regularly visit many of these once remote demi-paradises and going to live on one counts now as almost worse than no adventure at all.

Reading *Aku-Aku* the other night I was struck by the fact that adventure these days is so highly organized as to be practically prosaic. When you read of the vast preparations that were made for that investigation at Easter Island, you wonder why most of the participants didn't just sign up with the Cunard Lines and be done with it. The biggest danger they seemed to be running was getting mired down in a quicksand of paper work.

So since most of the thrill has been taken out of adventure by over-organizing it, I suppose the biggest adventure a person can go in for in America these days is to try to make a living as a writer or to start a small business. And I can testify—with no bitterness but with a sense of exhilaration—that that kind of adventure has no lack of perilous escapes, nerve-tingling suspense, and grueling trials of endurance. And best (or worst) of all is the feeling most of the time that this puny individual is pitting his solitary strength and mind against a fierce and hostile world full of wolves on the prowl and terrible unknown things that go bump in the night.

Yes, I think the great adventure of our time may be to give up the comforting assurance of the weekly pay check and strike out on your own. Someone, someday, will have the understanding to write the novel that will tell the story of this kind of adventurer but we will probably have to wait for the day when time allows us to see the nature of the hazards in a truer perspective. Meanwhile, we will have to content ourselves with the general opinion that the man who does it is just a damn fool.

But why is bookselling so hazardous? Well, as someone has said, it is just the nature of the beast. In the first place, there is really nothing so dead as a dead book. Think, if vanity and fond recollection will permit, of the days when *Gone with the Wind* was on everyone's lips. Not to have read it was even worse than having to confess in later years that you haven't at least a glancing acquaintance with *Dr. Zhivago*. And now I do well to sell one 75¢ paper edition of that rip-snorting best-seller once a week. Or take a more recent book like *The Caine Mutiny*. Go into any bookstore and ask for it—you'll be lucky if they can rake through a musty corner and disinter a second-hand copy. Books often come marked "Fragile"—in all justice, a good many of them ought to bear the legend "Perishable," as well. So it is hardcover—paperback—and the rest is silence except for those few books each year that make at least a bid for immortality.

And then, have you ever stopped to think of how books sell by location? Being near a university campus, I have had this brought home to me again and again and often to my most grievous cost. While John O'Hara will not move, I have trouble keeping in stock books on symbolic logic, Zen Buddhism, and Existentialism. Around Berkeley—I mean around the University—popular sociology as typified by *The Organization Man* or *The Lonely Crowd* has sold by the thousands during the past year. Its vogue seems now to be declining but there may be a few kicks of life in the old girl yet. *Dr. Zhivago* is stimulating an interest not only in Tolstoy and the other great Russian writers but in histories and studies of Russian literature. Psychology is still potent. There are fashions in books, as well as in clothes, and keeping up with them can be just as bewildering.

But the last thing I want to do is to discourage anyone from becoming a bookseller. First and foremost, I would put the fact that a bookstore exists for the purpose of putting books—any books—into people's hands. And I hope you will agree with me that that may fairly be considered a good thing, and that it is a sad town that has no bookstore. I know how teachers lament the fact when they visit bookstores in other towns and cities. For it does seem to me that a thriving bookstore in a town is a certain proof that there exists in that place a core of people whose minds are alert and lively and who demand the stimulation and the food for intelligent living that can only be drawn from the having and the reading of books.

Having a good public library, no matter how praiseworthy, is not the same thing as having a good bookstore. I think that in most cases bookstores and public libraries tend to support each other but one does not take the place of the other. In America today we usually measure the success of things by whether or not they are earning their way. And the point about a bookstore as distinct from a library is that in the bookstore the books are there to be bought. They are out there in the thick of it competing with all the other goods on sale in an enormously productive and competitive economy. "There," says the student as he buys the book, "goes my lunch money."

For it is one thing to borrow a book and another thing to own it. Owning it means that the purchaser has pondered over whether he wants to have this book near at hand so that he can consult it or study it now and in future. True, as time passes, books that once were prized will be discarded, but in the meantime they will have done their part in providing the fare that is needed to feed the developing mind.

All of this perhaps sounds rather exaggerated. Yet I think that most owners of small bookstores have something of this far back in their minds as they take care of the daily mass of detail. Most of them have a belief in books, some faint idea that books are still a vital force in people's lives, and that bludgeoning people into buying them amounts to something more than a crass commercial transaction.

The proof of this comes in that same day-to-day operation of a bookstore. It is true that most of the cranks and eccentrics will sooner or later turn up in a bookstore. What is infinitely more comforting is the fact that so do the liveliest and most creative people in the community. Once these latter see that the bookseller actually has some interest in and respect for what he is selling, the walls of reserve tumble down and there can be, and often is, good talk, and for the bookseller a growing number of contacts with people who are dynamic and productive.

From my own experience I would say that this is perhaps the most satisfying thing about being in the store. It may be that people are stimulated to good talk in a supermarket—I don't know—but I'm sure there isn't much opportunity to indulge in the urge at the checkout counter. No, there is something about a small bookstore that makes it an appropriate place for contemplation and talk. Here, at least, is a place where ideas count, where words have a certain importance and value, whether in a 25¢ paperback or a brand new magnum of a novel.

Believe it or not, I have had people tell me that they buy practically all their books through book clubs but they still enjoy coming to the store. There was a time when I made a somewhat embittered rejoinder. But the years have given me a certain philosophic tolerance. In the long run, I simply can't believe people will quit patronizing bookstores, even though we can't offer multi-volume sets of Sandburg or Churchill as premiums.

No, it seems to me that the retail book business—and the small bookstore in particular—is in somewhat the same condition as the theater, that fabulous invalid always on the verge of vanishing but always managing somehow to keep its head above the perilous waters. Bookselling has always, I suspect, been a hazardous way of making a living but, as I've said, it does offer rewards that make the risk worth taking.

So I don't take a gloomy view of the future of books. I notice how more and more people are getting together in informal groups to discuss the plays and the novels and the books on philosophy, public affairs, or other subjects. There comes a time, it seems to me, when people become sated with the whole array of mass diversion and say: No, television delights me not, nor my Jaguar, neither. So they come to reading and from that to the overwhelming desire to talk with other people who are of the reading kind. And even if books don't

lead to the desire to communicate with others, the ancient enchant-
ment of books still remains. When others fail him, someone wrote,
the wise man looks to the sure companionship of books. Between the
reader and the book there is a subtle communication that, once experienced, will always exert its power. For many I suppose it will
never be known, but every bookstore with an open door offers at least
the hope that the miracle may come to pass.

*The second expression of the place a bookstore can have is in an inter-
view with film producer Mark Kitchell in which Fred reflects on the events
in Berkeley in the 1960's:*

The early sixties were relatively uneventful, because you still had
the even political atmosphere, not very much happening in the university until the Free Speech Movement (FSM) in '64. People who
worked in the bookstore were active in FSM. It affected the kind of
books that were being sold. You know, that was kind of interesting
to watch over the years. The whole nature of what students were buying did change.

In '64, I can still remember when the kids came down after they
thought the FSM had won, and I guess they had, their great victory.
And they all came down the street, great streams of them, from their
victory rally, and you know, they were all in tears, and it was impossible for anybody to watch them, to see the kind of energy and commitment that they'd poured into it, not to be in tears with them. I just
stood on the corner and watched those kids coming down the street
and bawled like a baby.

And I think it was then that I first began to feel very strongly that
something was beginning to happen with young people in this country. Because, nothing remotely resembling that had happened to me
in college in West Virginia. I can remember almost furtive fund-
raisers for the Spanish Civil War and things like that, that a very few
of us went to. But beyond that, there was nothing on campus.

People tend to forget that the House Un-American Committee
hearings kind of set the stage for what was to come later in the FSM.
Students there literally got their feet wet in political action, and
learned that they could be a tremendous force.

It was perhaps the last time we saw any real idealism or any real hope in American political action. I don't think it's the same anymore. Now people do things politically, but it's a minority of people who have the hope, the belief, that it will count. They do it almost with a sense of desperation. Then, it was a real belief that if you got together and you got things moving, you would be able to move the country. You would matter. . . .

To me and many other people who were political, seeing young people begin to make waves, it was a feeling that, well, it was about time. We'd become very smug and complacent and self-satisfied about the state of things, and yet there seemed to be alarming gaps in the whole texture of American life; there was no sustenance. . . .

Much of the 1960's was confirmation of the belief both that man is an individual, and that he or she are social beings. On the one hand, a tremendous desire for an inner, personal life, which with the onslaught of the media and the standardization of everything in sight, is difficult. That was there, but at the same time, so was the whole social aspect, the gregarious aspect, the thrill and the satisfaction and the pleasure and nurture that comes from working with other people. That also we were deprived of. So the young people were, by and large, particularly vulnerable to any kind of philosophy or movement or people who would fill those kinds of needs. It was a dialogue of those two things going on together. The urge was there to get together, to feel something together.

What's bound to interest anybody who has a grain of sense in their head was that at the end, when they got together to celebrate, and they were all in a transcendent state of the highest kind of emotion, they didn't sing Solidarity Forever, they sang "We all live in a yellow submarine." Now what the hell does that mean? Part of the thing with somebody like me or an older person who had basic sympathies and yet who held back in a certain sort of way to try to stand apart enough to analyze it, was, what was going on there? There was a wonder in it.

Luckily they didn't want any advice. That was part of their whole posture: they were carving new ground, they were writing on a new slate, and everything that they were doing was completely new. Now that wasn't true of course, but that was part of what empowered them. That was something that disturbed me very greatly, but of course it was of the very nature of what was happening, and that was that the sense of history, the sense of continuity, seemed to me mostly lacking. Part of the mystique was that it was all new.

The great fear among Berkeley conservative types was that we would be absolutely inundated; we were so tolerant and so loving and so attractive, the streets were paved with pot and everything was just so sublime, that we would end up playing host to, you know, it would be another Children's Crusade and we would be the new Jerusalem. That feeling worked very strongly against things like the Free Clinic, that Pat and I had worked on, and the food program, and all the other kinds of programs that we pushed at various levels, state and local, to try to cope with this.

As to the influx of large numbers of transients, you could take that as a plague that had to be stamped out in some very punitive way, or you could take it in stride. So why don't we set up, in as voluntary a way as possible, really constructive ways to deal with this? And thus, things like getting the churches to open up a certain amount of their facilities to things like the Free Clinic. The beautiful part of it to me was to see people responding to their own needs. What amazed me was the number of young people who were willing for relatively long periods of time to make very serious commitments.

No one ever believes that anyone over the age of fifty is continuing their own personal exploration, their own personal challenge and development. And, in large part, I think I took this as a kind of challenge to myself to see whether I could deal with this in a creative and constructive way in personal terms, rather than allowing it to become a gnawing source of anxiety and corrosion of my energy and spirit. I wanted to take out of it what was really creative, that could give something to me, and it did.

By and large, I took off, well, during those years I was very fortunate to have other people to take care of business affairs, because most of the time, I was off doing meetings and working with people, and having a tremendous, by and large, a wonderful time. . . . If you kept a sense of humor about it, there is something inherently funny about a middle-aged person puttering around with younger people. The friendships that I made with young people then, many of them have hung on over through the years, you know, I've seen them marry and have their kids. . . . There was a lot of anxiety, particularly as far as the business was concerned, because at various times it looked as though it would simply be plowed under in the wake of all this. But you arrive at the point where you take that in stride, and you don't allow that to eat you up.

As to fears about the store, well, people wouldn't come anymore. Telegraph was too rocky for them, too dangerous. It went on for month after month after month. Window breakings and police using tear gas up and down the street. You could almost set your clock by the way it would work out: demonstrations at the university, getting off the campus and going down Telegraph, and then the police taking positions and playing cat and mouse, back and forth, up and down the street. You just have to close. And so business fell off terribly.

Once you let it be known that you have certain sympathies, there will be no lack of calls upon you to become involved. All you have to do is send up one signal, and it sets up a tremendous wave of reaction. And, I don't know, part of it was just being pulled in, by people who would come to you and say, Could we use the phone in the store for people who call who are interested, say, in organizing a free clinic? So you do that. Well, then, the first thing you know, it had inched along; they said, Well, could we use part of the space, set up a little office? So you say, Yes, you could do that. Well, could we have a phone installed? Well, yes, you could have a phone installed. Would you mind paying for the phone? And so on. It just snowballs.

As far as civic affairs, politicians here were terribly torn. On the one hand even those who would have used very rough methods were afraid that if they did that, it would produce such a reaction, that it would be far more destructive than to adjust. So there were a considerable number of people who were looking for somebody who could act as a mediator and interpreter, of both sides. And I played that curious, ambiguous role at various times. Anybody with a sense of humor and drama is bound to enjoy the spectacle of these dissimilar people coming together and the interaction; it was very funny at times.

It was people like Ray Jennings, pastor of the Baptist church, and myself and some other of the business people who came together; you see we had our own little community, our own little support group, if you want to call it that. Although we never met formally . . . years later we thought about how we had been very supportive of each other and that in a way we had kind of carried out a lot of the sort of underlying ideology of the movement ourselves in our own sort of peculiar way. The guy who ran the bakery, Eric Goodman, myself, Ray Jennings, a few of the other preachers, and some of the other business people: we could depend on each other, and we had a network of people who, when an emergency arose, we just naturally gravitated to each other.

There were situations like July the 4th. According to the mayor and according to the police, there was a belief spread from Washington, by Army Intelligence and perhaps by the CIA and the FBI, that there was going to be a national movement of taking over all the city halls of all cities over a hundred thousand population. You cannot believe that people actually thought that there was something in that. What city hall people basically told us, was, keep your hands off. Because you run a terrible risk, if you try to get out there on the street and you try to act as the monitor, because the police were determined to stay away until the point where it would be necessary to go in and really break heads, and that was what we were determined would not happen.

And so we set up a whole system of keeping the peace on that street, with tens of thousands of people on it. We worked with the people who organized it, and we were able to do it. But the whole emphasis on the part of officialdom, was to discourage this kind of voluntary activity. You would see these council people and the mayor himself kind of coming up and smelling out the action, and kind of furtively disappearing from the scene, unable to make a real commitment to stay there and fight the thing through.

But you know, if you want to regard it as such, that's a character-building activity. It adds a little bit of excitement to an otherwise dreary and routine life. We had some feeling between us at the end of the day, when we would have actually succeeded in going against the whole god-damned establishment ourselves. And maybe even going against some of the people who might have been antagonistic among the people who were there. Because I can remember, it would get very delicate at times. The balance would—things would hang by a pretty slender thread. There was that kind of wildness going on, so at any moment it could explode into something much more serious. Probably, we were innocents abroad. But what the hell, it was worth trying to do.

The other thing I was interested in, it seemed to me there was an awful lot of energy there. I've always believed very strongly that people should help themselves, people should come together. And there was a great deal of that in that time. A large part of the founding of the Berkeley Free Clinic can be attributed to that. Some of the leading people were medics in the Vietnam War, and carried little kits into the streets with the demonstrators, and took their chances. So you had that kind of thing where people were getting together. That appealed to me . . . I had nourished wistful hopes that perhaps a whole range of grass roots kinds of neighborhood medical organizations . . . I still think it should come about. . . .

To me, perhaps the most important thing about that period was the attempt of people to do things for themselves, to take back into their own hands the control over our personal lives, our destinies, our potentialities, to realize them, to work together in ways that break down all barriers. How to do that in a highly industralized, organized society is really the problem. Some of us had great hopes that that would be a springboard which would just go on from one little success to another, in a lovely cycle of movement. And I think to some extent, it did happen. You know, and it's still happening. . . .

It all is a kind of series of Eisenstein flashes in my memory, but this was a time when the police came roaring down the street. They were playing that cat and mouse game and a canister of tear gas flipped up off the sidewalk and bounced through the window and landed in the middle of the store. Well, we weren't there. We'd left some time before, as things began to get rougher. The contents of that can were disseminated in that store. So I started calling various people. First I called the fire department and I said, Is there any way you can come and put in blowers or anything? They said, Well, we don't do that. I said, Well, we might have to be closed for a week. Finally they brought blowers in and they ran them for about twenty-four hours. Despite that it was still unbearable in there. So then I started calling various people at the university and in Sacramento, Oakland, county offices and so on. Did anybody really know what this gas consisted of, and how long it stuck around and what was its effect on printed material? Did it cling inside the books? I said, What was the effect on our staff's personal health? Nobody knew anything. It became apparent that people were playing around with us the way they were playing around with natives in Vietnam. There wasn't that much difference. But the interesting thing was when we finally got the store open, then people came and bought the books almost as a souvenir. They loved the smell of the gas on the books. There was always that element, of fascination. As a matter of fact, I think that was what kept us in business. I always said that we ought to have started a campaign: Be adventurous. Take your life in your hands. Shop on Telegraph Avenue.

The city council, most of the time when it was chased into a corner, it took the right decision. It would hem and haw, and back and fill, and vacillate and procrastinate, but they would finally bite the bullet. For example, the closing of the street was a continual point of contention. Somebody would want to organize an all-day event, and close off the street. Now, the whole closing of the street, as the council came to realize, had a hidden agenda in there. There was something else going on in there besides the day's activities. The idea was to assert the people's right to their own street. A great deal of pressure would have to be put on the council before they would allow the street to be closed. Because they considered that they had suffered a defeat.

At times I was almost bitter about it, because it's no fun to be awakened in the middle of the night and told that five or six windows had been broken and you've lost your insurance and you're already so heavily in debt to publishers that you don't know whether they're going to take your house. Then you have to put out three or four thousand dollars to repair your windows. There was tremendous pressure to board up windows, or to eliminate windows. The Bank of America completely redid itself so that it wouldn't have any windows. I always resisted it, on the grounds that it was a confession that the society would end up a bunch of fortresses. That we literally wouldn't have an open society.

But you forget how much fun it was. Everything we did that caused us to break even or lose money was what made the store attractive when we wanted to sell it. We've had a succession now of students come through the university, for many of whom Cody's was a real part of their lives. They spent a lot of time there. They may not have spent a lot of money, but they spent a lot of time there, reading. It was their kind of headquarters. It was where they went to sit and read and absorb. I can go practically anywhere in the United States, and I'll be coming out of a hotel, and there'll be some damn grad student who knew the store, "Aren't you Mr. Cody?" And, "I lived in your store, and I want to tell you how much it meant to me," and so on. You know, it's very nice. It is possible to run a business, and have fun.

EPILOGUE

AFTER THE STORE   PAT'S NEXT CAREER   FRED'S ILLNESS
AND DEATH   TRIBUTE FROM ALAN SOLDOFSKY

Selling Cody's left a gap in our lives and our time. For my part, I had been a volunteer with DES Action. DES (diethylstilbestrol) is a drug that was given to millions of women from 1941 to 1971 in the mistaken belief that it would prevent miscarriage. I had a miscarriage in 1954, and when I became pregnant in 1955 with Martha, my doctor prescribed DES to me. Medical reports in the early 1970's told a grim tale: this drug had caused a rare vaginal cancer in some of the DES daughters.

Working with other DES mothers, daughters, and concerned health workers, I started to organize DES-exposed people in 1975 and to meet with the State Health Department about public and professional education on DES. When the store sold, I became a three-day-a-week volunteer, and later a staff member when we got a government grant for our program. Now—1992—I'm still with DES Action, which has grown into a national organization with chapters in twenty states and foreign affiliates in Australia, Canada, England, France, Ireland, Italy, and the Netherlands. Becoming a health educator turned out to be my third career.

Fred's creative energies turned to community service in a number of areas: host of a literary program on KPFA, one of the founders of the Radical Elders Oral History Project, president of Camps Inc. (a citizens' group that took over management of the faltering Berkeley city camps), co-founder of the Bay Area Book Reviewers' Association, regular essayist and book reviewer for the Berkeley Monthly, *the* East Bay Express, *and the* San Francisco Chronicle, *and active member of the Berkeley Citizens' Action (BCA).*

He had time for personal projects such as chapters for a proposed book on running a bookstore. Some of that work is in this volume, notably the section on calendars in Chapter 2 and on book travelers in Chapter 11. And, he completed and saw published in 1980 Make Believe Summer, *in which he took the illustrations of a nineteenth-century artist, Arthur Boyd Houghton, and wove around them a story of an English family at the seaside. Sad to say, he shared the fate of many of the writers he commiserated with over misadventures with publishers. His editor at A & W left that house so there was no one there to take care of it—and then A & W went bankrupt. That meant no promotion at all for this charming book.*

And now we come to the end.

Fred had always been a heavy smoker, and the letters from which I've quoted in this book often contained paragraphs of resolves to give it up. I was also a smoker, so we reinforced each other's behavior. He avoided going to doctors for check-ups because he didn't want to hear that he had to stop smoking.

In 1982 I began to notice that he never walked if he could drive, even three blocks to the market, and seemed to get short of breath quickly. He had a smoker's cough. Finally, late in December 1982, he told me that he had been spitting up blood for two months. We went to our doctor at Kaiser on January 4, 1983, and the first test was a chest X-ray. This showed a tumor in the middle of his left lung. We had no further testing done; we knew our next step.

Several years earlier, our friend Eric Goodman had developed cancer of the salivary glands and had used the Gerson diet therapy with complete success. We knew that the prognosis for lung cancer was poor. We both believed that traditional U.S. treatment of surgery, radiation, and/or chemotherapy had nothing to offer us. Fred's younger brother Mart had died in 1981 of metastasized lung cancer after a painful final year that started with lung surgery and ended with brain tumor and stroke.

We called Eric and through him made arrangements to go to the Gerson Hospital in Tijuana, Mexico. The hospital cannot be in the U.S. because it offers an alternative to the only treatments acceptable to the American Medical Association. We spent three weeks there, during which Fred began a drastic diet regimen and I learned how to prepare it. It is a rigorous system based on the work of Dr. Max Gerson, a German doctor who over many years developed his theory on strengthening the immune system through diet. This theory is described in his book A Cancer Therapy: Re-

sults of 50 Cases, *available from the Gerson Hospital, Box 430, Bonita,
CA 92002. We learned the practice. While we were there, severe winter
storms devastated the coastline of San Diego and Tijuana, and this violent
weather seemed to me a reflection of the rage and grief I felt.*

*Upon our return, our house became a one-patient hospital with a one-
person staff. Fred had freshly prepared organic vegetable and fruit juices
every hour from 7 A.M. to 8 P.M. as well as other foods and procedures.
Every six weeks a Kaiser nurse came to draw blood and gave us lab reports
on about twenty different factors, which we sent down to the Gerson Hospital. Fred lost weight: down from 185 pounds to 158, where it stabilized.
He was too weak to leave his bed and told me of dreams he had of such
simple pleasures as taking a bus ride.*

*The weeks went by and we felt we were making progress, since all the
blood reports were good. He was much cheered by carefully rationed visits
from friends. Our children drew about us with loving care. People asked
us if we were taking notes, so as to do a book on the Gerson system. Fred
said, "If I were to do a book, it would be about bonding," and he had Anthony get him Prince Kropotkin's essay on mutual aid.*

*On July 9, the day he died, he complained of nausea, and of feeling short
of breath. These symptoms persisted, and in the evening I called my friend
Ahna Stern, who had been a medical assistant. While we were talking with
him, he fell over in bed. We got him to the nearby hospital, where they re-
started his breathing, but to no avail.*

*My overwhelming feeling of loss was compounded by bewilderment:
how could this have happened? When I talked the next day with my sister
Sheila, a retired nurse, she said, "It sounds to me like a heart attack." I
had to know, so I had to have an autopsy. Kaiser Hospital would not do
one: "What do you expect? He had lung cancer." Fortunately for my peace
of mind, a cardiologist friend Ed Kersh arranged to have an autopsy done.*

*The report showed that his coronary arteries were 90% occluded, that
he had emphysema, and that the cancer was enclosed, had not metastasized, and had not even affected the Hilar lymph node which lay adjacent
to it. In short, the Gerson system had been working, and Fred had died of
undiagnosed heart disease.*

From the outpouring of tributes which followed Fred's death, I want to reprint this one, written by poet Alan Soldofsky in the monthly Poetry Flash *of August 1983:*

Fred Cody did not just sell poetry in his bookstore on Telegraph Avenue in Berkeley, he advocated it. In all of American letters and bookselling, Cody was something fine and rare and original. He embodied the tradition of Thoreau, Whitman and Muir. Their kindred spirits, along with his own, infuse the air inside the building he helped design and which bears his name. With his wife Pat, he created a living American literary institution.

Besides his public accomplishments, Cody had a special genius for being a person. Could anyone who encountered him stacking books in his store soon forget the rough-hewn face and fierce brow, or the passionate catch in his voice which trembled with emotion when his ire was raised? Meeting him for the first time, I recalled Shakespeare's line from the Sonnets, "How with this rage can beauty hold a plea." Yet Cody showed me more beauty through his words and deeds than I could have asked of one man. Cody taught us by his example, and our lives were good because daily we felt his presence among us. I shall feel that presence, wherever I am, as long as I live.

Cody nurtured the Berkeley poetry scene, an integral part of which—the Wednesday night readings—he housed in his store. He was as fierce in support of young, struggling writers as he was of his pure egalitarian politics. He felt solidarity with regional and small press publishers, particularly those that published poetry. After all, he too managed a small press. Many of us valued the Thoreau Calendar he published each year and sold for half a buck during the Christmas season, but we should also remember that he published the poetry of Julia Vinograd before anyone else would and also the play of Daniel Rudman. He was also one of the earliest financial backers of *Poetry Flash*. As national publishing houses consolidated and were bought up by conglomerates, Cody came to view the small press as the saviour of serious writing in America. He was once quoted in an interview as saying that Cody's would stock one copy of any small press poetry book, sight unseen.

His enthusiasm for independent publishing led, in 1975, to the organizing of the Inkslingers, who put on a printing and publishing fair at the Berkeley Adult School later the following year. The event brought Bay Area publishing to the attention of the public, but it had even a larger impact inside the publishing community. It brought people together. Cody was always bringing people together. And when he brought people together, he had a way of making each individual feel splendid and important.

Later, Cody served on the board of directors for the West Coast Print Center, organized by Don Cushman under a grant from the National Endowment for the Arts. Cody's influence in the publishing world was legend. It was well known, for example, that because he raved over Tom Robbins' first novel, *Another Roadside Attraction,* Ian Ballantine bought it and sold a million copies of it in the first year. But how many books of poetry, not to mention prose, would have gone unpublished or undistributed if it weren't for Cody's activism?

He had wide influence as a book reviewer. His columns in the *Berkeley Monthly* and *East Bay Express* helped readers discover wonderful books that might have otherwise gone overlooked. He was always doing that for his friends and customers. His taste was eclectic and extraordinarily far ranging, as was his knowledge of literature, philosophy, history and politics.

KPFA radio listeners were treated to hearing him often on the Morning Reading Program. Cody was, in fact, the only person suitable to m.c. the KPFA Poetry Festival on that sunny day in May, 1977, when 4,000 people assembled in the Hearst Greek Theater on the UC Berkeley campus to listen to the likes of Michael McClure, Bobbie Louise Hawkins, Jana Harris, Robert Bly, and Allen Ginsberg. Cody's performance was among the best of the day. I can still see him standing at the lip of the stage after Bly had finished reading, holding the poet's black engineer boots high in the air and clapping them together, calling Bly back on stage. They departed embracing, marveling in each other's company.

Because he exuded so much love for people, Cody engendered devotion, real personal devotion of the sort accorded to few human beings. He was one of the best among us—truly a man of his times. He was as great a friend to poets as we will ever know. That is why we must remember his life and hold it dear. His was an exuberant life, a life of strength and enthusiasm in an age of easy cynicism and despair. It is by no means hyperbole to say we shall not see his like again. He will be sorely missed.